A Touch of Treason

by

Vonnie Hughes

A Touch of Treason

Cover Art by *The Wild Rose Press, Inc.*

The Wild Rose Press, Inc.
PO Box 708
Adams Basin, NY 14410-0708
Visit us at www.thewildrosepress.com

Publishing History
First Edition, 2022
Trade Paperback ISBN 978-1-5092-4050-0
Digital ISBN 978-1-5092-4051-7

Published in the United States of America

Elverton swung around still holding Ariadne with one hand, and with the other he smote Helena hard across her face. She dropped the knife as her hands went instinctively to her face, and her head rang. Stumbling against the door frame she slid to the ground.

"Helena! Don't hurt me, Foxhyth!" Ariadne shrieked at Elverton as she dropped to her knees in front of Helena.

Through stinging lips Helena snarled, "You devil. Leave her alone."

"That's right, my dear. Sport your canvas! You are worth two of this sniveling child here. How I look forward to schooling you! We will have such sport together. In the meantime, I suggest you both cool down. I hold all the cards." He pushed them both to the far side of the room and slammed the door shut.

Ariadne began to cry in loud, gulping sobs.

Helena sagged against the wall, closing her eyes while she tried to gather herself together. Her whole face burned with pain. Her lip must have split again because she felt the warmth of blood on her chin.

She had known it would come to this but had not allowed for Ariadne's presence. All those years ago she had sensed that Elverton had it in him to do this sort of thing; that was why, without any just cause, she had mistrusted him. It stunned her that Papa had been impervious to this man's nature, but more to the point, *had her father been well aware of it yet still called him 'friend'?*

Praise for *A TOUCH OF TREASON*

"The first thing I noticed was how strong a writer Ms. Hughes is. I was immediately drawn into the world of 1811, Portugal; convinced by the vibrant period details and language. I've read tales set in this era, and have to say the author did an excellent job. If you're a reader who has never read anything set in the time of the English Regency, there will be expressions and words you'll have to gloss over or look up. Luckily though, this won't interfere with your enjoyment of the story."

~Long & Short Reviews

~*~

"This is a terrific read where the heroine is strong enough to face dangers, within the parameters of the Regency, and win."

~Cathleen Ross

Other Wild Rose Press Titles by Vonnie Hughes

Lethal Refuge
Innocent Hostage

Chapter One

A horse picked its way carefully among the shadows in a dark narrow lane leading to open ground above the cliffs. Overhead the night sky was surly with massing clouds. The rider cursed the inclement weather, worrying that the ship would not make the rendezvous on time. He did not want to be dallying near the shore at Dungeness in these difficult times. Above all, he had no wish to mistake a revenue cutter for the ship he was expecting. It had been known for the excisemen to set a trap. He fervently wished to be anywhere but this. His blackmailer knew this no doubt—would take a perverse pleasure in knowing his lack of courage when it came to things military.

He resolved to find a way out of this mess before his life was forfeit. Every trip to the coast laid him open to the chance of disclosure.

He halted his horse a safe way back from the cliffs and waited.

****

"Helena, we shall go for a walk. It's a lovely day, and I wish to see if Anna and Charlotte are walking in the park this morning," Ariadne Yardley announced to her companion.

Helena Marshfield placidly took a sip of tea before answering. "That sounds delightful, Ariadne. You will be able to show off your lovely new walking dress to all your friends."

Ariadne cast her erstwhile governess a sour glance, and her sister Caroline smothered a giggle. The late morning was breezy and warm—an ideal day for a stroll. Had Ariadne not suggested it, Helena Marshfield had been going to propose that very thing. Not, of course, for the same reasons as Ariadne. Helena doubted whether anyone would so much as even glance at her worn walking dress of sober lavender cambric and her plain bonnet. Nobody ever *did* notice a governess. They were invisible. And as she had no wish to cut a dash, it suited her to be invisible.

She would certainly enjoy a walk. It might help to dispel her looming worries, and hopefully a meeting with Ariadne's friends might put that young lady in a better humor. Ariadne's ill humors were the scourge of the household.

"We have plenty of time to tarry over breakfast. Ariadne will take at least an hour to get ready," Caroline remarked cheerfully when her sister had left the breakfast parlor. Helena smiled her agreement. Ariadne was exceptionally pretty, prettier even than Caroline, but her studied beauty was not obtained without a certain amount of devotion to curling-tongs and even occasionally to the judicious use of a haresfoot. In spite of her beauty, however, she was beginning her second Season without any favorable offer in sight. That could be because she was the much-indulged daughter of a Cit—an accomplished businessman and a warm man—but with no claim to being a true gentleman. However, it might also be attributed to the fact that Ariadne delighted in being the center of attention, even if the attention was sometimes adverse. A complete absence of self-discipline had gradually been replaced with a coating of 'manners' thanks to Helena's conscientious ministrations, but Helena knew that Ariadne would revert to her temperamental self the moment her will was crossed.

She said now as she rose from the breakfast table, "Dress warmly for the breeze, Caroline."

An hour later the young women left Russell Square and headed toward Hyde Park. It was a considerable distance away, and Green Park was much closer, but of course you did not walk in Green Park at this hour if you wished to be 'seen.'

Once there, they sauntered in an aimless perambulation which passed for exercise down The Walk. Occasionally they encountered acquaintances; more often they passed by members of the *ton* who ignored them frostily. No matter how rich Mr. Yardley was, there would always be some members of the *ton* whose only concern was breeding. Helena allowed herself a half-smile. She doubted that the Yardleys cared overmuch. They might emulate their 'betters' but they were not noticeably cast down by the snubs of people they did not know.

What a glorious spring day! How Helena longed for the Marshfield stables on a day such as this. There were many people riding this morning, but neither Caroline nor Ariadne enjoyed riding. They were city dwellers whose inclinations were to call for a hackney.

"Oh, drat!" Ariadne's attempt to keep the hem of her new, summery dress away from the dirt on the paved paths was not being met with success. Helena wondered how long it would be before the girl was forced to don her pelisse to prevent the wind from chilling her to the bone. However, as Mrs. Yardley had said as they departed, "The child does look a picture, don't she, Miss Marshfield?"

Ariadne's York tan gloves exactly matched the bunch of ribbons trimming her bonnet and the fawn of her walking dress was a color that only a young woman with a perfect complexion and bronze ringlets could carry off. Her lovely eyes sparkled with the anticipation of taking the shine out of those young ladies whose papas were not so well endowed with worldly goods.

Helena suddenly became aware that the 'child' was no longer walking alongside them. She had stopped to smile and nod to a well-dressed gentleman astride a beautiful bay thoroughbred. A pair of broad shoulders sprang to mind. "Caroline, who is that person? Isn't he...?"

"Yes, Miss Marshfield. He's the gentleman who opened the door at Hookham's Library for us yesterday."

Helena closed her eyes, feeling a blush heating her face. Heavens above! She would rather be anywhere else than here. She had spent a great deal of last evening chastising herself over her idiotic behavior yesterday at Hookham's. Merely because the gentleman had held the door open for her, she had behaved with something less than her usual decorum. It was unusual for men to bother with civilities when it came to companions and governesses. They were invisible.

Surprised at his kindness, she had cast a fleeting glance back over her shoulder. To her discomfort the tall gentleman had been standing, looking after her, his brows slightly raised. In response to her surreptitious glance he had gazed steadily at her, and Miss

Marshfield had cast her eyes down with all the natural embarrassment of a mere governess caught putting herself forward. She, who prided herself on correct behavior, had been caught out. So much for being the good example that the Misses Yardley looked up to.

Fortunately he had done nothing to discompose her. He had merely looked puzzled, as if trying to place her in his memory.

And now here he was again. Fate certainly had it in for her.

"Now, where was Ariadne introduced to him I wonder?"

Caroline laughed. "She probably hasn't been *introduced* at all! You know how Ariadne is sometimes."

Inwardly Helena shuddered. She must do her duty and would be unpopular with both Ariadne and the gentleman. Swallowing hard, she stepped forward and touched Ariadne on the arm. "Come, Miss Yardley. We must hurry if we are to meet with Anna and Charlotte."

Predictably Ariadne pouted. She could not be made to understand that, hovering on the fringes of the polite world as her family did, any unacceptable behavior could ruin her own and Caroline's acceptance to the untitled lower echelons of the *ton* and the Indian nabobs' and merchants' families which made up their milieu.

Helena gritted her teeth. She desperately hoped Ariadne would not defy her. A tantrum now would be embarrassing for everyone—except Ariadne.

The gentleman's big bay horse had stirred restlessly at Helena's approach and, without thinking, she raised a hand to gentle it. Curious, the horse stilled its shuffling and lipped at her gloved hand. A voice above her said, "Thank you, ma'am, for not startling him. He is a trifle resty. You are familiar with horses I think?"

Resty! Well, that was a polite term for a frisky, high-blooded creature such as this. Helena, forced to acknowledge the gentleman's presence, glanced up at him with a vague, artificial smile.

And found herself trapped in a steely gray gaze from eyes the color of the English Channel in winter. The severity of his Brutus cut emphasized the hard cheekbones and leanly sculptured face. His skin was lightly tanned and set off those eyes that could no doubt be exceedingly very, very chilly. At the moment they held only polite inquiry. Helena raised her chin.

"You need not keep your horse waiting, sir. We must be on our way."

She was astonished to hear him chuckle. "That may be beyond your powers. From what I've seen lately, this young lady might have other ideas. I don't envy you your task."

Ariadne stared at him with a half-smile, not one whit put out that the gentleman was not exactly complimenting her.

His eyes now held a distinct twinkle as he glanced from Ariadne to Helena and back again, with an invitation to Helena to share his amusement. She smiled ruefully in response. "Perhaps the cold wind may achieve what I cannot."

"Perhaps. May I introduce myself, ma'am? There appears to be nobody else to do so. Ivor Stafford at your service." He leaned down, ignoring Ariadne to that young lady's obvious annoyance, and clasped Helena's hand. Not an easy gesture with the bay on the *que vive*, anxious to be off and trotting. As he straightened in the saddle Helena's brain snapped to attention. Sir Ivor Stafford! She was doing Ariadne a disservice by assuming that the girl had scraped acquaintance with him in a hobbledehoy way, because it was common knowledge that Mr. Yardley and Sir Ivor Stafford had business dealings together. Well, that decided it. Ariadne had committed no indiscretion after all. Not this time, thank goodness.

That was why she had thought he seemed familiar. She had seen him occasionally from a distance. 'Sir Ivor' featured regularly in Mr. Yardley's conversation. He was always happy to let people know that he hobnobbed with the gentry.

She relaxed visibly, and Ivor Stafford's mouth curled upwards. "Happy now you've placed me? Liable to strike up acquaintance with all sorts of undesirables, is she?" he baited.

Helena's lips tightened, and she wisely ignored temptation. "Come, we had best not keep Sir Ivor's horse standing, ladies. Say your goodbyes, and we'll be on our way." She stepped back briskly, but at the same time Ariadne surged forward, bumping Helena to one side as she gazed meltingly upward. Her pretty face was raised to allow Sir Ivor to fully appreciate its finer points. The governess seethed silently and prayed that such blatancy would be overlooked.

However, it appeared that Sir Ivor was busy controlling his sidling horse, made nervous by Ariadne's heedless approach. Or perhaps he had the good manners to ignore so blatant an invitation. Helena knew from her salad days that many matchmaking mamas taught their daughters to gaze in just that way at susceptible gentlemen, although Mrs. Yardley lacked the subtlety to train Ariadne in such a trick. Ariadne was doing what came naturally.

This gentleman did not appear to be susceptible. Possibly he was experienced at fielding the approaches of over-eager young women. He hardly spared a glance for Ariadne, busy as he was controlling the bay. His horsemanship could not be faulted. After a little jostling, the bay stood still, flicking its ears.

"And you are?" he inquired directly of Helena.

"Oh—that's just Helena Marshfield, our companion."

Dear Ariadne. She did not fortunately say it in *quite* the same tone as she often used to her female acquaintances, but it was still said with an inflection which left the listener in no doubt about Miss Marshfield's station in life.

Helena gritted her teeth and preserved her calm but Caroline, who had moved closer in spite of her shyness, said hotly, "She is our good friend, not just our companion!"

"Hush, Caroline," Helena murmured softly, placing a gloved hand on Caroline's arm to prevent further outpourings. Caroline blushed, and Helena smiled to soften the blow. She knew that Ivor Stafford was watching the by-play.

"Oh yes…well…I'm *so* sorry! Sir Ivor, this is our 'friend,' Helena Marshfield. As you can see, Caro and Helena are boon companions," Ariadne snapped. To Helena's experienced eye, Ariadne was working herself into a petulant snark which meant the end of a peaceful walk.

"Oh," said Sir Ivor vaguely. "I had thought her name was Athena." Ariadne looked completely blank. Caroline giggled, and Helena blushed painfully again. Damn the man!

He held his head to one side consideringly, as if he were judging horseflesh. "Yes…the Marshfield is rather an anticlimax, but I agree wholeheartedly with the 'Helena.' It suits you."

How *dare* he? Just because she was a companion, he was baiting her. "Thank you." Helena knew she sounded as though the words were painfully extruded from between her teeth.

"Not at all, Athena."

The Yardley sisters were watching the sparring match wide-eyed. Helena had not bantered with a man like this for some years and was sadly out of practice. She was not able to think of a single stinging retort to put him in his place. Athena indeed! She had nothing but contempt for a man who toyed with the feelings of a governess who was, because of her station in life, unable to answer back. She turned to the girls. "Come," she said firmly. Ariadne glared at her. Fortunately, Sir Ivor was gathering his horse's reins together preparatory to departing and did not appear to notice the mutinous expression on Ariadne's face. Either that or his manners were excellent—except when it came to governesses.

They all stood well back from the horse's hooves. He raised a hand and the bay trotted away, playfully sidling and jerking its head.

"I don't know what Sir Ivor must think of you, Ariadne, staring up at him like that." Helena purposely used Ariadne's first name because she knew it irked

Ariadne to be spoken to as if she were still in the schoolroom.

"Good heavens, Helena. At least I wasn't blushing and stammering as you were. Anyway, we are in fact quite *good* friends," Ariadne stated grandly, smirking. "I took tea with him only last week in Papa's study."

Oh? Although she was aware of the social ambitions of the Yardleys, Helena had not realized that Mr. Yardley was as assiduous as Mrs. Yardley at matchmaking. His business acquaintances would feel every bit as hunted as did the titled gentlemen of the *ton* during the Season, if Joshua Yardley continued to throw his daughters in their way.

She shrugged. No doubt Sir Ivor could look after himself. He seemed on short acquaintance to be an intelligent man, and even if Ariadne's beauty appealed, he was awake to her disposition.

Helena thought none the worse of him for that. She felt sorry for any young man who aspired to Ariadne's hand, but Sir Ivor was not young enough to be strongly affected, as were some of the youthful, naïve town beaux when they first set eyes on Ariadne. Her incandescent smile and abundant curls inevitably floored them. Some even saw her vanity as justified and her uncertain temper as 'fire and spirit.' Fortunately for them they did not have to live with all that 'fire and spirit,' and as for the man who eventually *did* marry her, he was much to be pitied.

****

Helena would have been startled to know that that was precisely Ivor Stafford's opinion too. He rode away, an amused smile curling his lips. So she was a companion. He had never seen eyes that shade before—

a deep purple-gray. The goddess Athena was reputed to have had eyes like those. He recalled that unconsciously 'come hither' backward glance at Hookham's Library and smiled. Miss Marshfield might try to be the soul of decorum but there was a strong character beneath that façade.

Then he caught himself up short. Forget about the woman. He had not escaped the clutches of hordes of ambitious mothers and daughters for the past ten years in order to fall under the spell of a young woman at this moment. *Not now* when he had almost succeeded in the most important task of his life.

The young woman's station in life would not worry him if he were hanging out for a wife. He wouldn't care if she were a washerwoman. He was not of the *haut ton* where such a thing was unthinkable. But he was not looking for a wife. And that lady with the mesmerizing eyes was destined to be a wife, not a *chère amie.* Breeding showed in every inch of her from her glossy hair down to her cheaply shod feet. What had happened that she should be reduced to chaperoning Joshua Yardley's daughters? Totally absorbed in worrying the conundrum, he completely missed seeing poor Harry Cargill, one of his closest friends who was sauntering alongside the carriageway.

****

The Yardleys did not encounter Anna or Charlotte Morris, so Ariadne was unable to dazzle those young ladies with her expensive new toilette. As the breeze freshened, they turned back for Russell Square. Ariadne, having been balked of her prey, was savage in her disapprobation of Helena's 'untoward behavior.' She would not let go the topic and was like a terrier at a rathole. "Sir Ivor must not have known at first that you were just our companion or surely he would not have talked to you as he did. Next time we meet him please remember that it is *I* whom he wishes to converse with. It was not well done of you to keep him talking in that manner, Helena."

Helena closed her eyes for a second. A governess or companion was at the beck and call of whomever employed her and was sometimes unjustly accused of all sorts of peculiar things. But to accuse her of attempting to attach Sir Ivor's interest was ridiculous. It was Sir Ivor's fault for singling her out. Heaven help her for the next few days until Ariadne found someone else to torment.

For the past five years she had relegated herself to the ranks of the employed, never once putting herself forward, for she had seen what happened to those who displeased their employers. A natural strength of spirit allied to the self-confidence of having ordered a household from the tender age of sixteen served her well. But oh, she had to struggle to remember her place sometimes when Ariadne Yardley tried her patience.

Her self-confidence had taken some vicious blows since she had begun governessing, not to mention the buffeting it had taken at the hands of her erstwhile 'friends' when the scandal of her father's death had first come to light. She had to struggle to hold her chin high on bad days. It would have been better for her had she been born a meek and mild person, but she had not been.

"And another thing—" Ariadne began.

"Oh, be quiet, Ariadne!" Helena had come to the end of her tether. Ariadne opened and shut her mouth a couple of times.

Caroline giggled. "You look like a baby bird, Ariadne."

"How *dare* you!" Ariadne gasped, presumably to Helena.

"I dare because you are an unprincipled little baggage. There! I have said it at last. If you stopped to think for a moment, you would be aware that Sir Ivor was merely playing a joke on me. What else would he be doing with a governess? The poor man has no doubt been hunted and haunted by hundreds of young ladies such as yourself. From what I hear it is no fun being an eligible bachelor these days. No doubt he thought I was of an age where I could share his joke. As well as being a mere governess, I am past the age where I might take his joking seriously. As you appear to have done," she added for good measure.

"Dear Miss Marshfield," Caroline said, tucking her arm through Helena's. "You are only a few years older than Ariadne."

"Thank you," Helena said dryly. She might only be four and twenty but after two years of dealing with Ariadne she felt more like a hundred.

Already she was regretting her luckless tongue. Ariadne would of course run straight to Mr. and Mrs. Yardley to complain. Would she be dismissed? Would she have time to find another position before she had to leave? Mr. Yardley was a fair man, but the Yardleys were inordinately proud of their daughters and spoiled them outrageously. She hoped desperately that they would not condemn her for losing her patience with Ariadne. After all, *they* had found it impossible to curb her behavior and had left Helena to be the arbiter of all decisions pertaining to Ariadne's upbringing.

She had nowhere to go if she lost this position. Well, not quite true. She could always return to Miss Fichton's Academy for Young Ladies in Bath. Back to stultifying boredom.

Her throat sore with the sharpness of unshed tears, Helena raised her chin. No, she would *not* let that little baggage see how badly she was hurt. Drat Sir Ivor Stafford or whatever his name was. He might be the possessor of a wonderfully wide pair of shoulders, and he might be kind enough to converse with a mere governess, but she wished he had left her alone. No doubt he had not considered what a mare's nest he had stirred up. It was Helena's experience that gentlemen rarely considered the consequence of their actions. Her own father had certainly not done so when he had killed himself, leaving her brother and herself alone in the world without a penny.

"Cheer up, Miss Marshfield. Nothing will happen." Caroline, a great deal more sensitive than her older sister, could see that this argument had shaken her governess badly. "I promise I shall tell Papa exactly what happened."

"Caroline, it is kind of you to intercede on my behalf, but I must face your father's wrath alone."

"What are you two whispering about?" Ariadne demanded.

"Nothing," they both chanted in unison. Caroline smothered a giggle, but Helena could only smile wanly. Dear Caroline. Ariadne might be a thorn in Helena's side, but Caroline was a sweet young woman and Helena was proud of her young charge. She was lovely, but set next to her older sister she lacked sparkle. She was quietly enchanting but still a little naïve. She would learn. She was a quick learner. Caroline would be the ideal helpmate to a young budding politician or a wealthy tradesman with ambition.

And most important of all, Caroline and Helena were friends—in fact, Caroline and Miss Fichton, her old governess, were the only true friends Helena had.

How strange that after years of being her father's spoilt darling, and that one fascinating Season where she'd felt she had all the time in the world to worry about her future, that her once interesting world should narrow down to this focus of just two real friends.

"I shall speak to Mama and Papa as soon as we reach home." Ariadne's sharp eyes bored into Helena's. "You might be turned off, Helena." Her gleeful, self-righteous expression made Helena's hand itch. She stared straight ahead, saying nothing. Did it not occur to Ariadne that if she were dismissed, another companion would take her place? No, probably not. Ariadne was not overly endowed with intelligence. It would serve her right if the replacement companion was a real bitch. It would give Ariadne some competition.

Helena struggled to maintain her usual placid demeanor. She had no intention of letting that little horror know how badly her temporary loss of self-control had startled her. She sighed. If it had not been for her father's untimely death, she would probably be mounted on a horse from the Marshfield stables right at this moment going down The Ride. She would have the right to acknowledge Sir Ivor Stafford as an equal, or anyone else for that matter. She did not know why she felt so desolate today. She had had five years to come to terms with the knowledge that her future probably held many charges like Ariadne—young women who would, no doubt, be insolent, hot to handle, possibly even downright vindictive—so why should she feel today, suddenly, that she could not bear it?

She became aware that Ariadne's pace had quickened. The young woman was determined to get to her parents before Caroline did.

"Mama! Papa!" Ariadne practically ran up the front steps of Yardley House, ignoring the butler. Stalley raised his eyebrows. Helena stripped off her gloves and remained in the foyer.

"Caroline, I shall wait down here for your father. If he is at home, he will want to speak to me immediately, I should think."

"Oh, but Miss Marshfield, you only told her to be quiet and—"

"No. I should see him straight away. He may want to dismiss me formally. I hope to see you later, darling, to say goodbye." She swallowed.

Stalley, who had been on his way to the butler's pantry, stopped dead in his tracks. He swung around, but before he could speak, Helena chivvied Caroline up the stairs. From halfway up, Caroline hung over the banisters.

"It's not fair, and I shall tell Papa so, Miss Marshfield." Her lovely eyes were swimming with tears now that she saw how seriously Helena regarded her own conduct.

Helena remained standing, staring into space. It was an unspoken rule that no matter how insolent one's charges were, no matter how difficult they were, a mere governess had no rights. She must never retaliate.

"Miss Marshfield!" Stalley hissed. "What

happened?"

"Miss Yardley finally tried me too far."

His lips folded firmly together. "How you have tolerated that young woman for two years, I don't know. Well, if you go, then I go."

"Good heavens, Stalley, no! You must not."

"Miss Marshfield, *you* run the household. Mrs. Yardley is not capable of doing even half of what you do. I could not work here if we had to go back to having Mrs. Yardley ordering the household." He shuddered. "Before you came it was bedlam. Housekeepers came and went. Housemaids came and went. Then you arrived, and within a month all was serene. I'm sure Mr. Yardley won't want to lose you."

"I hope not, Stalley. Thank you for your confidence." She felt better knowing that at least somebody appreciated her efforts. Stalley never forgot that he used to be employed in a titled gentleman's residence. His contempt for the Yardleys was kept barely within bounds. He had never questioned any of *her* orders, but she had not realized until today that he actually respected her.

She waited, not knowing what to do. "Stalley, is Mr. Yardley at home?"

"As far as I know, Miss Marshfield."

"I had best stay here then." Her nerves had all congregated in the pit of her stomach where they scrabbled to maintain a balance. She could feel her palms sweating, and a trickle of moisture dribbled down her back. She tried to make her face as expressionless as she could as she crossed the foyer to wait at the door of Mr. Yardley's study.

Upstairs a door slammed, and heavy footsteps

tromped to the top of the staircase.

"Miss Marshfield?" Josh Yardley leaned over the banister. "Would you be so good as to step into my study? I shall be down directly."

Stalley whispered, "Good luck" and disappeared into the butler's room.

Well, here it was. She might have to go back to Miss Fichton's if she could not secure a new position in London. At least she had Miss Fichton's excellent reference that might find her a position somewhere in the shires, but it was doubtful she would get another job in London again if the Yardleys turned her off without a reference and traduced her character to any possible employers. The Ariadne Yardleys of the world were responsible for ruining many careers.

Mr. Yardley thundered downstairs in his usual manner. "What's this I hear?" He had a habit of talking and moving at the same time. He rarely sat down before he burst into speech. "I have heard two conflicting stories from my daughters and would like to hear your version."

Suddenly, Helena was weary. Weary of everything. Weary of worrying about her brother; weary of Ariadne Yardley; weary of trying to steer Mrs. Yardley away from social faux pas. She really didn't care anymore. Even if he asked her to stay, she would visit the agency to see about another job. Enough.

"I don't think my version will vary from your daughter's, sir."

"Ah, but which daughter? Did you really *insult* Ariadne? And you flirted with an eligible man who had been talking to her and forced your attentions on him? My goodness, Miss Marshfield, you *have* had a busy morning." His eyes twinkled.

She smiled wanly. "It was not like that at all. But I suppose I did insult her."

"Hmm. All this can easily be overcome by an apology. And then we can all forget it."

Forget it? Ariadne would bring this up time and time again. She would have no compunction in telling all her friends how her companion had been forced to apologize to her. She would dine out on that tidbit for weeks.

Her heart promising to gallop from her chest to her throat, Helena raised her chin. "No, Mr. Yardley. I don't think I shall do that. I have borne many insults from Ariadne over the past two years, and she has never once apologized. I cannot therefore bring myself to apologize to *her* for merely one incidence of rudeness on my part. I think it would be best if I remain in my position only until you find another companion. Unless you prefer me to leave immediately," she added. She was fairly sure he wouldn't want her to do that. As Stalley had said, her place in the household was a responsible one.

****

Josh Yardley was not surprised at her refusal to apologize. She was a proud woman, for she had little left in the world except her pride. And he knew darned well that his little Ariadne was remarkably hot at hand. He would have to work quickly here. He was surprised at Miss Marshfield's vehemence. Most uncharacteristic. He peered closely at her. She was neat as a pin as usual but there were dark rings under her eyes, and she seemed to lack her normal vitality. Fretting about her brother, no doubt. She must have read the papers and seen that his regiment had been engaged in the retreat on Corunna.

When he had first approached Miss Marshfield at Miss Fichton's Academy for Young Ladies where Ariadne and Caroline had been boarding, he had been prompted by the enthusiasm of his daughters for their favorite tutor. But she had rejected his offer of private employment on the grounds of loyalty to Miss Fichton. He had been much struck by Helena Marshfield's cool elegance and her loyalty to her employer, and had set out in his usual way to garner as much information as possible about her. What he had found out had satisfied him greatly. This particular young woman would give his daughters the town polish that he and his wife could not.

He was sorry that her circumstances had forced her into the life of a governess, but he was pragmatic. He intended to profit from her misfortune. Nobody amongst his acquaintance had such a well-born young woman as a governess.

He knew she worried about her brother, which was not to be wondered at, as she had no other family. He was aware that Helena scanned all available newspapers for army news, and the latest news was very bad. He was himself extremely interested in the war news. He had a vested interest in the outcome of the Peninsular campaigns. He could not help but think that Miss Marshfield's unusual conduct was the result of hours of worry about her brother.

"I did not expect *you* to apologize to Ariadne. From Caroline's description of the incident, the boot is on the other foot. The apology should come from Ariadne." He hoped she believed him. As a face-saving trick it lacked subtlety, but he had to move quickly. He had not expected her to seriously consider leaving their household.

She stared blankly at him.

"Ariadne is presently penning an apology to you. It may not cover *all* incidences of her bad behavior over the past two years, but as many as Ariadne considers to be 'bad'." His eyes twinkled again. "Mrs. Yardley and I are well aware that you have done wonders for our daughters, Miss Marshfield. As well as that, you have the ordering of the household. We have no intention of letting you leave our employ."

****

She looked up. He had made it sound almost like a threat, and his face was shuttered. "Furthermore, I wish to talk to you about Caroline's coming-out."

Poor Caroline. She was sweet and shy and something of a bluestocking, all traits that Helena had fostered to a degree as the question of Caroline's coming-out was to have been deferred until the following year. But Helena was afraid that the influence of an empty-headed mother and a vain older sister would gradually erode that bright intelligence and replace it with a fashionable passion for à la modality and nothing else. God knows Mrs. Yardley and Ariadne had scarcely any thought in their heads apart from morning visits and clothes, and it had been extremely difficult during the past twelvemonth for Helena to focus Ariadne on anything except folderols.

It was "Helena, don't you think this dimity is absolutely divine?" from Ariadne, or, "Miss Marshfield, may I see you for a moment? What do you think of this villager bonnet in La Belle Assemblée?"

from Mrs. Yardley.

Was Caroline now to be dragged into that milieu?

"I know you do not feel that Caroline is ready yet, Miss Marshfield. But I am aware that my daughters will need all the polish they can get in order to make good marriages even though my money will gild the lily." His acerbic tone made Helena's lips twitch. "I'd like them to enter the shoals of the social whirl as soon as possible to gain experience and polish before they attach themselves in marriage. There are some charming but impecunious and untrustworthy men in town at present, and I want Ariadne and Caroline to be able to make shrewd judgments. *That* can only come from experience."

"You intend to let them choose for themselves, sir?"

"I should prefer it if I could guide them but not coerce them."

"Your daughters are very fortunate, sir."

"Then we are in concert." Josh Yardley just had to have the last word. No, Helena thought rebelliously, they were *not* in concert. She thought that Ariadne had been brought out at least two years too soon; her lack of maturity proved that, and now they were doing the same thing to Caroline. Fortunately they could trust Caroline's intelligence, and Helena was determined to guide Caroline much more firmly than she had Ariadne. Ariadne had spent most of her time with her mother since her coming-out.

Presuming that her interview with Mr. Yardley was at an end, Helena dipped a curtsey.

"Have you had any correspondence from Sir Robert recently, Miss Marshfield?"

She paused. "No. I have heard nothing for three months. I am extremely worried."

Josh Yardley still persisted in calling her brother Sir Robert. It was an empty, useless title but the Yardleys adored titles.

"Shall I make some inquiries of my own?"

Helena's spirits lifted. "Thank you, sir," she said with real gratitude.

"Now I believe Ariadne wishes to speak to you upstairs." He bowed his head over some work on his desk, and she was dismissed.

As Helena climbed the two flights of stairs up to her room she wondered if amongst all the polite platitudes she had heard an unspoken plea from Mr. Yardley. Well, she would stay a little longer, but if Ariadne's jibes became unbearable, she would move on before her self-respect lay completely in tatters.

On reaching her room she discovered that there was, as yet, no penned apology from Ariadne. She *might* still be writing it. Her penmanship was not speedy. But Helena did not really expect to receive an apology from the young woman. In the three years she had known Ariadne, she had never heard her apologize to anyone for anything, not even at Miss Fichton's Academy. No doubt Ariadne had pretended to begin writing an apology and had screwed it up the minute her father was out of sight.

Helena sighed and threw herself down on her bed. What *fun* the Season was going to be! It had only just begun, and already she did not see how it could possibly get any worse.

Chapter Two

In Eaton Square the two Stafford brothers sat down to luncheon.

"Ned, do you remember the Marshfields?"

"Of course. Robert is the best of fellows. We were at Magdalen together. His father shot himself in public—well, practically—in one of the writing-rooms at Whites, actually. Horrendous business. Gambling debts, I believe. I doubt there was anything left for Robert. Daresay the family is all to pieces."

And he had gone on to say that he would like to meet up with Robert again but that he had heard nothing from Robert since he had joined the army. "Why do you ask?"

"There is a Miss Marshfield who has apparently been governessing the Yardley girls. I presume it is the same family."

"That would be Ellie or…"

"Helena."

"That's right. Robert used to call her Ellie. Poor woman. How long has she been with the Yardleys?"

"No idea. I've only just met her. She spends most of her time with the younger daughter."

"Hmm. I know you and Josh Yardley do business together, Ivor, but I have to say I sincerely pity Miss Marshfield. From a pleasant country seat at Oxford with a house in town, to chaperoning the Yardley chits.

Ghastly. The Marshfields had an excellent estate you know. Marshfield invited a group of us there at half-term break once. Don't remember meeting Miss Marshfield though. She may have been in town."

"I'd think you would remember her if you met her."

Ned looked quickly at his brother. "Really?" He selected some more slices of roast beef. "If you see Miss Marshfield again, ask her how Robert is, would you?"

"I'm sure I shall be seeing her again."

Ned hesitated. "This is a bit awkward Ivor but… just remember that she's the sister of a friend of mine. I realize that recently you haven't lived up to your er… past reputation, but I should think a woman in her position would be fair game." He shook his head. "Wouldn't like to see it."

"Is that what you think I'd do? Give her a slip on the shoulder?" Ivor felt as though Ned had punched him.

Ned persevered. "No idea what you'd do. As I said, you've changed."

Ivor reflected grimly that Ned was quite correct. Three or four years ago he would have had no compunction in sounding out Helena Marshfield to see how far their relationship might progress. Had the attraction been mutual he might have set up the governess as his latest flirt. Ingénues had never been his style, but the elegant governess with the unusual eyes was exactly the sort of young woman he had once pursued. Both of them would have known the ropes, of course. She looked to be past her first prayers, and he had never believed in leading on innocent young

25

women.

But deep down he knew he was maligning her. It was true that she held herself with a ladylike assurance, but that was belied by the innocence and uncertainty in those purple-gray eyes. He had *never*, to his knowledge, seduced an innocent.

All the same, he wondered if she had any idea what a complex mix of signals she had given him.

No, he was certain she was innocent. And therefore he must, as Ned had said, leave her alone. He knew how to deal with experienced women. And there abounded in the *ton* some very experienced women who had selected him from amongst those youths leaving the hallowed halls of Cambridge, and who had taken it upon themselves to complete his education.

Ned changed the subject. "I say, Ivor, did you hear about Dalrymple?"

"No. I don't get about town as much as you do."

"That's true. I say, Ivor, why…? Never mind." He continued with his *on dit*. "Well, it appears young Dalrymple is enamored of one of this year's crop of delectable débutantes. Unfortunately, before pursuing her, he did not check to see if his feelings were reciprocated. Apparently at the Marchington soirée he seated himself beside her, and the next thing everyone heard was her piercing voice shrilling, '*Please,* Lord Dalrymple. Remove your hand or I shall call Papa.'"

Ivor snickered. "Poor devil, to have made a fool of himself over a witless seventeen-year-old. What happened after that?"

"He left the soirée abruptly with a red face and has gone back to his country seat. I daresay we shall not see him again until next Season."

"What happened to the young woman?"

"Nothing. We've all been steering clear of her. I can attest to the fact that Miss Trevor certainly has a penetrating voice. I danced the boulanger with her last month at…oh…I forget where…and she carried on a loud conversation even when we were separated by the turns. Unnerving. Her mother should have a word to her."

Ivor grimaced. "Thank God I've chosen to leave all that behind me. More to the point, I'm glad I'm not an earl or some such. Poor old Tolly told me that this Season he has employed a smoke screen by hinting he is interested in an unspecified woman who is rarely in town. Even then he is still besieged."

"God, yes. Even I, a mere second son of a baronet, have had to be downright rude in order to avoid ambitious mamas."

"At least most of the mothers have respectability on their side. The young matrons, on the other hand, are worse than the veriest trollop."

Ned shook his head. "Well, they are safe if they get pregnant, so they throw out lures to all and sundry and pass off the offspring as their husband's."

"Hmm." Ivor reflected on the knowing looks and clever hands of the married women who had been willing to service his needs. Gradually he had become contemptuous of their easy virtue. Perhaps as he neared the time when it became necessary to take a wife for himself, he shrank from finding himself a cuckold.

He had *never* under any circumstances lain with the wife of one of his close friends, yet he knew many who could only achieve sexual satisfaction with the added *frisson* of knowing how close to the line they stepped. He had a sense of honor that decreed he could not call 'friend' the husband of one of his lovers. But just as important to him was his intention never to raise false hope in an innocent débutante's bosom.

At least the embarrassed Dalrymple was not in Ivor's shoes. He did not have a sword of Damocles hovering over his head, determining his every move. Ivor gave a mental shrug. Now that he had succeeded to his father's shoes just in time to avert the family fortunes from a fate precisely like that of the Marshfield family, his interests lay in keeping his estates entire. His days of wine and roses were far behind him now and would have been curtailed earlier had his profligate father taken him into his confidence. Now Ivor had responsibilities in the shape of his mother, brother and two sisters, not to mention Stafford Place itself. As soon as he discovered just how deep his father had dipped into the family coffers to keep his ruinous drinking and gambling fever fed, Ivor had eschewed as much as possible both those fashionable occupations. Concerned that he may have inherited a tendency toward profligacy, he became more temperate in his lifestyle. He now indulged only in the occasional minor bet at Whites so as not to draw attention to the change in his circumstances.

He could still hear their solicitor's unctuous tones. "I regret to tell you, Sir Ivor, how time and time again I warned Sir Theo that he was overdrawing the budget, but..." and he had shrugged negligently. Ivor had quickly realized that the solicitor did not give a damn, nor did he expect the son to be any better than the father.

Their steward had been browbeaten to the point of

despair. "I am sorry, Sir Ivor. Over the past couple of years, no matter what I did, your father remained uninterested in the estate." Ivor was forced to conclude that his father had knowingly run the estate into the ground, leaving the pieces for him to pick up. Stafford had been an unloving, distant father, but their mother had adored him, so Ivor had held his tongue and begun the uphill struggle to restore his inheritance to the prosperity he remembered from his grandfather's day. So far, so good.

He knew damn well that his contemporaries had commented that he was no longer to be found at his old haunts, and they had shaken their heads in puzzlement. It amused him. Did they not realize it would happen to some of them?

Matchmaking mamas suddenly approved of him. Polite Society saw that yet another young man, on succeeding to his heritage, had set aside youthful excesses and settled down to get his estates in order. Ivor, however, had disappointed those matchmakers by ignoring the charms of their daughters and grand-daughters. They could present him with all the young women they liked, but he was too damned busy to worry about paying court to some sweet young thing who demanded all his time and who would probably bore him to boot. Yes, he knew everyone thought he should beget himself an heir. Well, he had time enough to spare and frankly, none of the young ladies straight out of the schoolroom had caught his eye.

His tastes had always run to older women, but of course what one chose for one's paramours was *not* the sort of woman one chose as a marriage partner. No, Ivor would continue to hold his cards tight to his chest.

Let them think he was too nice in his sensibilities. He had responsibilities way beyond the claiming of a wife.

For the past three years he had been struggling to restore the Norwich estate to its former glory to ensure that his mother and siblings would never realize how close they'd come to penury. The Staffords were no longer as close to debtors' prison as they had been, but he still needed to be careful—exceptionally careful.

He smiled grimly to himself. Had some of the matchmaking Mamas who had tried to foist their daughters on him known the true state of the family fortunes they would have been less pressing. And he certainly did not need a demanding spendthrift for a wife. As far as he could see, most of the last few years' débutantes came into that category. Heaven only knew what this spring's lot was like. He recalled Ariadne Yardley and rolled his eyes.

****

Ned watched his brother and wondered. He felt helpless to understand why, since taking over the reins on their father's death, Ivor had changed so dramatically. His large group of friends had dwindled to a select few. He seemed to find little joy in the sporting pursuits and round of social entertainments that had once been his whole life. He took far more interest in their lands and investments than Theo Stafford ever had, and though Ned was not as much the countryman as his brother, he knew that their lands had never been in better heart. What drove Ivor? He was as close as an oyster. Ned had tried once or twice to winkle out of his brother the reason for his abrupt change of lifestyle but to no avail. Ivor had seemed to be amused, as if he were dealing with a playful puppy, which had irritated Ned vastly. When Ned had persisted, Ivor had become implacable. "There's nothing for you to worry about, Ned. Just enjoy yourself. The Stafford holdings are my responsibility."

And Ned had been firmly excluded. But with no real interest in the estate at Norwich and having been on the town for several years and finding the endless round of pleasure becoming tedious, Ned knew he needed an occupation. He had no inclination to join the army, or to take orders. In short, he did not wish to be beholden to his brother, but he was not trained for anything of any consequence. However, he had done well at Cambridge, if he said so himself. Latin and mathematics had been his favorite subjects, and one of his tutors had once mentioned that he would make a fine physician. He had therefore turned more to scientific studies rather than the classical topics he had previously undertaken.

He sought now for words to explain himself to his brother. "Ivor?"

"Hmm?"

"I had thought I might take the Licensing Exam at the Royal College."

"Ned!"

"Is that a 'Ned' of surprise or a 'Ned' of horror?"

"Surprise, I assure you. Are you tired of being a man about town?"

"Very much so. As we have just been saying, evading the jaws of matrimony and the endless repetition of the entertainments has begun to pall. There is no *purpose* to anything. And it was suggested to me once that…well, I think it might suit me to be a physician. What do you think?"

"It is not for me to think, Ned. It is *your* future."

31

"Yes, but Ivor, you're the head of the family. Oh, you know what I mean." Ned gave up, laughing. "It sounds so stuffy to call you the 'head of the family' as if you were fifty or sixty."

"Thank you, brother." Ivor grinned. "Seriously, Ned, I am honored that you confided in me. Are you certain about this?"

"Yes."

"Then you have my congratulations." Ivor stood and came around the table to his brother. "I am proud of you, Ned. It is an important decision."

Ned flushed. "And once I go into practice, I shan't be a cost upon you anymore."

"Surely you are not doing this merely to gain an independence?"

"Of course not. To have an occupation, unfashionable as it may be, suits us both. We Staffords are not made to be idle. And you must admit that one less responsibility will make your life easier."

Ivor placed his hand on his brother's shoulder. "I must know, Ned. Do you *sincerely* wish to do this?"

"Yes," Ned said simply.

"Excellent! When will you take the entrance exam?"

"I can take it next week if I wish, or leave it till June for the next intake."

They began discussing the future in earnest, and for the first time in four years Ivor felt that the sword of Damocles hanging over his head was lifting. It might have been better to discuss the future with Ned a couple of years ago. He needed an ally within the family. "Ryewolds is almost free of encumbrances," he explained, "and two of the five farms including the home farm yielded their highest ever this past autumn. Replanting is already under way."

Ned was not particularly interested in that aspect of his heritage, but he was worried about his sisters. "Is there any money put by for settlements for the girls?"

"Yes. Not as much as I'd hoped but…"

"Our father was as careless of his family as he was with money," Ned burst out. "You must have had a dreadful time of it, Ivor. I've often wondered how you managed."

"It could be worse. Nerida has already been brought out and there's a small dowry available for her, thanks to Mama's marriage settlement. It was tied up for her daughters, and Father couldn't touch it. By the time Erica is ready to be brought out, there'll be sufficient in the coffers for that, too."

Thank God for Mama's marriage settlement. There was a mortgage on the townhouse, but there was scarcely a townhouse which wasn't mortgaged. Best of all, a minor investment which he had tentatively taken up last spring had succeeded beyond his wildest dreams. Unlike his father he was not a natural gambler, so his cautious nature had prevented him from investing as much as he might have. Importing goods was a notoriously dicey way of making money. But the shipload of tea he had invested in had not foundered, nor had the tea moldered as had happened to so many other shipments. The English had an undying thirst for tea, for which he was grateful.

And now Ned might one day be in a position to reduce his expenses even further. Naturally he would still make Ned an allowance of some sort or other; that went without saying. But for the first time since their father had died, Ivor felt he could breathe freely again.

Soon he might be able to find the time to do more work for the Committee, to contribute his mite to the war. He burned to come out of the shadows of the half-life he had been living, not to rejoin the amusements of the *ton* but to make a difference in the war effort, and to live a less secretive existence.

He had thought to give himself another year before he could afford to relax. But maybe six months might do it... Involuntarily his hand clenched, and he inhaled sharply. Light at the end of the tunnel.

Chapter Three

The gentleman was dressed from head to foot in black. The only exception was a carelessly tied cravat at which he tugged from time to time as if it bothered him. His feet were propped on a leather footstool as he lounged in an armchair with crude abandon. His housekeeper drew in a breath as she placed before him a decanter of brandy. He sneered at the woman. "Where is Hopkins?"

"In bed, my lord. 'Tis past three o'clock in the morning, and Hopkins is an old man."

"Curse all old men. But I'd rather have him than your Friday face around me. Get him out of bed. I have need of him."

****

Josh Yardley was as good as his word. He made inquiries at the Horse Guards regarding one Robert Marshfield, and wished he hadn't.

"His company was in the thick of it at Astorga. It sounds as though Marshfield was wounded at Lugo on the retreat to Corunna. Paget's division had the job of fighting a rearguard action including blowing up bridges. There's no record of what happened to Marshfield after that. He probably made it to Corunna because he was aide de camp to General Edward Paget, and the General looks after his staff. But where he is now, we have no idea." Ned Yardley's contact at the

Horse Guards was a pragmatic man and not given to hyperbole. If Robert Marshfield could not be found, he could not be found. Josh Yardley dreaded reporting this to Miss Marshfield.

But when he reached home there was a surprise awaiting him. Miss Marshfield had apparently received a letter from General Edward Paget himself, so his wife informed him. Ned Yardley decided he would not go out to any of his clubs that evening; he joined his ladies for dinner in order to find out more about the mysterious letter.

But he was doomed to disappointment. Miss Marshfield did not appear for dinner at the usual time and did not send down an apology. When dinner had been twice deferred, Caroline was deputized to hurry upstairs and knock on the door of Miss Marshfield's bedchamber to inquire if all was well. To Caroline's consternation she heard muffled sobbing coming from within.

"Miss Marshfield! May I come in?"

No answer.

Pushing open the door, Caroline found Helena face down on the bed, desperately trying to stifle her sobs with a pillow. Caroline was horrified. She had never once seen her efficient, collected governess in such a state.

"Miss Marshfield! Oh no…is your brother…? I mean…dear Miss Marshfield, *tell* me."

Helena struggled to control herself. She sat up. "No, Caroline. Not dead. But the poor boy may well wish he were. He was badly wounded on the retreat to Corunna. It is his kind general, Sir Henry Paget, who writes to me. Not Robert himself. So I can only deduce how ill poor Robert must be. Here, read it for yourself."

"Oh no, pray…'tis your letter Miss Marshfield. I could not."

"Please, Caroline…I cannot think clearly at present."

Deeply concerned, Caroline took the letter and quickly scanned it. "*Poor* Sir Robert," she whispered. "The shoulder *and* the leg." She raised her head. "It says he is returning. Where will he recuperate?"

"When the letter was written, the wounded were waiting to evacuate. I don't know when he will arrive, and I don't know what we shall do. I cannot think of anywhere he could recuperate. Perhaps when my mind clears I will be able to come up with a solution. Would you make my apologies to your parents, Caroline?" Her face twisted. "I could not possibly eat anything at this moment."

Caroline laid a gentle hand on Helena's arm. "No, of course not."

But Caroline had Betsy bring up some tea and bread and butter just the same.

Mr. Yardley, as soon as the news was told him, bade Betsy take a glass of brandy to Miss Marshfield, saying that would be more acceptable.

****

Helena sipped the brandy gingerly. It had finally come. The letter she had been dreading for the past year. She picked up the general's letter again. How she missed her brother. They had always been very close, she and Robert. Twenty months ago he had unexpectedly come to see her at Bath, where she taught the senior classes at Miss Fichton's Academy for Young Ladies. He had not seen her for many months and was concerned that she seemed to feel no joy in life—that she had no expectations of a happy future.

"Dear Ellie, the army life suits me well. But I am not convinced that teaching is your *forté*. You seem depressed."

"No, Robert. It is just that I have the cold. Miss Fichton is very kind to me. Now tell me all your news." And that way she had managed to fob him off. In spite of his regular letters, she hardly knew him from the boy she had farewelled as she left for Miss Fichton's Academy. He had then been bowed down by the weight of their father's deception. He was now upright, strong and self-possessed whereas she felt diminished in stature and had lost her self-confidence. She was proud of Robert. His unexpected advent at the Fichton Academy had evinced sighs and murmurs of approval from a handful of young ladies who had the good fortune to see him as he strode in his striking red uniform down the hallway to Miss Fichton's drawing-room.

Helena had been well aware of the titters and giggles emanating from the corridor, but to her he was just Robert, her big brother. She did not see him as the answer to a maiden's prayer. But for several weeks after his visit she was amazingly popular with her charges.

She had made it easy for him because she knew his visit could mean only one thing. "Have you come to say that you are off adventuring overseas?"

She instilled enthusiasm where there was none. She knew that his regiment would be sent to Portugal to assist in the routing of the enemy, Bonaparte.

"We sail next week, Ellie. I am to be aide de camp

to Sir Henry Paget. I trust I shall distinguish myself."

"Of *course* you will, Robert." Helena was quite sure he would acquit himself favorably. And every day since, she had watched and waited, fearful of receiving a letter like the one she held in her hand.

She composed herself and went downstairs to thank the Yardleys for their kind thoughts. She attempted a smile although she could feel it wavering. "Thank you, Mr. Yardley. There are not many employers who would care about the sensibilities of a governess, sir."

"Tosh, Miss Marshfield. You are well aware we regard you more in the light of a friend than a governess. When we persuaded you to leave Miss Fichton's Academy we saw you as a positive influence over our daughters. Now, I am firm in my resolve that Sir Robert must recuperate with us, isn't that so, my dear?"

Mrs. Yardley was equally effusive.

Preparing to disclaim, Helena hesitated when she realized that not only regard for their plight ruled the Yardleys' feelings. Mr. Yardley was positively avuncular with the prospect of entertaining 'Sir Robert' in his household. It was churlish to point out that Robert's title was no longer of use without any estates or holdings to sustain it. And more to the point, Robert's wounds could well be of a long-lasting nature. Even the most indulgent employer would tire of endless philanthropy involving a relative of one of his employees.

But she would know more when Robert arrived. They would just have to deal with any setbacks as best they could. They had coped with horribly disheartening difficulties after their father's death. No doubt they would manage again this time. There was a good prospect that Robert could sell out and they could invest the proceeds. It might be possible to subsist on the income from that for a short time. Perhaps. It took all her resolve to maintain a tranquil façade.

The topic of conversation in the drawing-room changed to discussing plans for Caroline's dress-party. Unlike Ariadne, Caroline was not excited at the prospect of attending her own coming-out party. The Yardleys' townhouse boasted a small ballroom, and although his daughters were not of the *haut ton,* Mr. Yardley felt he could "show the world a thing or two when it came to entertaining."

Caroline cringed. "Oh, Papa! Need we invite such a large number of people? Why not just a few close friends?"

"Now, my dear, we will invite just as many as will fit in the house and then some. We must not be seen to be ungenerous. Remember, the more people we invite, the more chances you and Ariadne have of making useful acquaintances."

Helena flinched slightly at his use of the word "useful." Of course he was no more at fault than his social superiors—those members of the *ton* whom he sought to emulate. Usefulness was often their prime motivation for cultivating certain acquaintances. Helena didn't know which was worse—Mr. Yardley's attitude or the attitudes of the *ton* whose morés she had long left behind. She knew who she'd far rather deal with however. Mr. Yardley's pound dealing was preferable to the unctuous mannerisms of some of her erstwhile friends.

Poor Caroline dreaded meeting so many people all at once. But she was overridden, as had been many a young lady in similar circumstances.

"Caroline!" her mother expostulated. "We must have all your papa's particular friends and Ariadne's new friends she has made since her coming-out. We could not possibly have 'just a few friends' to celebrate your coming-out."

Caroline shrank back in her seat. She pinned a nervous smile on her face. Helena sympathized and thought that they might just as well put poor Caroline on a block at the meat market and have done. At least in Helena's own circumstances her father had had the taste to leave all the details to his socially polished sister.

"Just enjoy your first Season, my dear. There's no need to make any lasting commitments," he had advised her at the outset. "Of course, if you meet someone you are sure you cannot possibly live without..." and he had laughed at her, twitting her affectionately in the way he often did. Had she known what was in store for her future, she might have behaved differently. Perhaps she would have seen marriage as a career as most young women did, rather than merely an alternative to a pleasant spinsterhood in her father's home.

Her father's advice and her own natural reticence were responsible for her present circumstances. She had whistled two perfectly respectable suitors down the wind. Now when she thought of those two suitors, although she could not possibly imagine herself married to either of them, she still felt betrayed by her father. Had he been more honest about their circumstances she would have behaved less light-heartedly.

Helena smothered a smile as she thought of herself as Mrs. Bonhaven. Her most ardent suitor had gone by the unfortunate name of Beresford Bonhaven. He had been a kind youth with, unfortunately, nothing except his kindness to recommend him. Robert and several of his friends had twitted her mercilessly about her tongue-tied, extremely overweight suitor, saying that she would certainly find a very *big* 'haven' in his arms. Out of pity for him she had not dissuaded him as strongly as she might have. It had taken a frosty set-down from her aunt to finally dampen his ardor, and although Helena regretted the manner in which it was done, she was grateful not to have ended up as Mrs. Beresford Bonhaven.

Her father's sister had, as a matter of fact, routed nearly all the gentlemen who had shown the slightest interest in Helena. She presumed her father had told his sister the same thing he'd told Helena—that she need not make any major decisions in her first Season. But every now and again Helena wondered if perhaps her father had planned a very different future for her and that he had instructed his sister to warn off any serious suitors. For when Giles Foxhyth, third Lord Elverton had visited Marshfield Manor, her father had gone to considerable trouble to leave them alone together, not something a loving father would normally do. She suspected that he wished her to see Lord Elverton in the light of a suitor, but Helena had been terrified of Elverton. He purposely brushed up against her as he walked past, rather like an offensive tomcat. Or he would take her hand to greet her, then retain a firm grasp so she could not free herself. The more she struggled, the tighter he held her, grinning all the while.

She had learned not to struggle, just to let her hand lie quiescent in his, fighting to quell the shudders that rippled down her spine. His behavior indicated that Elverton was a cruel man to whom it was best not so show any fear, in order to discourage his predatory instincts. He affected to dress always in black and often behaved in a very uncivil manner. Sometimes he had ignored her father completely. One moment Helena suspected that he held some sort of power over her father, and the next moment she decided that she was too fanciful. Sometimes Elverton and Papa had discussed the war results amicably, then the next minute Elverton would rant about how England didn't understand what Bonaparte was trying to achieve. Elverton's mother was French, and the man had spent several years being educated in France until his English father had requested his presence at their country seat. Elverton had said with a sneer, "Father wished me to learn how to behave liked a 'civilized' Englishman. Pah!"

Robert had been away most of the time and had no idea of the many shifts she had been put to in order to avoid Lord Elverton. When Foxhyth entered a room she left it on the pretext of "checking with Cook about the meals" or "to see the gardener about the flowers." She had rarely used the same excuse twice, so she did not think he was suspicious. But he said acidly to her one day, "Such a *busy* little lady as you are, Miss Marshfield. Never still."

She had quickly responded, "I *hate* to be still, sir. All my friends will tell you so." With a convincing laugh she had made her escape, but after that she found it more difficult to elude him. He had redoubled his efforts to accost her till she asked her father outright if he had given his permission for Elverton to court her. Her father had hemmed and hawed and finally said, "If you do not wish it, my dear, then it shall not be so."

"Father, he frightens me. He treats the Manor as if he owns it. He neglects to have himself announced by Peebles, and I unexpectedly find him all over the house. Yesterday he was in the conservatory. Today I found him looking up the stairs to the maids' quarters. *Please* don't make me stay here whilst he is visiting. May I go back to town to be with Aunt Tinsley?"

Her father had finally realized the force of her fear and after that Elverton had disappeared for a while.

But just before Robert joined the army, long after all their father's debts had been cleared up, she came upon a promissory note in the shape of a carelessly penned message stuffed into a drawer in her father's escritoire. It was written in such an obscure fashion that its meaning was unclear. Neither Robert nor their steward understood the details of the debt. It was a vowel scrawled on a scrap of notepaper and said, "We two only are cognizant of the details of this debt. Value decided. To be collected at will." The only signature was an indecipherable letter, presumably an initial. It could be an E, or possibly a G. It looked as if it had been scribbled hastily in a gaming hell. The penmanship was not that of John Marshfield.

"Don't worry about it," Robert had advised his sister. "It is indecipherable, and the writer has not approached us so…" He had shrugged, and their steward had agreed.

But that unclaimed debt kept Helena awake at nights. She had her suspicions. There were many nights in her little sanctuary above-stairs when she found it necessary to count the proverbial sheep. She was almost certain that a deal had been struck between her father and Lord Elverton and that she had been the bargaining chip. But something must have gone wrong.

Now, in a deep bond of fellow feeling with Caroline, also to be a sacrifice to parental ambition, she ventured to intervene. "Perhaps sir, a smaller gathering might assist Caroline to become used to—"

But Mr. Yardley knew what was due his daughters. "No, Miss Marshfield. If my girls don't catch good husbands, it will not be for want of effort on my part. I trust I am a good father?"

"Of *course* you are, sir. I have said often that your daughters are very fortunate." Helena hastily soothed his ruffled feathers for Mr. Yardley undoubtedly had his daughters' best interests at heart. Indeed, unlike many members of the *ton* who had titles to consider, never once had Helena seen Josh Yardley express a wish to have had sons instead.

Ariadne was unimpressed to hear that Caroline's coming-out dress-party would take place earlier than originally planned. "But I have only had one Season! 'Tis *unfair*! Caroline is only seventeen. She can wait another year, can't she, Mama?" Ariadne's lovely voice held a distinct whine.

Miss Marshfield felt rather like whining herself. Struggling to exert a semblance of quality on the Yardley household whilst keeping various warring factions apart—Poppy the Cook and Stalley the butler were constantly at loggerheads—Caroline's dress-party was an added responsibility. She, too, felt that this event could well wait a twelvemonth.

Caroline, seeking to smooth troubled waters, hastily intervened. "Yes, Papa. Ariadne is right. I can delay my coming-out. Truly, I am not sure how to behave just yet. I have to rely on Miss Marshfield."

"No, my dear. Your mama and I have decided." So that was that.

Ariadne, unable for once to twist her parents around her little finger, knew when she was beaten. With insufferable condescension she informed Caroline, "I shall guide you. After the initial greeting of the guests and the first dance with Papa, you may then do as you wish."

"Now, my pet," Mrs. Yardley hastily interrupted. "Miss Marshfield will see to it that Caroline understands her obligations."

"Yes, young lady," Mr. Yardley agreed. "We'll concede to Miss Marshfield on all matters of social usage."

A pouting session looked imminent, and Helena hastened to divert attention. "That's settled then. Now who would like a game of lottery tickets?"

Mrs. Yardley nodded in approval, and the ladies became engrossed in their game whilst Mr. Yardley sat quietly by the fire, watching them. Helena's concentration was fractured. She was easily beaten by both Caroline and Ariadne and even once by Mrs. Yardley. Her brother was foremost in her thoughts. She was anxious to get to her room to re-read her letter. When Caroline began to look tired, Helena was finally able to excuse them both. Lord, she could not endure another hour of the Yardleys *en famille*. Even Caroline's wistful sympathy grated, for she was one to lick her wounds alone.

In her room she re-read the General's letter, trying to read between the lines. Just how ill was her brother? Would it be possible for him to take up some genteel occupation in the future?

Oh, how she resented Papa! Thanks to him she was forced to live a featureless, cloistered existence, and now poor Robert was severely injured. Damn their irresponsible father for consigning Robert and herself to the membership of an overcrowded, penniless, minor aristocracy.

They had had such a wonderful childhood. Their father had denied them nothing. Perhaps it might have been better had he done so. It would at least have prepared them for the difficult times ahead.

On her father's death, Helena had been heartlessly deserted and crushed underfoot by people she had considered to be her friends and acquaintances. She particularly remembered the measured, sarcastic tones of Lord Elverton. "Perhaps now you will learn to behave with the humility that befits one of your station."

How his tone had smarted! For months he had treated Marshfield Manor as if he owned it, yet suddenly he had turned on her, vindictive and haughty, so sure of his own worth and so scathing about her lineage. She was thankful that Robert had not heard *that* conversation.

She should not cling to the past. She knew that. It was a form of self-indulgence. Yet her father's betrayal was the one shattering incident that had shaped her life for the past few years. She well knew the ways of the *ton*. She knew that they latched on to tidbits of news such as the misfortune of others with the tenacity of bulldogs. Many of them had very little to do except discuss each other. They fed on any piece of juicy gossip they could unearth.

But more important than the shame she bore, she missed her brother. Fortunately, both she and Robert were assiduous letter writers. His letters, penned amidst the noise and dirt of war, were redolent of the warmth of the Iberian Peninsula. In his last letter he had written, *"You would love the countryside here, Ellie. Vast tracts of arable but empty land broken only by cork trees. And the people! They have had a terrible time, but they still have their stiff-necked pride. Far more prideful than any Englishman. The French swept through, appropriating food, stealing horses and, well...you can guess the rest. And that has not encouraged them to trust anyone, even their 'allies.' As a result, the Portuguese are not above betraying us. It is common for local bandits to sweep down from the hills and attack English and French alike."*

Robert had asked Helena to retain his letters so he could formulate a travel diary on his return. She had faithfully followed his instructions and wrapped his letters in a square of fine cambric. A few tears had been shed over the letters, and some of the ink was smudged.

She smiled now, thinking of Robert's cleverness with a pen. If it weren't for their father's mistakes, Robert might have held a position in the diplomatic corps. He had been fortunate to purchase a commission in General Edward Paget's cavalry division. She suspected some influence at work there, possibly from their uncle. Even when the aunt who had supervised her coming-out had shown no interest in the fate of her niece and nephew after their father's death, she suspected that her kind uncle-by-marriage had maintained a watching brief. Once, on her birthday, she had received a small parcel from him. He had made no pretense that her aunt had co-signed the pleasantries on the attached note. He was very much under the cow's thumb in that household.

She sighed. Thanks to their father, all of Robert's education, charm, and bright intelligence had been put to use parlaying instructions back and forth between the English and Portuguese armies in a hot country far away, pursuing the ever-acquisitive French.

She had shown Caroline one of Robert's letters, and Caroline was astounded at the penmanship. "One can almost see the horses and the mud!" she had cried. "You are so lucky to have a brother, Miss Marshfield."

But now Helena wondered whether she did indeed still have a brother. "Please, God," she prayed, "spare Robert."

Chapter Four

"What a dull afternoon!" The weather was behaving inconsistently as spring was wont to do, and Ariadne was disgruntled. The prospect of sitting with her family beside the fire held no appeal. It was too inclement to go for a walk and so far, no intrepid visitors had called.

Then Stalley, in his usual bland tone announced, "Sir Ivor Stafford."

It had an electrifying result. Mr. Yardley glanced up from his newspaper and tossed it aside. Caroline and Mrs. Yardley looked mildly polite. Ariadne squeaked and patted a wayward curl. Miss Marshfield, repairing a hem on one of Ariadne's flounces, blushed unaccountably.

"Show him in. Show him in," Mr. Yardley said impatiently. So instead of showing Sir Ivor to Mr. Yardley's study as usual, the butler brought him to the withdrawing-room. Helena signaled to Stalley to await her instructions. As she left the room, she met Sir Ivor in the doorway. He bowed slightly in Helena's direction. "We meet again, Miss Marshfield." Helena, her mind distracted by thoughts of refreshments suitable at four o'clock in the afternoon, smiled vaguely and bobbed a quick curtsy. It was to be hoped that Poppy the Cook was not in one of her disagreeable moods.

On her return to the withdrawing-room she was amused to hear Sir Ivor chaffing Ariadne on her summery attire. "Tell me, Miss Yardley, I hope you did not catch cold the other day?" he inquired solicitously.

"Oh, no, Sir Ivor! I am very healthy you know, and I never catch cold," Ariadne replied in a far from innocent tone.

Unfortunately, Mrs. Yardley promptly began rattling on in the same vein, pointing out to Sir Ivor Ariadne's obvious vitality making Ariadne sound like a brood mare. The conversation had definitely entered the realms of bad taste. Caroline wriggled in her seat, as embarrassed as Helena, and Sir Ivor turned to her politely. "And you, Miss Caroline, did you enjoy your walk?"

Miss Marshfield mentally blessed him for his good manners in both changing the subject and including Caroline in the conversation.

Caroline blushed but commented, "Miss Marshfield and I enjoy walking, although I prefer walking to a specific venue such as the library, rather than just strolling through the park."

"Yes. I saw you and Miss Marshfield at Hookham's recently, did I not?" He smiled. "You both looked very intent on your business."

Helena colored again, remembering that backward glance which Sir Ivor had returned. She dipped her head.

Mr. Yardley broke in. "These two are always filling their heads with that Italian and French stuff." He sounded very proud of them both, but also insinuated that he did not necessarily endorse education for females.

However, Sir Ivor appeared to be interested, or perhaps he was merely being polite. Turning to Helena where she was presiding over the tea tray he said, "That's interesting, Miss Marshfield. I would that my young sisters had the felicity of having such an informed governess. I believe they spent most of their time exasperating ours. My mother was firm about their devoting as much time as possible to studies, but I doubt they ever learned much beyond the pianoforte and a little poetry. Naturally they would tell you otherwise." He laughed, obviously very fond of his sisters just the same, and Helena liked him all the more for it.

"Where are your sisters at the moment, Sir Ivor?" Mrs. Yardley, never one to stand on ceremony, asked.

"They are at Ryewolds, in Norwich, with my mother. They are coming down for the Season in about two weeks. Nerida has just become engaged to the Honorable George Chiswick so they are in no hurry to leave Norwich. His father's lands lie adjacent to ours. So our Season this year will be busy. Incidentally, Miss Marshfield," he said turning to her, "I believe my young brother was up at Magdalen with your brother, Sir Robert. My brother is Ned Stafford," he added by way of explanation.

"Oh yes, of course! I remember Robert mentioning Ned and…Tally Wishart, was it not? It seems they were all particular friends." Helena hoped that here was one person who would be au fait with the Marshfield difficulties but perhaps not so critical of them.

"Hmm. I gather some of their exploits don't bear mentioning in mixed company."

Helena tried to keep smiling but the smile became

strained and mechanical as she turned away from him to hand around the tea things.

Mrs. Yardley interposed in the tones of one wanting to settle down to a good gossip, "Sir Ivor, isn't it dreadful about Miss Marshfield's brother?"

Ivor Stafford looked startled.

"Injured," Mr. Yardley explained succinctly.

"Miss Marshfield...I *do* apologize. I didn't know. Ned wondered how he was. We heard only that he had gone to the Peninsula."

She bent her head. "I heard from his commanding officer," she murmured. "Sir Henry has been very kind when you consider—"

"We've told Miss Marshfield that Captain Marshfield is most welcome to come to Yardley House to recuperate," Joshua Yardley interrupted. He had cut across Helena's conversation, but she had become quite used to that. However, as she had made no decisions about Robert's future—indeed that was up to Robert, not her—she was embarrassed. She did not wish to give Sir Ivor the impression that the Marshfields were going to make themselves at home at Yardley House in the manner of poor relations. She opened her mouth to object, then subsided. It was not at all the thing for her brother to come to her place of employment to recuperate. There were so many problems inherent in that idea! She had already resolved to say nothing further but keep her own counsel and await developments.

On the pretext of replacing his cup, Sir Ivor moved to her side. "Miss Marshfield, forgive me. I had no idea that your news was so recent. Not that it makes a lot of difference whether such news is recent or not. But I had no intention of distressing you."

She gazed up into the concerned gray eyes and said simply, "Thank you, sir. I shall rest easier when I have heard further about his condition. At the moment I am somewhat distracted."

"'Tis not to be wondered at. Have you any relatives where your brother may convalesce?" Helena noted that he, too, considered it unsuitable for Robert to convalesce at Yardley House.

"None who care to own themselves our relatives anymore," she answered bitterly.

There was a short silence.

"I see."

Ariadne felt she had been ignored for long enough. "Sir Ivor! Tell us what you think about Papa's proposal to purchase a country estate."

Considering Sir Ivor spent a good part of each year at his ancient, elegant family seat in Norfolk, and that Ariadne's idea of a country seat was of a faux baronial manor no more than twenty miles from Town so that she would not miss any of its entertainments, this debate was doomed to failure from the start. Caroline wisely chose not to enter the discussion, and when Helena's opinion was sought on what she thought constituted the ideal country seat she demurred, saying that both Sir Ivor's and Ariadne's opinions had their merits but that she did not feel qualified to proffer any fresh ideas. Predictably, Ariadne pouted.

Helena caught Sir Ivor's eye at that point and saw the lurking twinkle. "Very diplomatic," he murmured quietly, for her ears only. She dimpled and turned away.

"What did you want to discuss, Sir Ivor?" Mr. Yardley inquired.

Stafford rose to his feet again. "It's best discussed in your study, I think." The men left the withdrawing-room, and Helena and Mrs. Yardley had their hands full in coping with what Ariadne saw as Sir Ivor's defection. Had there been any other men in the room she would have had no hesitation in playing one off against the other, but there being no other amusements to hand, she had enjoyed being the center of Sir Ivor's attention.

"Not fair, Mama," she railed. "Why must Papa take Sir Ivor away whilst we were having such fun?"

"Hush child, 'tis business," Mrs. Yardley expostulated. Helena wondered idly, as she often had, what business Mr. Yardley and Ivor Stafford had in common.

Happily for them all, a messenger arrived with a card from Ariadne's particular friends, Anna and Charlotte Morris, begging her attendance at a hastily contrived early turtle dinner followed by a get-together of young people to be chaperoned by Mr. and Mrs. Morris themselves. Mrs. Yardley had no hesitation in approving this scheme because, as she confided to Helena, "I am finding her a proper trial lately, Miss Marshfield, as I'm sure you are too. I'll be glad of a comfortable coze by the fire, and we can discuss your plans for your brother and plan some of Caro's dress-party in peace, without Ariadne's interruptions."

Helena would far rather have retired to her room to be alone with thoughts of her brother. But her duties came first. Fortunately during her coming-out year she had perfected the art of appearing to listen attentively to aimless social discourse whilst thinking her own thoughts. That way she needed only to attend to part of any conversation in order not to lose the thread. It was a gift that had come in very handy since she had moved into the Yardley household.

Taking up her needlework she drifted away in her thoughts, speculating about the association between Sir Ivor Stafford and Mr. Yardley. She automatically came back to her senses when she heard Mrs. Yardley frame a question.

"My dears," Mrs. Yardley said. "How would it be if we decked out the entire house in green silk?" Seeing the puzzled looks on Helena and Caroline's faces, she elucidated, "To represent spring of course!"

"Oh...er, charming."

"Now Miss Marshfield, I can see you are not happy with my little scheme." She sighed. "Mrs. Everton draped silk all around her foyer and it did look ever so lovely."

Helena reflected that Mrs. Everton had had the taste to decorate only her foyer and not the entire house.

"My dear ma'am, you *know* you want to be a leader, not a follower. Confess now."

"Dear Helena, you are quite right. Where would I be without you? Well...what do you suggest then?"

"Ah, I'm not sure, Mrs. Yardley. Perhaps something elegant and uncommon. Let us think." She recalled her own coming-out ball just after being presented to Queen Charlotte. "Mmm...fresh and green. What about decking the receiving room and the ballroom in willow buds or fresh flower buds if there are any to be had? That could be interpreted as 'just out' don't you think?"

And within a few minutes, Mrs. Yardley was convinced that the decorations had been all her own notion.

"How clever of you, ma'am! I know it's going to be all the rage. Caroline and I noticed in *The Lady's Magazine* at Hookham's last week that the Duchess of Arumchester employed the use of hundreds of potted ferns at her daughter's dress party. So we are in vogue!"

There was nothing Mrs. Yardley enjoyed more than knowing she was joining a trend set by her social superiors. She oozed enthusiasm. "Well, my dears. Ours will be one of the most successful dress-parties of this Season I am sure, even if the nobs don't get to hear about it. Now Caroline love, we must consider your dress."

Naturally Caroline's dress was very important. Although she did not show to her best in white, it was the most unexceptionable and appropriate color for a young lady at an informal coming-out. Mrs. Yardley had made an appointment for the morrow with Madame Yvonne Férant in Bond Street. Mrs. Morris had recommended this establishment to the Yardley ladies, saying that if one wished to cut a dash, it was *essential* to frequent this establishment.

Madame Férant was apparently an *emigrée* from France. Her exceptional dressmaking skills had earned her the patronage of many aspiring hopefuls to the *ton*. Her true talent, apart from flair and artless sophistication, was that of individual design. It was said that with just a few lines on her sketchpad she could alter the line and fall of fabric to suit an individual's form, so that even the most difficult figure was successfully disguised. And Caroline's was by no means a difficult figure. It should not be too arduous a challenge for Madame Férant to create a delightful confection for such a well-proportioned young lady.

As Caroline and Helena went upstairs, Helena asked Caroline if she had any particular preferences for the trimming of her dress. "Caroline, this is the dress you will remember all of your life, so you must make your wishes known to your mama and Madame Férant. Don't feel that you have to fall in with Ariadne's ideas, or anyone else's for that matter," she added diplomatically.

Caroline clasped her hands together. "Oh, Miss Marshfield, truly I don't mind. I shall be guided by you."

Helena laughed. "Caroline, you will have Madame Férant to guide you. Let us accede to her advice."

"Miss Marshfield, tell me about your coming-out gown. What was it like?"

"Oh…" Helena was flummoxed. Being presented to royalty was a far cry from Caroline's party. She had no wish to seem superior and struggled to describe her experiences which all seemed so far away now, even though it was only six years ago.

"Let me see. It had a train of course, and one had to back out of Her Majesty's presence which made it difficult. I was terrified I would trip over the train. We were not presented to the King but to Queen Charlotte. I believe the King was going through one of his bad spells at the time. And we all had to wear feathers as a headpiece—somewhat old-fashioned but that was the stipulation. I remember that my hair was my biggest problem. It is so thick you see, and the feathers just would *not* stay in properly."

Caroline looked taken aback that Helena could

regard her glossy, dark tresses with disfavor. "How can you say that? Your hair is perfect!"

Helena rolled her eyes.

"And did you wear any jewelry?"

"Hardly any. It is not really considered the thing for young women only just out to deck themselves liberally with jewels, my dear. Also, one has to make sure when being presented to Royalty that you do not exceed the value of *their* jewelry. I remember my aunt was rather scathing of that dictum. My father had presented me with a beautiful diamond pendant for my coming-out, but of course I could not wear it on that particular occasion."

"Oh, how lovely! Do you still have the pendant?"

"Oh…I can't remember," Helena said vaguely, knowing full well that Rundell & Bridge had been ecstatic to receive such a distinctive and beautiful piece of jewelry on behalf of the estate.

Unable to drag any more information out of her governess, Caroline took herself off to bed to dream of angoulême lace and spangled gauze.

Helena went to her little room at the top of the house hoping that Caroline would not be too strongly influenced by those of lesser taste. Preparatory to pulling the pins from her troublesome hair in order to give it her customary one hundred brush strokes, she opened her precious hoard of Denmark Lotion and spread a little over her face. After all, she might be only a companion, but that was no reason to let her complexion become ravaged before its time. She despised women who simply did not try. She leaned into the mirror. No, she was not a mean bit yet. One could not say the expenditure of an inordinate sum for the jar of lotion was precisely *wastage* because one had self-respect, after all. Naturally, going about town, all the ladies tried to protect their skin from the dust and grime of London. Then she smiled a twisted smile. Who did she think she was fooling? Her father had spoiled her dreadfully and brought her up to adhere to certain standards. That was the crux of the matter.

Pushing away the worrying news of her brother, she tried to think what Mr. Yardley and Sir Ivor might have in common that they should discuss so much business together. She understood from Ariadne's artless conversation that though now a respectable member of the *ton* and a responsible landowner, in the past Sir Ivor had had quite a reputation as a man about town. Ariadne described him as a "rake" with wide eyes. She was obviously not fully conversant with what "a rake" signified.

but she knew it was something daring and exciting. Miss Marshfield could well believe it. She had seen for herself how agreeable he could make himself, with very little effort. She had found herself responding to the glint in his smile without any hesitation. She had met a few rakes during her coming-out year, and without exception they were all charming men. They were not for débutantes but were best left to entertain themselves with ladies of questionable virtue. Some of those rakes eventually matured and over time became responsible citizens, but Helena was of the opinion that once a rake, always a rake. And the rakes of the world were not for the likes of her either, tempted though she might be to be drawn into witty discussions where innuendoes were dropped to see what resulted. *Any* witty conversation would be acceptable at times, as two schoolroom misses did not precisely sparkle with witticisms.

And whatever Sir Ivor's salty reputation as a rake had been before he succeeded to the title, he had today undoubtedly been kind to her, a mere companion. Nice manners, she decided briskly, blowing out her candle. But it wasn't his manners that stayed in her mind as she drifted off to sleep.

Chapter Five

Inside an office at the Horse Guards, a secretary pored over a map. He did not understand or recognize any of the place names, nor did he care particularly. All he needed to do was to verify that this map was the one he had been instructed to copy. Yes, it must be. He had found it in the specified drawer, carefully left unlocked so he might complete his task.

Hastily he withdrew a sheet of paper from his pocket and, after locking the door of the office, set to work to copy the map outlines. Laboriously and diligently he copied the strange place-names and the unusual shape of the coastline.

Once he paused, rigid with fear, at the sound of voices outside the door. But whoever it was moved on, and he breathed freely once more.

When he had finished his task, he carefully replaced the original sketch in its allotted drawer and folded his copy into the specially made lining of his jacket. He returned the standish to its usual position. He blew gently on his pen to dry the nib, then slid it up his sleeve. He would replace it in his own office. There had been no pen on the desk in this room when he'd arrived. Its occupant had the reputation of being fussily careful about such things. He drew in his breath and set his ear to the door. No sound outside. He unlocked the door and slipped out.

****

The promised visit to Madame Férant threw the Yardley ladies into a fever of anticipation. Even though the tyrannical ogre Napoleon was everywhere condemned, French seamstresses certainly were not, particularly when they designed as well as this lady did. It was rumored that prior to the revolution Madame Férant had enjoyed all the trappings of one of the privileged class. No doubt the harrowing tale of her escape to England by being smuggled on board a boat owned by one of her English relatives had been exaggerated, but she was undoubtedly a dress designer of the first order. Once through the little blue door in Bruton Street the Yardley ladies found themselves in Aladdin's cave. Rolls of cloth of every hue were strewn over stools and tables. Accessories such as ostrich feathers and pearl encrusted evening gloves were arranged artfully in one corner. Ariadne darted ecstatically from one corner to another, dragging the other ladies behind her.

"Just look at this lace, Caroline! Oh, Mama, did you ever see such a sweet pair of evening gloves? I simply *must* have a pair."

Several attendants rushed hither and yon offering sweetmeats and coffee to all and sundry whilst the clients awaited their turn with Madame. She alone made all final decisions. It wouldn't do to take the word of a mere assistant dressmaker.

This was the world Helena had known for such a short time. As she kept her charges entertained by pointing out various fabrics and colors, she wondered what she had seen in this fussy, overheated atmosphere. Having new clothes was one thing, but being poked and prodded and turned this way and that had been a trial. She knew that Caroline would not like it either.

Eventually they were rewarded with Madame's full attention. In spite of her airs and graces she knew what she was doing and was able, with a few strokes of a pen, to sketch for them precisely the sort of dress Caroline most wanted.

Helena reflected that Madame Férand knew that if she were to establish herself as a leading dressmaker to the *ton*, she had first of all to start with the wealthy tradesmen and nabob's wives and daughters. They would provide the financial base for her to advance herself to the more influential members of the *ton* who were not always as conscientious about paying their bills as were the bankers and business people.

"Simplicity, ma'am," Madame Férand said to Mrs. Yardley firmly. "That is the thing when one is young. There is time enough later for more complicated designs and adornments, *n'cest pas?*" thus putting paid to Mrs. Yardley's flights of fancy.

Helena was amused to note that Madame Férand was distinctly tyrannical, but as it bade well for Caroline she was satisfied. Madame also persuaded them that a cream color would become Caroline better than stark white. "Everyone has white, even when it does not suit their skin, my dear," she said, waving her hands. "But you—you are such a pretty young lady. We must make the best of your assets." Caroline shyly smiled.

Madame Férand's sharp business sense fastened on Ariadne's charms next, and she hinted to Mrs. Yardley that of course "the so beautiful sister must have a new gown too." Naturally this took up the rest of the morning. Ariadne was in heaven and was much inclined to wonder why Madame Férand had not been commissioned to make her own coming-out dress the previous year.

"But you looked *beautiful* at your coming-out, Ariadne," Caroline said in awe, and the awkward moment passed.

Helena had her own problems to overcome. When she had mentally reviewed the contents of her meager clothes closet, she wondered which of the dresses she had salvaged from her salad days could be refurbished to do justice to the reputation of the Misses Yardley. It was unlikely that anybody would notice the dress of a duenna, but it would still not be the thing to wear exactly the same gown to Caroline's dress-party as she had to Ariadne's. Dear Ariadne would be the first one to point it out. She wondered if she might resurrect a pastime of long ago and sew herself a simple sarcenet over-dress or even a new satin under-dress.

On their arrival home Mrs. Yardley was thrilled to find Mrs. Morris and her daughters being plied with refreshments by Stalley. "My dears! Such news! Let's be comfortable, and we shall tell you all about the salon."

"Good day, Miss Marshfield," Mrs. Morris said, and her daughters bowed slightly in the governess's direction. Mrs. Morris might come of similar stock to the Yardleys, but she had infinitely better manners.

"And how did you find Madame Férand, Caroline?"

"Oh Mrs. Morris, she was so kind to us. She…"

Taking advantage of her charges' preoccupation with their visitors Helena went to her room and pulled out an old sketchbook, endeavoring to outline some of the ideas she had seen at the dressmaker's. A simple dress was all that was required. Her evening slippers would suffice. After all, they were not used often, but a new pair of evening gloves was essential. Helena sighed wistfully thinking of how many pairs of evening gloves she had in the past put aside for her lady's maid. She hoped Nanette had gained a good price for them at the markets.

Since the predicament their father had left them in, Helena had had many such deliberations with herself. She stringently adhered to the rules she had set for herself. It would not do to be noticed or be seen as putting herself forward, especially with her family history. Tongues would wag, and her life would become even more difficult. She still cringed inside when she remembered some of the whispers she had overheard in the months following her father's demise.

Although the Yardleys were very kind, it was apparent that they had chosen her for her name in spite of that name being besmirched, a fact which Mr. Yardley seemed to have disregarded. Not being of the *haut ton* it did not occur to him that the Marshfield name was best forgotten. But the sad fact was that the Yardleys' kindness did not make up for Helena's sense of estrangement from her former life. She was employed as a governess/companion, and that was all she'd ever be. She was not one of the family, no matter how much the family tried to make her feel at home. All the family with the exception of Ariadne that is. Toward Helena, Ariadne was bumptious and uncivil. She had none of the sweet ways of Caroline, nor was she prepared to learn the lessons of decorum that

Helena tried so hard to inculcate. Ariadne was sure that her beauty alone would carry any situation. She had no sense of duty toward dependents, and it was unlikely that she would ever be able to deal fairly with servants. She would make somebody a very bad wife.

No doubt endeavoring to improve Ariadne's behavior was good for Helena's character, but she'd always considered that strengthening one's character was highly overrated.

Now there was the new problem. How would she cope with Robert if…when he came home from Spain? Perhaps there would be a pension. She was hazy about the actual amount he would receive on retirement from the army, should it come to that, but she doubted it would be little more than a mere pittance.

She had heard dreadful stories about injured soldiers reduced to begging. And to think that the monster Napoleon had improved conditions for his old soldiers by continuing the refurbishing of Les Invalides that the late king had begun! It made one wonder if perhaps he were as barbaric as he was painted.

Later that afternoon whilst the young Yardley ladies were visiting their cousins in the company of their mother, Helena applied herself to the agreeable task of shopping for dress fabric at the Western Exchange where she knew she would find the prices to her liking. It was fun to venture out alone, not having to check Ariadne at every turn from ogling young men, nor prevent Caroline from making unsuitable purchases. Now that she was a member of the working class it was acceptable for her to go shopping alone in areas such as these, something she could never have done were she still 'Miss Marshfield.' Life had some compensations.

She hovered pleasurably over an array of poplins, muslins, crêpes, taffetas, cambrics, sarcenets, and satins as she faced the entrancing task of choosing which she most admired.

"Do you require evening gloves to go with that, miss?" the bored shop assistant asked after she had finally selected a length of soft blue sarcenet.

"Yes, please. They must match the fabric exactly." She could not return to select another pair if the shade was wrong. Not on £90 per year, most of which she hoarded, not having any idea what would happen to her at the end of her tenure with the Yardleys.

The bazaar was crowded, and the hum of conversation mingled with the cries of hawkers and the distant sound of carriage wheels. Helena was enjoying herself hugely. It was only when she was away from the Yardley household that she felt alive. In the townhouse she felt half-suffocated and effaced. She had the terrifying feeling that life was passing her by as she marked time in a half-world where she was neither servant nor master, but something in between. She had heard from other governesses that this was how most of them felt. A governess had nobody to confide in at the end of her working day. Loneliness was the overwhelming factor in their lives.

But here she was one of the throngs. It was hard to be lonely among such a disparate group of people. Around her cries of "a farthing for a crossing!" and "the best Brussels lace over here!" competed with the murmurs and exclamations of the shoppers. She was lucky to have this hour to herself.

With her purchases dangling in a string-tied

package from her fingers she headed for home, well pleased. The hard work would now begin. And perhaps more difficult than the finicking stitchery would be the effort to keep her work secret. Even Caroline had no real idea how scanty Miss Marshfield's meager wardrobe was. Helena still had pride, cold comfort though it was.

Whilst his family was busy, Mr. Yardley had spent the afternoon closeted with several government gentlemen, but he emerged from his study at dinner time ready to tell the ladies all about his plans for the dress-party.

"One of my associates has recommended an excellent orchestra, so I have already followed his advice and hired it. Now, my dears, I've settled on a date which I'm sure you will all agree with."

Naturally his ladies agreed with him, but Caroline gasped when Papa mentioned how soon her dress-party would be taking place. "You must know, my dear, that to be one of the earliest of the Season's entertainments is very important," her father pointed out.

And the Yardleys were determined that although they might not be of the *haut ton* and still "smelt of the shop" as the phrase went, they intended that their daughters, and therefore of course their grandchildren, would be respectable.

As Helena knew to her cost, polite society was a fickle thing, needing always to be courted, and offering little by way of solace should one offend against its unspoken tenets. She prayed that the Yardleys would not be rebuffed by too many as they clung to its fringes.

The invitations were to be left to Helena. "You have the most magnificent copperplate, Miss

Marshfield. And we would be grateful for your help as to whom to invite. Your knowledge of the proprieties will assure us of acceptances from the right people."

Helena bit her lip. She doubted it.

The following morning saw Caroline and Helena in Mr. Yardley's study designing invitations and the guest list. Helena was pleased to see that both Sir Ivor and his brother Ned Stafford were to receive invitations, but her face blanched when she saw Mr. Yardley add one particular name to the list. Lord Elverton. Please God, no!

Since Lord Elverton had, three years ago, vociferously condemned her father out of hand, Helena had not once seen him. He had ignored Robert and Helena since their father's death. Yet prior to that date he had been her father's greatest crony. In fact, Helena would have said that it was he who had introduced her father to the gaming tables where the steepest stakes were available. But perhaps she was doing him an injustice. She had been too young and heedless to be fully acquainted with the facts; even Robert was not privy to his father's secrets. But a certain promissory note in her armoire nagged at her conscience. She had often wondered if that scrawled signature was an 'E.'

For some reason the man gave her the horrors. There was something sinister about him that she was unable to define.

Why on earth had the Yardleys invited Lord Elverton to Caroline's coming-out? She had not realized they even knew him. Hopefully he would ignore their invitation. What was Mr. Yardley's connection with Lord Elverton? For Mr. Yardley was not naïve, and in spite of his ambitions for his daughters, he had no illusions about the attitude of the *ton* to people such as himself. When Helena had first come to work for the Yardleys, she had thought of Mr. Yardley as an amiable, middle-class businessman, but the longer she worked for him, the more puzzled she became about his wide variety of contacts and knowledge of politics. His acquaintance spread over a vast range of people such as members of the House of Commons and the House of Lords, bankers, nabobs who had made their fortunes on the Indian continent and many other business people such as merchants and shopkeepers and even the owners of several manufactories. Although Helena seldom accompanied the Yardleys *en famille*, she understood from Caroline that Mr. Yardley rarely appeared in public without encountering somebody he knew.

Helena ran her eye down the list of invitees. The Yardleys had noted all their especial friends on the list along with nearly every eligible bachelor present in London in the Season of 1809. There were a few people who would be hard put to it to recall the Yardleys at all, and for many young men, Ariadne would be the draw card. Some might be curious to see if Caroline matched Ariadne's beauty. Most were probably well aware of the excellent dowries attaching to Helena's young charges. She sincerely hoped that both daughters would become suitably riveted to young men of some substance so that they would not be married solely for their money. Of course Mr. Yardley would do his best to put a stop to that! Helena was particularly worried about Caroline who should be valued for her intellect and gentle nature. Naturally Ariadne would hold her own in any matrimonial disagreements. But Helena's heart ached for little seventeen years old Caroline who had rarely been scolded because she had never needed to be, and who had a headful of dreams wherein her heroes resembled something out of the Greek legends.

Then Mr. Yardley confounded her by saying, "Now, Miss Marshfield, you must enjoy yourself too. We have invited Ned Stafford so that you will have at least one acquaintance to converse with."

"No, no, Mr. Yardley. You mistake the matter. I have *heard* of Mr. Stafford but never met him. He was one of my brother's friends. Besides, I am to keep an eye on the girls, not—"

"No, Miss Marshfield. At Caroline's coming-out it is for us to chaperone our daughters. They are under our roof and so under our care. Mrs. Yardley and I expect you to simply enjoy the evening. You will have the initial organizing to do, so you will *need* some jollification after your exertions." And Mr. Yardley laughed heartily.

With mixed feelings Helena sincerely hoped that Mr. Yardley would not force poor Ned Stafford—or anyone else—to acknowledge her. If Ned Stafford had the good manners of his brother, then he would probably offer her a civil bow. She prayed that he was not, like Lord Elverton, high in the instep. The Yardleys did not understand how society now viewed Helena and Robert. She herself had found it difficult to understand at first, but she had *almost* become inured to it.

A fever of activity now invaded the Yardley household, so much so that Mr. Yardley, when not at his warehouses in King Street, often had recourse to his club in order to gain peace and quiet. Ariadne maintained a steady bad-tempered irritation since she was no longer the center of attention. Her incessant cries of "Betsy? Betsy?" drove everyone, especially the unfortunate upstairs maid, away from whichever section of the house Ariadne was in.

Since Ariadne had been made much of for the past year, to now discover she was not the center of attention was a shock. Her mirror told her she was arrestingly striking. Her skin was that of a perfect peach, and her hazel eyes glittered when she was excited. She had tiny hands and feet "just like a doll's" as a besotted Mr. Harold Simpson had said when he first espied her. Mr. Simpson was one of the faithful swains who flocked about Miss Yardley on all possible occasions.

Helena had observed that those "tiny doll's hands" were capable of grasping anything Ariadne particularly desired, especially to the detriment of her younger sister. The governess sincerely hoped that some acceptable young man would make an offer for Ariadne soon, in order that Caroline could enjoy her time in the sun without her older sister's inhibiting presence. Perhaps Ariadne would meet someone eligible at Caroline's dress-party.

After several days of domestic upheaval, Mrs. Yardley admitted to Helena that she was unable to prevent Ariadne's ill-tempered freaks. "Please, Miss Marshfield, see what you can do."

When a particularly petulant outburst greeted a morning visitor to the house, Helena took Ariadne aside and in trenchant terms pointed out a few disagreeable facts. "It is my duty to tell you that you are making yourself universally unpopular. What if Mrs. Trewes chooses to tattle about you? She pretended to ignore your behavior, that is true, but she is not deaf." This particular crony of Mrs. Yardley was a well-known gossip. Helena followed up her short homily with a shrug of her shoulders and commented, "But I notice that lately you don't seem interested in what others think of you. It's such a shame that a beautiful girl like you should ruin your own chances. However, when Caroline is married, I'm sure you will be a comforting companion to your parents in their old age."

"What are you talking about, Helena? I shan't be here. I shall be married too, of course."

"Oh, I shouldn't think so, Ariadne. Most gentlemen dislike having to deal with temperamental young women. I have often observed that it is kind, placid young women who are popular with everyone, even if they're not particularly beautiful."

She refused to discuss the matter further but hurried away to confer with Mrs. Yardley about decorations for the ballroom. Ariadne seemed to take very little notice of Helena's homily at the time, apart from showing the governess a cold shoulder. However, over the next few days she tried to be helpful and even managed to enter into the spirit of her sister's coming-out, albeit with a condescending and forced gaiety. Helena Marshfield was not optimistic that the acquiescent mood would last, but she hoped it would endure until after Caroline's party at least. It would be dreadful if Ariadne were to treat everyone to one of her tantrums on that evening. Not only would it color Caroline's recollections of her dress-party forever, it would also result in gossip dangerous to both girls' reputations. Well did Helena Marshfield know just what a parcel of idle gossips could do, no matter what their station in life was.

For Helena, the days leading up to Caroline's dress-party were frenetic. What with conferring with the cook, housekeeper, various tradesmen and food suppliers, as well as the dancing master, she was kept on the trot from morning till night. It was "Miss Marshfield, where should this go?" from Stalley and "Miss Marshfield, here is a message just delivered," from Betsy or Katy.

Her greatest challenge was the dancing master for whom Ariadne had a decided *tendre*. It would be wonderful if she had not. Mr. Ferris was a tall, graceful young man of respectable breeding who knew just how to ingratiate himself with gullible mothers like Mrs. Yardley. He also knew how to charm susceptible young women. Ariadne was entranced with the man, because although Mr. Ferris was charged with teaching Caroline the steps of several country-dances, he often used Ariadne as a partner in order to demonstrate. Whilst Miss Marshfield played the spinet, more often than not Caroline found herself watching rather than participating.

"Isn't he *divine,* Helena?" Ariadne enthused.

"Who?"

"Why…Mr. Ferris of course!"

"Of course, Ariadne. *All* dancing masters are divine," Helena returned, laughing. "My dear, they are *paid* to be pleasant to young women. That is what their career demands."

Ariadne pouted. "Spoilsport!"

"Not at all. I do not spoil your sport. Enjoy the young man while you may. Just remember that he is impecunious and your Papa would not look to see you riveted to a dancing master. After the end of next week, you will most likely never see him again."

Ariadne thought for a minute. "I do not think I should like to marry a dancing master. He would always be with other women."

"Precisely."

Helena took Mr. Ferris aside. "Mr. Ferris, may I ask you to spend a little more time with Miss Caroline, who is, after all, the young woman Mrs. Yardley hired you to help? Thank you." Mr. Ferris reddened, and his eyes followed Ariadne as she left the salon. Reflecting that Mr. Ferris would not last long as a dancing master if he made sheep's eyes at the daughters of the houses where he worked, Helena found tasks to keep Ariadne away from the salon while the dancing lessons took place.

And she had enough on her plate without worrying about Ariadne, for as Mr. Yardley had predicted, his wife handed over the reins to Helena. Mrs. Yardley retired to the chaise longue in her boudoir content in the knowledge that Helena would cope with the myriad details necessary to bring off a successful evening.

And cope Helena did, although late at night in her 'spare time' she nodded over her stitchery as the candles guttered. As she sewed, she reflected that although life with the Yardleys was not particularly onerous, and indeed much of the time it was incredibly boring, it could on occasion be exciting, as it was now, organizing Caroline's coming-out.

She smiled as she recollected how Mr. Yardley had first approached her when she had been employed at Miss Fichton's Seminary for Young Ladies in Queen's Square in Bath. He had bounced up to her without any introduction and put to her what he saw as a simple business transaction.

"Miss Marshfield, we are very impressed with the way you've taught our girls since they've been here at Miss Fichton's. And they are very fond of you. It's been 'Miss Marshfield says this' or 'Miss Marshfield says that.' "

He laughed heartily, but she saw the determination underneath the façade. "However, they will leave here at year's end. What would you say to coming to us in London, to governess Caroline for one last year and to act as chaperone for Ariadne when she comes out next month? Of course your wages would be of the highest." She gained the impression that Josh Yardley had already inquired into governess's wages. When she knew him better, she realized that the conditions and wages he offered her were nicely balanced—generous, but not quite at the top of the scale.

She had said no to his offer at first, because Miss Fichton had taken her on as junior mistress only as a special favor. It had taken Mr. Yardley some time to prise Miss Marshfield away from the safety of the seminary.

Miss Fichton had been Helena's own governess prior to her coming-out. She was a talented and outstanding woman who had inculcated Helena with the pleasure of learning. Helena had been instructed in the Italian and French languages and the pianoforte, but above all she had learned to show a pleasant and serene face to the world.

These were attributes that had appealed to the Yardleys. They were searching for someone who could imbue their daughters with a layer of sophistication.

Mr. Yardley had managed to elicit from Miss Fichton the information that Miss Marshfield's family was now by way of being defunct. Her father, unable to face his debts, had chosen to dispatch himself with his expensive Henry Nock pistol—unpaid for—thereby leaving his son and daughter to fend for themselves. Apparently the man had committed the social solecism of doing so in a public place, namely Whites. He was not the first to do so, and he would not be the last. He had drunk a final glass of port, retired to the writing-room, and shot himself. Presumably he had decided that his heir could face the consequences of his unpaid debts.

But Mr. Yardley did not know all the facts.

Throughout the weeks following their father's death, Helena and Robert had struggled to maintain their dignity. Helena decided that there was only one choice open to her: she would have to earn her own living. And there were precious few ways for a young, gently bred woman to do so. Much as her brother tried to remonstrate with her, she had known it was impossible for him to maintain a household whilst he was in the army, liable at any moment to be posted overseas.

"Darling Robert," she had said to her anxious brother, "thank you for trying to assist me, but there is no need. It is in no way incumbent upon you to take over the responsibility that Papa abdicated. Yes, I *do* resent what Papa has done to us, but that must be overcome."

She had had to work hard to convince Robert that he would be better off in barracks whilst she pursued a career. She knew he could not support her in lodgings as did some of the officers. To her brother, Helena showed a determined but serene face. Inside herself she was extremely frightened. The prospect of going into service was terrifying, and without anyone in the world to support her or show her how she should go on, she was desperately lonely. During her childhood she had not noticed the absence of a mother, but on the death of her father she had yearned for a loyal, loving mother such as some of her erstwhile friends had.

At first she had planned to become a companion to an elderly lady. But she had been out for only one year and discovered that young women of nineteen were not the sort of companions that older ladies required. Not only was Helena too young and attractive for any lady with susceptible male relatives to employ, she had also to live down the stigma of her father's name. As one elderly Woolhampton resident had explained after Helena had wasted several preciously hoarded shillings for a seat on the stage to Woolhampton, "My dear, you are far too lovely. I have a very susceptible nephew who lives with me. He is betrothed to a young woman of my choice. Belinda is a sober, steady person, just the sort of young woman he needs. I don't mean that you are not sober and steady, Miss Marshfield, but it has taken me several years to bring the boy under my thumb, and I do not wish to place temptation in his path. He has too much of his father in him. I'm afraid I need a biddable middle-aged spinster who will *enjoy*— not politely tolerate—the subdued jollifications of Woolhampton."

She had then advised Helena to "Go to Bath or London where you may find a husband, my dear. So much more fun for you!" Unfortunately the dear lady had not specified how that was to be achieved.

In desperation Helena had applied to her old governess. Miss Fichton, recalling the pleasant years spent with the Marshfields and the large sum contributed by John Marshfield toward her purchase of Fichton's Seminary for Young Ladies, happily agreed to assist.

Naturally, after three years of grinding boredom in the Queen's Square establishment Helena was excited when Mr. Yardley offered her the post of governess/companion to his two daughters. Yet in loyalty to Miss Fichton, Helena had to demur. Many employers were fickle. Miss Fichton was not. She had offered Helena a place for life, whilst also expressing the hope that Helena would at some stage find more congenial employment. "My dear Helena, I urge you to seek a post where you may go out into the world a little. If you become known by the best families, one of them may find a role for you where you can obtain some of the niceties of life. I hate to see you like this."

Helena had suppressed a shudder and thanked Miss Fichton. She had no wish to re-enter the world she had known. She now feared that world. Not one of her erstwhile 'friends' had made more than cursory inquiries of them after her father's death. Most of them had cut her dead if they passed her in public. For months she had lived with a seething anger that was difficult to control. How *dared* they pass judgment on her and Robert? As though what their father had done was any of their doing! And many of those people condemning the Marshfields were living on tick by cheating their providers and tradesmen of their fees.

For Helena the loneliness was unbearable at times.

Helena, Robert, and their steward had paid off all Sir John's debts as soon as possible. However, Helena dreaded the day that a stranger approached her, producing a duplicate of that promissory note she had found in her father's desk. What would she do? She had no assets left, and no way to pay this last, mysterious debt.

****

On receiving a wary reception from Helena, Mr. Yardley had approached Miss Fichton. Miss Fichton strongly recommended to Helena that she take this golden opportunity. "My dear Helena, I am not comfortable with you burying yourself here in Bath. A Queens Square ladies' seminary is not for you. Go to Mr. Yardley's establishment. His family is not of the first stare, but you have said you do not wish to be part of the *ton* any longer. And the Yardleys, though their money comes from trade, are respectable enough. This might lead to other opportunities. Well-born, well-educated governesses are highly sought after. If you give satisfaction—and I *know* you will, my dear—you will probably be offered a position with another employer in the future. I shall write you a reference so that you may be easy in future. And of course you may always return here. You know you will be most welcome."

So Helena had swallowed her pride once more— indeed, it was wondrous she had any left to swallow by now—and gone to the Yardleys. They had greeted her advent with pleasure and relief, and Mr. Yardley was well pleased with his bargain.

Helena had had very little cause to regret it. Both Mr. and Mrs. Yardley were as pleasant as they were ungenteel. Though sometimes Helena shuddered at some of Mrs. Yardley's notions of what was proper for young ladies, and if Mr. Yardley tended to judge a man by his bank balance, well…there were those of the *ton* who were not so particular too. Thus, Helena re-entered the fringes of a life she had once enjoyed, albeit as a duenna where she was unlikely to chance a meeting with an old acquaintance.

Now that Robert was coming home with no prospects, the best she could hope for was that Caroline would become riveted to some respectable young man and they would require her assistance with their nursery. Helena grimaced as she stitched. She knew nothing about babies. No doubt she would learn.

Then on the eve of the party, Betsy toiled upstairs to Helena's room. "Miss Marshfield, here. Another of those army letters," she panted.

"Thank you, Betsy. So good of you. You should have waited till I came downstairs."

"Oh no, miss. I thought you would want it at once."

Full of dread, Helena broke the seal, and to her surprise and delight the letter was addressed 'Portsmouth Hospital.' Robert had written it himself, if it could be termed writing. It was a barely legible scrawl which he explained away by saying that he was temporarily learning to write with his left hand, his right being 'out of commission for a short time.' He said that he was gradually getting better. It seemed that so far the surgeons had not felt that amputating his leg was necessary as was first thought. Helena shuddered and read on. However, Robert did not think he would be likely to dance or ride again. He admitted to being very pulled by his injuries.

She wondered how long it had taken Sir Henry Paget's letter to reach her. It had been undated, but Robert described in his letter how it had taken them two weeks' sailing to return to England due to inclement weather. After putting out to sea they had had to return to shore to wait for storms to abate and had run out of stores early in the piece. She put the letter down and gazed out her casement window with unseeing eyes, imagining the appalling suffering of the injured crammed into the hold, and some no doubt on the open decks, all with very little medical assistance available. Robert did not specify the extent of his injuries, but she had no doubt that her brother had suffered terrible pain during the last few weeks.

'Have faith and remember that every day that passes improves my strength,' he wrote. He had apparently been injured when, acting as a messenger between his own and a Portuguese division, they had become engaged with the French in a rearguard action. Paget's instructions from Sir John Hope were to demolish bridges as they retreated in orderly fashion to prevent the French army from following. Robert had been grazed by a spent musketball as he shepherded the remains of a Portuguese regiment toward the tail end of his company, but most of his injuries were caused by his horse, startled and terrified, rolling on top of him. According to him this was a common occurrence. 'I shall write again in a few days when I am more myself. I very much look forward to seeing you again, my dear sister.'

He had glossed over the seriousness of his injuries and made no mention of the appalling losses the army must have suffered to instigate such a retreat.

"How will we manage?" she said to herself as she heated the iron to press the new sarcenet gown. Although at present her responsibility was to the Yardleys, she had an important responsibility toward her brother too. Unless he had made firm friends with some of his fellow officers, she did not know where he planned to recuperate. Irritated by the ceaseless worry, she clicked her tongue and concentrated on her ironing.

Betsy was very taken with the new dress. "Ooh, Miss Marshfield. Don't it look pretty! You *will* look a picture!" She oohed and aahed so much that Helena became embarrassed. However, she had learned that the underservants took pleasure in the small favors sometimes extended to upper servants, so she showed Betsy the evening slippers and gloves too. Betsy would probably relate all the details to Cook and the kitchen maid, thus enlarging her own self-importance. Four years ago Helena would not have understood the importance of the hierarchy. Now she did, and she was always careful not to wound feelings. A governess had to tread carefully that thin line between the employers and the servants. Anyway, it was stupid to upset the lower servants because they could make life impossible for a governess if they chose. Instead of hot water in one's washing bowl, cold water would be delivered, not a pleasant thing in early winter mornings. Lack of respect would show itself in little ways such as pretending not to hear requests from a governess, or unexpectedly shutting a door in her face. No, Helena knew better than to upset the lower servants. Besides, nearly all the servants at Yardley House were pleasant people, although Cook and Stalley were not easy to deal with. They took their tone from their employers and as a result Yardley House was often in an uproar over some minor domestic dispute.

She shook out the finished dress. Holding it against herself she peered into the cheval glass, the only mirror her room boasted. She would just have to trust to Providence that her stitching was as good as it used to be. After all, she could not change her mind at the last minute and wear something different as she had done in her salad days. She had nothing else suitable to wear.

"Anyway, nobody will notice you, Helena. All eyes will be on Caroline," she admonished her reflection. Traitorous thoughts of steely gray eyes must be quashed immediately. It was useless to cherish false hope.

She collected all the incriminating pieces of thread and her needles and put them in the sewing basket in her closet.

Chapter Six

"Miss Marshfield! Miss Marshfield!" The Yardley household was in an excited uproar. Everyone looked to Helena to organize them on such an important day, which was just as well. Mrs. Yardley had taken her smelling salts and retired to the chaise longue in her boudoir. She had no intention of fatiguing herself and was conserving her energy for the evening's entertainment.

Helena smiled wryly to herself. She might not be paid to be chatelaine, but *somebody* had to be responsible. Left to their own devices the servants would simply mill around looking for direction. Reining in the pandemonium as she went, Helena took time to talk to every one of the staff individually, letting them know what was expected of them. "Thank you so *very* much," she soothed. "I know I can trust you all to do your best. If you have any further questions, please come and see me."

Discussions with Stalley were all preceded with a sniffy "I have been used to dealing with far larger gatherings than *this*, Miss Marshfield" until Helena thought she might scream with vexation. Certainly, Stalley could cope. But was he prepared to obey her requests to the letter? He tended to disobey the Yardleys' instructions if he did not consider them appropriate. Sometimes he obeyed them with an insolently challenging air. Helena understood that in his own way, Stalley tried to bring the Yardleys into line with acceptable behavior. She could understand his exasperation with Josh Yardley's bluff heartiness and Mrs. Yardley's misguided attempts to be 'ladylike.' Stalley was not impressed with people who flouted convention. But he really should remember who paid his wages, although it was unlikely he would be dismissed. No matter how truculent he became, the Yardleys would ignore it because they were thrilled to have as their butler an ex-employee of Lord Penningstone.

By dint of imploring him, "*Please*, Stalley, I do so rely on you," Helena managed to garner his cooperation. Together they calmed the ebb and flow of hired helpers as Yardley House echoed to the sound of busy feet.

By mid-afternoon Helena was feeling limp, and had she been in the fortunate circumstance of being able to do so, would have lain down upon the sofa with her smelling salts. However, companions did not do such a thing, and anyway she didn't own smelling salts. Instead she took a deep, calming breath and consulted the next item on her list.

By the time everyone had repaired to their rooms to dress, everything seemed at last to be in order. Helena prayed she had not overlooked anything. Hastening to Caroline's room to offer encouragement, she checked on the threshold when she saw Betsy and Caroline peering at a card that had been delivered along with a pretty posy of flowers. Caroline turned shining eyes on her governess.

"Miss Marshfield! The flowers are from Sir Ivor.

Was that not kind of him? And the card is so prettily penned too."

Helena glanced at it, smiling. The message on the card could not be faulted. Sir Ivor begged to be allowed to offer a small token in respect of a young lady's coming-out. The posy was of the palest pink and white rosebuds, not yet out. A subtle message most likely not understood by Caroline.

"How lucky you are, Caroline! The flowers have probably come from Sir Ivor's succession houses. Your papa has often told us about Sir Ivor's succession houses at his estate in Norfolk." It seemed that Sir Ivor was interested in the propagation of rare and interesting flowers and fruit. As it was far too early yet for rosebuds, these would have been forced under cover.

But in spite of all the excitement, Caroline looked wan.

Helena managed to get Betsy out of the way. "Now Betsy, I want you to go and fetch Miss Caroline a hot chocolate and a wafer biscuit. Then when she has composed herself, you may help me to dress her hair." Helena turned to Caroline. "My dear, how do you feel?"

"Miss Marshfield, I am so nervous."

Poor Caroline. She looked as if she were facing the guillotine.

"Sweet girl, just take some deep breaths and relax for a few minutes. When your hot chocolate arrives, sip it slowly." Helena rubbed Caroline's shoulder. "Now, let me see to your hair. Are we still agreed that à la Sappho is the style you want?" She soothingly brushed Caroline's hair preparatory to styling it in a fashion which was not so very different from the girl's every day one. The slow brush strokes and Helena's calm manner soon settled Caroline into her usual placid self.

The bronze tresses were artfully curled around Helena's fingers and with a judicious tweak here and there from the hot curling tongs Betsy had earlier prepared on the fire, Caroline's hair was styled.

"Caroline, you are still a little pale."

Caroline gasped. "I'm all right, really. It is just when I think about…tonight…that I get worried." The lovely eyes were over-bright.

"Could I suggest a tiny dot of color from the rouge pot? Because, my dear, on this night of all nights, you daren't look haggard."

"But, Miss Marshfield! Will not people notice?"

"No. People only see what they want to see. Nobody will notice. Just a little dab here and there. Now we shall rub it in with the haresfoot. There. Perfect." Helena swiveled Caroline around to face the mirror.

As they laid the spangled gauze dress out on her bed there was a scratching sound at the door. It was Mr. Yardley with a special gift. "Oh, Papa! Thank you so much. Look, Helena!" Caroline stood on tiptoe to shyly kiss her father's cheek.

He laughed and pinched her chin. "You'll do, missy. You'll do," he told her proudly. He fastened the double row of pearls around her neck with the silver clasp that exactly matched the spangles on Caroline's dress. A lot of thought had gone into that gift. Josh Yardley had consulted with Helena as to what would be the most appropriate coming-out gift for his daughter. She had suggested pearls. He must have managed to find a skilled jeweler to design and craft the exquisite necklace.

Many a father would not have taken the slightest notice of a daughter's coming-out, Helena thought. Even in this enlightened age there were still a number of men about town who cared only for their sons—or at least for the son who would succeed to a title or an estate or business holding. Josh Yardley was not only an indulgent father; he was a conscientious and caring one.

Helena duly admired the magnificent pearls and adjusted the necklace so that the cleverly wrought silver clasp was to the side of Caroline's throat where it could be seen to advantage but was not the cynosure of all eyes. Little tricks of style made all the difference. Josh Yardley grunted his satisfaction. "Excellent, Miss Marshfield. Chin up, my dear," he whispered to Caroline. "You will take the shine out of them all."

"Oh, Papa!"

Helena smiled and hurried to her own room to shake out her dress. As she began to untie her day dress, there was a loud crash and a raised voice from Ariadne's room. Helena cast her eyes up and hurried, along with Mrs. Yardley in her wrapper, to see what had happened. They opened the door to the overpowering smell of a virulent perfume.

"Oh, dear. What now?" puffed stout Mrs. Yardley.

It seemed that Ariadne had spilled her favorite toilet water and she could not possibly, *no, not possibly*, wear any other perfume. Betsy must go this minute to Clarges Street to the perfume mixer's shop to fetch a fresh phial.

"But it's nigh on six o'clock!" expostulated Mrs. Yardley. "Won't another do as well?"

However, Ariadne's cooperative behavior of the last few days had come to an end. She had decided to audition for the role as Mrs. Siddons's understudy, and the entire household was treated to a histrionic display of talent hitherto unsuspected. Mrs. Yardley, ineffectually wringing her hands, begged Helena to do what she could.

"Yes, ma'am. Obviously Miss Yardley is too ill to attend her sister's dress party. What a shame! She will have to go to bed of course."

"Bed? At six o'clock? Absolutely not!" Ariadne stopped her shrieking and looked daggers at Helena.

"I'm afraid so," Helena said. "My dear, you are obviously unwell. I shall have Thomas fetch Dr. Amos. Lie down, Ariadne, and wait for him." Firmly she pushed Ariadne down on to her bed. Then she plucked Mrs. Yardley's smelling salts out of her hand. Ariadne found herself lying down in her wrapper with smelling salts being waved under her nose.

"Take that away! I am *not* unwell, Helena. I will go downstairs just as soon as I am ready."

"Then you had better make haste. It wants only an hour till the first guests arrive." Lingering for a precious moment to check that Ariadne's sulky mutterings were merely idle threats, Helena thrust a scared Katy back into Ariadne's boudoir. She sped back to Caroline's room where, fortunately, all was serene. Caroline was admiring herself in her new dress as she twisted and turned in front of the mirror, peering first at the front, then at the back. Betsy stood with clasped hands admiring her.

"Don't she look lovely, Miss Marshfield?"

"Very pretty." Helena ran a practiced eye over the

details of Caroline's dress. It was delightful, and its effect was precisely the desired one—that of an untried, sweet girl in her first evening gown. After a final primp Caroline followed Helena to her room so that Helena could scramble into her dress.

Caroline was very impressed with Helena's new gown. "Why, Miss Marshfield! I didn't know you had this. How lovely!"

As she fought with her wayward hair, struggling to tame it into submission under a cap, Helena remembered something she had meant to talk to Caroline about. She was about to broach the subject when Caroline asked, "Are you uh…going to wear a cap, Miss Marshfield? I've never seen you wear one before."

"Yes, I think it is time. Caroline, my dear, I need to discuss something with you. Now that you have officially come out, I can no longer be considered your governess. You are a young lady, and I am by way of being a sort of servant, well…a companion." Inadvertently Helena's mouth twisted, and she hastily composed herself. "You must call me 'Helena', and I will now call you 'Miss Caroline' the same as Betsy does."

"Miss M…Helena! You are my friend, not a servant. How uncomfortable! You must call me 'Caroline' the same as ever."

Helena took Caroline's cold little hands in hers. "My dear, now that you are 'out' there is more of a gulf between us. It is kind of you and typical of that kindness to wish to treat me as a friend, but it must not be so." She smiled reassuringly. "We will leave your parents to decide the niceties."

But when she descended the stairs behind Caroline, holding back to give her family and servants the chance to see Caroline at her best, Helena could not help but feel a certain tingling anticipation. It had been a long time since she had attended a gala party such as this. At Ariadne's coming-out she had been just one of the chaperones. This time she would be part of the celebrations.

Mrs. Yardley exclaimed, "Eh, Caroline, you are *beautiful* dearie. Like a little dream, isn't she Miss Marshfield? And Miss Marshfield, you look ravishing! But I'm not sure about the cap." Mrs. Yardley glared at the offending article. "Look, Josh, doesn't Miss Marshfield look a picture?"

Helena drew in a breath. She hadn't meant to stand out in any way.

"Indeed she does." He patted his daughter's arm, but his eyes assessed Helena as though seeing her for the first time. "Now, Miss Marshfield," he began, "Mrs. Yardley and I are quite decided on one thing. If any gentleman should ask you to dance, you must do so. We don't like to see you sitting amongst the chaperones as though you were an old antidote. We are chaperones enough for our daughters in our own house. We shall be extremely angry with you if you relegate yourself to the background. And you will most certainly be asked to dance, no doubt about that, provided you take off that cap." He guffawed at his little joke.

Helena felt herself blushing. What should she say? These kind people had always been unorthodox, and of course she wanted to dance, but what of the gossips? Just *being* her father's daughter had been enough to cause some of them to shun her. Fortunately, there would be very few of those people here tonight. There would be bankers and merchants and a few minor baronets such as Sir Ivor Stafford. Then she remembered Lord Elverton. Pray he did not come.

Caroline whispered to her parents, and to Helena's further consternation Mrs. Yardley plunged into speech. "Now, my dear. We understand you think it's '*the thing*'"—Mrs. Yardley humorously emphasized the words—"to address Caroline as 'Miss Caroline' from now on. Well, you can stop that straight away. And if you would give us your permission, we could all be comfortable and call you 'Helena' as Ariadne does." She stared archly at Helena, daring her to disagree.

Helena opened her mouth and shut it again.

"That's settled." Satisfied, Mrs. Yardley patted Helena's arm, then bustled away to find her smelling salts. Helena had had the ground cut neatly from under her. Mr. Yardley grinned knowingly.

"I am ready on time!" trilled Ariadne, and everyone duly turned to admire her as she descended the staircase. She was striking in her new apple green overdress, though hardly demure considering that she had lavishly damped her chemise. There was a stunned silence. The Yardleys and Helena all stared at her aghast, but nobody made a comment. Not only was there no time to do anything about it—as Ariadne well knew—but nobody was prepared to face the consequences of scolding her. A tantrum now was not to be borne. Caroline instinctively edged closer to Helena.

Helena was mortified. She had been so busy caring for Caroline that she had completely forgotten to check on Ariadne before she came downstairs. She cast a harassed glance at Mr. Yardley. To her relief he merely shrugged. Helena bit her lip. In another household she could have been dismissed for such a dereliction of her duties.

The first guests were announced just then, and, wishing to make a good impression, Ariadne hastened to her parents' side to be part of the welcoming party. Helena had had quite enough of the young baggage. She took Ariadne firmly by the arm and marched her into the ballroom, delivering a stiff lecture on the way. "We trust you will not catch your death of cold with those damp chemise and petticoats, Ariadne. Frankly it makes you look like a class of woman who—oh, never mind. Now, I want you to help by making sure that Stalley and the caterers have all the final details under control. Also, please see that the card-room has been set up satisfactorily. Send for me if there are any difficulties. I shall be here in the ballroom."

"Isn't that Mrs. Yardley's job?" a well-remembered voice asked. Sir Ivor was an early arrival.

Drawing in her breath, she turned to greet him. "Good evening, Sir Ivor. No, Mrs. Yardley detests organization, and I'm happy to do it," she explained.

"So, you are governess, companion, chatelaine, advisor and…what else?"

She smiled and shrugged. "Whatever needs doing, I am happy to do. The Yardleys are the kindest and best of employers." Oh, how fine he looked in his evening breeches and cutaway coat. Many a young man would wish to emulate his ability with the intricate folds of his neck cloth. However, unlike some of the younger men, it seemed he did not slavishly follow the Prince of Wales' style of ridiculously high, stiff shirt points. He was tall enough to look well in anything he wore, and of course those shoulders...no extra padding needed there. No doubt he spent many hours in Jackson's Boxing Saloon and Cribb's Parlor and all those other ghastly places that Robert used to hold so dear. Strange how such violent pugilistic sports appealed to normally nice men, she mused. She wondered if Ivor Stafford had intentions toward Caroline or Ariadne, or if he was in reality exactly what he seemed—a business acquaintance of Mr. Yardley's who was well disposed toward the family.

Helena was curious about that point. She knew Sir Ivor had never been involved in trade, having inherited his title and lands from his father, his father having done the same before him. And she knew the Staffords featured in all of the histories of the gentry because she had surreptitiously searched the available reference books in both Hookham's and Mr. Yardley's miniscule library. Her family had featured in the *Billington's Almanac* too, but all newer editions would merely make mention of their name. There would no longer be a description of their land and holdings. The Staffords' lands were larger than her father's had been, and Ryewolds near Norwich was cited as one of the best examples of early Georgian architecture available, though no doubt inconvenient and drafty as some early architecture was wont to be. Somehow, though, Helena couldn't see Sir Ivor accepting lukewarm dishes and cold shaving water. He had a well-bred air of authority, which displayed a calm certainty that nothing in his household was expected to go wrong. Probably very comforting to those working for him. For that type of person nothing usually *did* go wrong. It wouldn't dare.

She smiled to herself.

"A penny for them?" Sir Ivor asked.

"Good gracious, no!" Helena blurted.

He smiled slowly then rescued her by saying, "I'm sure you are quietly deriving amusement from Mrs. Sowerby's appalling coiffure," but his eyes glinted. He knew darned well that he'd been the subject of her thoughts. She reminded herself that this man had been a great success with the ladies until he succeeded to his title, and he was much more experienced than she in the art of flirting. She took his offer of a polite gambit. "Yes, Mrs. Sowerby's latest creation is certainly startling. Please excuse me, Sir Ivor. I must see to Ariadne and Caroline." She had no wish to become fodder for the gossip mill and turned away from him. They should not be conversing like this, apart from other people. *He* had no need to worry about things like that. *She* did.

"Just one minute, Miss Marshfield."

She paused.

"When you have done your duty by your charges, I should like to introduce my brother to you. We would like to talk to you about Robert, if we may. Perhaps we can find a secluded area away from the general mêlée? One where we could be undisturbed for a few minutes?" His glance scanned the room.

"Oh! Mr. Yardley's study would be best," she answered. What could Sir Ivor and Ned Stafford want to ask her about Robert? She smiled, always ready to talk about Robert. "I had another note from him last evening. He seems to be much better."

****

Ivor Stafford smiled back, wondering if she had

97

any idea how totally unsuitable she looked to be anyone's governess or chaperone. As she was now, animated and dressed as well as any of the other young ladies in the ballroom, she looked every inch what she was—a beautiful, gently-bred young woman. He reminded himself to tread carefully. He had no wish to raise any expectations, nor was he seeking a permanent relationship of any sort. But he found it hard to think logically when he was close to her. "Excellent. Now remember that you must save me a dance."

"Oh no, Sir Ivor," she said, looking stricken. "I-I don't think…" She indicated her cap. He glanced disparagingly at it but forbore to comment.

"You don't need to think. I have already asked Mr. Yardley's permission since he stands in loco parentis to you."

Dammit. Now he'd have to mention it to Josh. What had made him come out with such a thing? What would the old biddies say? But God knew, he wanted to dance with her, to see that animation return to her face and watch the graceful body move through the steps of a sedate boulanger or cotillion.

He almost chuckled as he realized it was the first time he'd asked a lady for a dance and had them look at him aghast. She fiddled with her reticule.

Dependent on the hierarchy of the assembled guests, he might be obliged to stand up with any titled lady present for the first dance of the evening. Anyway, Miss Marshfield would have her hands full as the dancing began, chivvying young couples into position.

"It must be the second dance, I think. I expect you know what it is since you no doubt had the organization of the whole evening."

She flicked him a glance. "It's a cotillion."

"Very well. Shall we meet here?"

****

She nodded, unable to do more, then thankfully escaped to see if all was well with Ariadne. But on her way she made a detour to stand quietly for a few minutes behind the conservatory door to fan her heated face. He made her feel like a tongue-tied schoolgirl. Her pulse raced like an uncontrolled horse, and it was not only her face that was heated; she felt excessively warm all over. Not just warm, either, but as if she had swallowed a hot pepper that needed a water hose to extinguish the flames. She might not know much about being bedded, but she had an inkling of what this heat was about. She would do best to keep well away from Sir Ivor Stafford. Her head told her that, but her heart and various other parts of her anatomy seemed to be in full rebellion. "Pull yourself together," she admonished herself sharply.

She reminded herself that he had much experience in the art of dalliance, whereas she had experienced only one Season where she had been kept firmly under her aunt's chaperonage and well away from any rakes. She sighed. She seemed to have a marked predilection for rakes.

By the time she caught up with Ariadne, that young lady was enjoying herself without caring one jot about anybody else. She had left several young ladies to their own devices as she chattered excitedly to two young men. The young men looked dazzled both by her beauty and her animated conversation. Ariadne was giving them no chance to interpolate comments or questions. Helena gathered up the abandoned young ladies and smoothly introduced them into Ariadne's group. "Miss Yardley, do you remember Miss Charlton and Miss Greaves? We have not seen them in an age. And of course, the Misses Goodenough came on our trip to see Lord Elgin's marbles recently." She nodded firmly to Ariadne to follow her lead but was not optimistic. Ariadne was rarely interested in pursuing social chitchat with young ladies. She had always shown a marked preference for the male of the species. Women bored her, unless they were sycophantic.

"Oh, yes," she said carelessly, leaving her audience in no doubt that she neither remembered nor cared about Miss Charlton, Miss Greaves or the Misses Goodenough. Helena's heart sank. Miss Greaves flushed with embarrassment and anger.

Fortunately, good manners on behalf of the youths saw to it that everyone was included in the conversation, and after a short time Ariadne tired of the competition and drifted away. To the young gentlemen's credit, their eyes did not follow her. That might have been due to the fact that her behavior had been distinctly overpowering. She was apt to be overbearing when in full flight.

Helena shuddered. If they only knew what Ariadne was like in one of her temper tantrums!

She found Caroline conversing painfully with a group of young people and as she approached, Caroline gratefully excused herself murmuring, "I really don't think I enjoy this sort of thing Miss…Helena."

"It will get better, I promise you," her mentor replied. "You'll see. I was dreadfully shy for the first two or three weeks of my Season, but then I became used to the way people conversed, and their usual topics of conversation. After that it became easier." She reflected that the easy-going socialization which the Yardleys and their friends practiced would help Caroline find her feet a lot more easily than Helena's environment had.

At that moment a blushing young man approached Caroline to ask her for the second of the country-dances. He said that of course he knew she would stand up with her father for the first one, but he would deem it an honor to lead her on to the floor for the second. Caroline blushed too and whispered "Yes, thank you."

The musicians began to strike up their instruments, and Helena moved to Mrs. Yardley's side to check that all was well. As they conversed, they caught sight of Ariadne taking her first champagne of the evening from one of the hired waiters moving amongst the throng. "Lord!" Mrs. Yardley hissed. "If she gets any more excitable, we shall have to send her to bed with a dose of laudanum."

"I shall keep my eye on her as much as possible, Mrs. Yardley. But first—would it be possible for me to meet with Sir Ivor and Mr. Stafford in the study? They have requested me for news of my brother, ma'am. I feel I must talk to them, particularly Ned Stafford, since he used to be a friend of Robert's."

"Of course, my dear! Mr. Yardley and I will watch out for Ariadne, and Caroline don't need much attention." Joshua Yardley had heard the gist of their conversation and smiled encouragingly over the top of Mrs. Yardley's head.

With a clear conscience Helena hurried to Mr. Yardley's study where Sir Ivor introduced her to his brother. Helena smiled at Ned and said, "I know you must be Sir Ivor's brother. You have the look of him."

"Everyone says that," Ned responded cheerfully, shaking her hand.

"I wonder whether that could be termed a compliment or not," Sir Ivor mused, apparently to himself.

His brother playfully punched his arm. "Ivor! Take no heed of him, ma'am. Now sit down and tell me all about Robert."

It seemed that Robert, like Helena, had not kept in touch with old friends, feeling that the chill winds of disapproval so common in their acquaintance might also have extended to their closest friends. It was only when Ned had read in the Observer that Robert had been posted to the Peninsula that he discovered where Robert was.

Apart from their steward and Miss Fichton, nobody had expressed any interest in Robert or Helena since their father's demise. She was touched that this young man, who must have many friends, should remember Robert with kindness and affection. Overcome, she blinked rapidly as tears threatened. Knowing that most gentlemen became extremely uncomfortable around watering pots she raised her chin and attempted a misty smile. A large gentleman's handkerchief was pressed into her hand, and Helena gratefully wiped her eyes.

"What do you know about your brother's injuries, Miss Marshfield?"

"Hardly anything, Sir Ivor. He is reticent at the best of times, and I know he would strive not to worry me. I believe his shoulder was badly wrenched, may in fact have been dislocated and is taking some time to heal. I understand his leg is broken in more than one place. He said in his letter that he did not think he would ride or dance again." She sat for a moment with her hands folded in her lap.

She saw the brothers exchange looks.

Sir Ivor broke the silence. "Have you made arrangements for Robert to see a surgeon?"

She swallowed. "I have done nothing at all yet, and indeed I don't know which way to turn." She pleated and re-pleated Sir Ivor's immaculate handkerchief until it resembled one of Ariadne's attempts at stitchery.

"Then that is easily settled," Ned said firmly. "Ivor and I have decided that Robert must stay at Stafford House until he is well enough to be shifted to Ryewolds. I have lodgings in Duke Street and can see him often. Ivor has a huge staff standing around doing nothing because Mother spends most of her time at Ryewolds. It's only when our sisters come to town that she spends any time in London. She prefers the country. Our sisters will not be up for the Season for another couple of weeks. Ivor can arrange for Robert to spend a few weeks at Eaton Square. It's a peaceful part of town, too peaceful for my liking anyway," he laughed, "so it will suit an invalid. And you, Miss Marshfield, may come and go as you please. Isn't that right, Ivor?"

"Yes. All is arranged, Miss Marshfield, provided that is what you wish, and what you think your brother would wish for?" queried Sir Ivor.

"I-I scarcely know what to say," she murmured. She looked from one Stafford to the other. "Your unexpected kindness…"

"Pho!" Ned clicked his fingers. "Robert was a good friend to me. And just wait till I tell Tally that Robert is back! We will have some good times again!"

She smiled uncertainly at him and turned to Sir Ivor. "Sir Ivor, is this *really* what you wish? It must be an inconvenience. Robert is a stranger to you."

"Not for long, Miss Marshfield. And remember, 'tis but a short walk for you to Eaton Square, and you may visit your brother every day, circumstances permitting. I expect to see you often—no polite excuses. As Ned says, you may come and go as you please."

Helena was overwhelmed by their kindness. She fluttered her hands nervously, knowing that she should not accept the invitation but deeply grateful that they had offered her and Robert such an excellent solution to their problems.

"Robert would do the same for me," Ned averred, and suddenly she knew this to be true. She and Robert would be beholden to the Staffords for a time perhaps, but one day it might be in their power to repay the debt. Time would tell. She relaxed a trifle, then not wanting to detain them any longer, rose to her feet. "I think you gentlemen must be the kindest men in all London," she told them unsteadily.

"Enough of that," Sir Ivor said abruptly. "Now, Miss Marshfield, don't forget that cotillion you promised me."

Bemused, she realized that the dancing was well under way. Quickly she hurried to introduce some of the youngest couples to each other. Caroline and her father were the first couple on the floor, and there were six other couples lining up. With such a number of people going through the set pieces, it would be a long while till her dance with Sir Ivor.

She stood to one side, watching the Morris girls

and quite a few other young women eyeing Sir Ivor. It had not occurred to her before, but Sir Ivor was undoubtedly the target of many an ambition. Seeming not to notice, he adroitly sidestepped the attempt of a matchmaking mama to snaffle him as he passed. Helena stifled a giggle. She was close enough to hear part of the conversation.

"Sir Ivor! Do you not remember us?" Very coy.

"Of course, Mrs. Brentwood. How could I forget you and your charming daughter? But I had not realized she was out of the schoolroom yet."

Helena blinked. But Mrs. Brentwood was on the hunt and was impervious to insult. "How naughty of you, Sir Ivor! You know very well that Harriet has been out of the schoolroom for some time. Is such a charming complexion and a neat figure found on schoolroom misses? Hardly."

Sir Ivor however had bowed and moved on. Lord, if Helena had realized how every eye followed his progress around the room, she would never have been so stupid as to agree to stand up with him. Not that she had agreed, precisely. His invitation to dance had sounded suspiciously like an order.

Half an hour later she found herself with her hand through his arm going toward the ballroom to join the next set. She glanced back over her shoulder at Ned who nodded and smiled and asked her to keep him a dance too.

"Do not fret, Miss Marshfield. Your employer has given you permission to dance. You have a very expressive face, you know. It is bad for my confidence that you evince such concern about dancing with me." Ivor Stafford's pained expression pretended chagrin, although Helena doubted he was serious. She couldn't help it. She giggled like a schoolgirl then hastily pressed her gloved fingers over her mouth. She blinked with surprise at her own exuberance.

"Much better." The glint in his eyes, looked for but rarely seen, flashed for a second. Dimpling, she curtsied as the cotillion began, then stepped gracefully into the movements of a dance she hadn't danced for almost five years. Lately of course she had assisted the dancing master by demonstrating to Caroline various country dances, but she had not danced publicly since her father's death. She gave herself over to the pleasure of each stately measure, meeting with Sir Ivor at the end of each promenade. How she had missed it! She hadn't realized how much until the dance came to a close and Sir Ivor escorted her off the dance floor. She withdrew her hand from his arm, smiling shyly up at him, her inhibitions about the differences in their status temporarily forgotten. "Thank you, Sir Ivor. I wouldn't have danced except for your persuasion."

"That would have been a pity. You are an elegant dancer, Miss Marshfield," he rejoined. "Seldom have I danced with a young lady who is able to look at me when I speak rather than down at her feet as she counts the steps, and who can actually converse rationally. Most refreshing."

From which she judged that he must have had a hard time of it with some of the débutantes he had danced with. Then she blushed, wondering if he was insinuating that she had been perhaps a little too exuberant or if he just meant the compliment as it sounded. She was aware that *sometimes* she felt her circumstances deeply and was apt to read hidden meanings into perfectly polite conversations. Naturally, that didn't happen often. Did it?

"I have a question, however."

"Sir?"

"You are a beautiful woman." He stated it as a fact, not expecting any dissension, and she felt herself blushing an even deeper crimson. "Why do you think you should pay for your father's sins by hiding yourself away?"

"I don't. But I have had experience of…well, governesses are not expected to—to put themselves forward in any way." She took a deep breath. "It was a hard lesson to learn. I think I must have been much indulged when growing up."

He clicked his tongue impatiently. "I doubt that. Social usage need not turn you into a wallflower. Perhaps now that your brother is returning you will be able to set up house together and you could leave this companion business behind. Obviously, life may never again be what you were used to some years ago, but it could be more tolerable than this half-life you seem determined to live," he said. "Mrs. Yardley is a pleasant lady, but it irks me to see you like this, well educated, and with far more breeding than the woman employing you. You are passing your life as a drudge, at everyone's beck and call."

She stared at him in surprise. "Not at all!" How dare he? "In spite of your kindness to Robert and myself, Sir Ivor, I fail to see what business it is of yours. The Yardleys spoil me as you can see." She spread her hands to demonstrate that with very few employers would she be allowed to engage in social discourse or dance at a soirée.

"If you say so." He did not look convinced.

Helena discovered that it was disconcerting to be grateful to someone yet be annoyed with them at the same time. She was not only angry on her own behalf, but also for the Yardleys. What right did this man have to dictate how she lived her life? Had she made a dreadful mistake in accepting his hospitality on behalf of Robert? That comment of his was insufferably condescending. Perhaps he thought she should have remained in a boarding house somewhere, politely awaiting Robert's return whilst attending to her stitchery. A lot of good that would have done her. She would have been hungry within a se'ennight.

There was a burst of laughter from across the room, and she was reminded of her duties. "Excuse me, Sir Ivor. I must go." And she fled to the familiarity of duty, her feathers ruffled, still puzzling over the enigma that was Ivor Stafford. After checking the card-room, then ensuring that no wallflowers had been left to wilt alone in the ballroom, she signaled the caterers to begin serving supper. The Yardleys of course were renowned for their generous spreads, and although Helena had endeavored to tone down the large and somewhat vulgar variety of refreshments originally proposed, there were still cold meats, hot vegetable pastries, smoked oyster patties, sweetmeats, jellies, and candied fruits ready to spread before the guests. Josh Yardley, frustrated at what he saw as Helena's cheese-paring notions of an elegant array of foods, had balked at being denied his smoked oyster patties.

"Miss Marshfield, we *must* have smoked oyster patties and cold meats for the men. We must. Otherwise as usual we shall be left with a sticky sweet array such as you ladies prefer. But gentlemen don't like that sort of stuff."

Helena, well used to catering for large gatherings of males at Marshfield Manor had laughed and assured him that oyster patties and cold meats were already on the menu.

The ballroom was busy with murmured conversation and the muted sounds of the orchestra. So many couples were joining the dancing it was unlikely that anyone would be departing for many hours. The card-room was alight with laughter and the click of dice. When supper was brought in ceremoniously on huge trays, the seal of approval was final. The evening was a success.

Too nervous to eat anything, Helena checked here and there, ensuring that all the guests were looked after. She threaded her way through the throng and was accosted by Mrs. Morris, Anna and Charlotte's mama.

"Congratulations on an excellent evening, Miss Marshfield. I know full well who had the ordering of all this." Mrs. Morris twinkled. She was used to Mrs. Yardley's indolent ways.

"Thank you, ma'am. I have been dreadfully nervous," Helena confided. Mrs. Morris smiled. She was a sensible woman, always civil and generally liked.

"Don't worry, Miss Marshfield. If Josh Yardley had had any doubts about your ability to carry this off, you can be sure he would have hired somebody else to do the job."

That was true, Helena thought. She turned to check that Mrs. Sowerby's plate was laden with the fruit jellies she so enjoyed. Mrs. Sowerby of the strange coiffures was a bosom-bow of Mrs. Yardley and was an inveterate gossip. Helena usually evaded her sharp tongue by treating her with an air of deference. At the moment the woman's mouth was crammed full of sweetmeats and she could not therefore chatter about any of the other guests. Helena smiled and moved away. She had found that it was always best to be extremely busy when the Mrs. Sowerbys of the world wanted her attention. Having been the subject of much gossip herself, Helena shrank from discussing others.

She turned as a plate was pushed into her hand. Ned Stafford's voice whispered, "Ivor and I thought you might be able to manage a little ham, Miss Marshfield. We realize you're busy, but you must eat something." She smiled gratefully at them. A few slivers of wafer-thin ham would be just right. No doubt they were used to looking after their mother when she entertained. They would understand that anybody who had the organizing of an evening like this would be extremely nervous and unable to eat heavy foods.

Just then Mr. Yardley pushed through the crush of people toward her with a glass of champagne in his hand. "This is for you, Helena. You've done us proud, young lady. Such a success! Isn't she a right one?" he demanded of Sir Ivor who, with his brother, had propped his shoulders against the wall.

Embarrassed, Helen fought to suppress a blush. Sir Ivor had perforce to agree. The poor man had no option. Mr. Yardley was practically *throwing* her at him. She didn't know which way to look and effaced herself by murmuring softly and drifting vaguely away to check on Ariadne. Vulgarity could be viewed with amusement when she was not personally concerned, but it became unbearable when it involved a person whose good opinion she valued.

"Miss Marshfield!" She was accosted by one of the musicians. "Is the new waltz to be played this evening? We have had several requests for it."

Here was a quandary. Although the waltz, recently introduced from the continent was popular in some quarters, it was still considered by many to be not quite the done thing. Normally, a young girl's coming-out was not the place for it. However, that had to be balanced against the fact that the Yardleys were not of the top rung of society. Probably nobody except the highest sticklers would consider it noteworthy that the waltz had been danced at the private dress-party of a merchant's daughter.

Helena chewed her lip then shrugged and guided the musician toward Mrs. Yardley. This was not a decision for her to make.

"Oh, dearie, we should have thought of that. Of course they should have their fun! Why not? We'll ask Mr. Yardley, but I'm sure he'll agree. Won't you, my dear?" she demanded as she approached her husband. She had literally cut a swathe through the people thronging about the supper tables. She sailed along in her puce gown like a fat little sailing ship with Helena trailing behind her.

"Yes indeed, Helena. A capital idea! Instruct the musicians to strike up an impromptu waltz after the next country-dance. That will keep our guests happy, eh?" Josh Yardley was full of bonhomie, or perhaps he was full of some of the contents of his excellent cellar below-stairs.

Ned and Ivor Stafford watched from the sidelines. "Stands out from the mob, doesn't she?" Ned murmured.

"Who?"

"As if you didn't know. Miss Marshfield, of course."

"Mmm."

"Like a lily in a field of daisies."

"Good Lord, Ned! You're waxing poetical. Some men prefer daisies."

"Yes, but not you."

Ivor tried to look bored and refused to rise to the bait, but he approached Helena with intent as soon as he saw she was not busy. "Do you waltz, Miss Marshfield?"

"Not very well. I've not really had the chance."

"No you don't, Ivor. It's my turn," interrupted Ned who had sauntered up behind him. "Please let me have the first waltz, Miss Marshfield. Remember—you promised me."

"I did?" She smiled at Ned. "If you don't mind a clumsy partner then. But I must talk to my charges first."

She rounded up Ariadne and Caroline and, directing a quelling frown at Ariadne, said, "I don't want the waltz turned into a mad romp, Ariadne. Otherwise your father may forbid us any more waltzing this evening." Well, anything was possible.

"I love to waltz," Ariadne said, almost bouncing in her dancing slippers. "Of course they will play more than one."

But Caroline held back, looking miserable. "I have only a sketchy knowledge of the steps. We did not think…"

No. Nobody had thought it necessary that a girl not

yet out would need to know the steps of the infamous waltz. Helena hesitated. "I think the best thing for you to do is to sit the first waltz out. If any young man requests you to dance, why not suggest that your first one is taken? Then watch to see how it's done. You will see how the steps you practiced with the dancing master look when danced properly. But as this is your first evening out, much will be forgiven you."

Caroline nodded, committing this to memory, then bubbled over with laughter. "Oh, Helena. That gentleman over there said that my eyes were like diamonds! Did you ever hear anything more ridiculous?"

Helena chuckled. "My goodness, he *did* empty the butter-boat over you, didn't he?"

Caroline giggled and would have continued but Helena raised her finger. "Tell me all the details tomorrow, my dear. Now is not the place."

"Oh...of course."

When Helena took the floor with Ned Stafford she discovered that she felt awkward and embarrassed to have his arm about her in the style of the new dance. The waltz was so...intimate. Even though Ned was a nice person and she trusted him, she did not feel quite at ease. It had been a long time since she had stood this close to a man. Perhaps if it were Sir Ivor that she was to waltz with she would feel a little safer. For some reason he imbued her with a sense of security that no other person had ever done. Even her father had been more her indulgent friend than her protector. She had no idea why Ivor Stafford should have this effect on her.

And it was such a shame really, because Ned was

by far the nicer man. It was strange how one could feel so anxious and yet inwardly excited with one gentleman, and yet feel nothing but polite acceptance of another. Ned had plenty of address and was a likable young man. Like his brother he dressed well, although he had not quite left behind a young man's leaning toward dandyism. His shirt points were a trifle too high, and his cravat was a complicated affair. As they'd arrived she had heard his older brother quizzing him. "Good God, Ned! What do you call that?"

"It is an invention of my own." Said with dignity.

"I think you'd better work a little more on your invention."

"Ivor! It's not so bad. I was in the devil of a hurry this evening though."

"Yes. That's precisely what your cravat looks like. Perhaps you'd better name it 'Vite, vite'."

"What do you mean?"

"Quick, quick."

Good-natured Ned exploded into laughter.

Helena had smothered a smile and purported not to have overheard. She decided that Ned was an engaging scamp and was very like Robert. He would be fun to have as a brother.

However, she could not see Sir Ivor in the light of a brother at all. It was obvious he had had plenty of experience in engaging the emotions of young ladies. He was a man who understood women. He was different from Ned. Ned was not like that at all. His jaw was every bit as square as his brother's, and he certainly was just as determined. He had organized Robert's homecoming very efficiently. But he seemed to be of a more easygoing nature than Ivor. That was the way of many second and third sons. They knew they would not have to succeed to their father's responsibilities, and their lives were far less complicated than those of their elder brethren.

Helena cast a swift glance around, wondering if Sir Ivor intended to dance the next waltz with her as he had said. At present he was not dancing, just leaning against a pillar, deep in discussion with a man she had never seen before. He was, however, looking in her direction. Quickly she looked down, pretending an inordinate interest in the polished parquetry as it spun past.

As the first waltz finished and Ned stepped back to bow, Sir Ivor took his place. It was as smooth as that. She tensed and was immediately very aware of him. He held her exactly as Ned had done but... She steeled herself and fixed her gaze on his cravat—*not* 'Vite, Vite' but an elegant Waterfall—and endeavored to appear serene. It seemed that they danced together extremely well. For once she was glad she wasn't a little dab of a thing, that she was quite tall. In fact, several couples around them fell back to give them room. When she realized this, Helena blushed painfully. Again. Thanks to Ivor Stafford she had blushed more this evening than she had in her whole life.

As the waltz drew to a close, Ivor Stafford glanced down at her and said, "You dance beautifully, Miss Marshfield. In spite of the wretched cap, you will be inundated with partners after this."

"I had not expected to dance, you see. I wore the cap because I am a chaperone."

Nevertheless, his words turned out to be prophetic. As soon as she had finished one dance, a partner would approach her for the next one. Had that been Ivor

Stafford's intention to make his point about not withdrawing from the world? Had he only danced with her in order to establish her as a desirable partner? Well, he had certainly succeeded.

An hour later she swung breathlessly into the third and last waltz with Mr. Yardley. Mrs. Yardley watched them fondly, and when the dance was finished, she clapped her hands saying, "Eh, but you two do look elegant! You must give these girls of ours more lessons in the waltz, Helena. Now, here is Lord Elverton waiting to lead you into the country-dance."

Helena's euphoria came crashing down as, stricken, she looked up into the haughty face of her father's erstwhile 'friend.' Fear had her stammering. "M-my lord...I must decline, I'm sorry. My first d-duty is to my charges." She had no desire to brangle with this man in public. She mistrusted him intensely and knew that if he criticized her father as he had done before, she would not be able to contain herself. Even though her father had seemed to like him, she had never been able to stomach the man. He had treated her with a haughty but indulgent air, much like an adult with a child. It had always raised her hackles. Underneath that smooth, polished address she sensed a harsh, unforgiving nature allied to an overdeveloped sense of self-worth. Confirming her opinion he snarled, "It didn't seem to bother you a moment ago that you had duties to attend to."

"I was given permission, but now I must go." She would have brushed past him, but he gripped her arm painfully.

"Yes, and you have just been given permission to dance with me by your employer. I say you *shall* dance with me *now*," he hissed, his swarthy countenance furious.

Helplessly Helena looked about her for aid. She could no longer see the Yardleys. She tried to tug her arm away. His fingers bit painfully into her skin, and she pulled harder. The puffed sleeve of her carefully sewn gown tore as she wrenched herself from his grasp and hurried away. Embarrassed and horrified, she heard his raised voice follow her. "Forgetting who you are, Miss Marshfield? I knew your father, remember that. I still hold one of his vowels."

She hesitated, then turned and unwillingly retraced her steps. Several people had overheard and were staring at the two of them, avid for gossip.

"Not so hoity toity now, are you, Miss Marshfield? Surely you realized I'd come to collect one day?"

Holding fast to her torn sleeve, she stared up at him, stricken, unable to gather her wits. Was he speaking the truth? Could it be "*the*" vowel over which she'd spent many sleepless nights? Was he talking about something else entirely, or was he trying to terrorize her?

She inhaled deeply, trying to gather her thoughts. His statement did not ring true. With his vindictive nature he would surely have approached her before now to collect from the estate. He had become one of her father's most vociferous critics and had been on their doorstep even before Papa was buried to collect monies owed. Why had he not then declared this other debt he was talking about?

Grabbing a fistful of courage she blurted, "I don't believe you."

"*What*?" he roared.

Oh God. She should not have said that. Desperately she sought for an innocuous phrase with which to pacify him. But her mind was a blank and she stood at the edge of the dance-floor, her hand clenched over her sleeve, staring at him as people brushed past.

As usual he was dressed in black. Only his cravat was white. It looked sickly against his swarthy skin. She had always thought of him as a malignant crow. His sloe-black eyes bored into hers. *Why* had Mr. Yardley invited this terrible person to his house? Probably because Elverton had a title, and the Yardleys, in all their naïveté, adored titles. Helena bit her lip, conscious of a hushed murmuring as a circle of people began to form around them.

"Is everything all right, Miss Marshfield?" a voice asked.

Thank goodness! Sir Ivor. Without thinking, she turned blindly toward him, trying to summon up a wavering smile. "Sir Ivor, Lord Elverton and I—" She looked imploringly at Sir Ivor, willing him to understand.

He did. One minute Lord Elverton was sneering down at her; the next he was being moved firmly through the throng by Sir Ivor in the direction of the conservatory.

"This way, Foxhyth," she heard Sir Ivor say briskly. And that was the last she saw of Lord Elverton that evening.

It was much later that she heard from Mrs. Yardley what had transpired. Sir Ivor had apparently escorted Lord Elverton only as far as the conservatory where he had asked him to leave the premises. After some sharp questioning as to what right a Stafford had to evict a

Foxhyth from premises that did not belong to either, Lord Elverton had dismissed the whole incident with a shrug and sauntered away, leaving behind his cloak, hat, and cane. Mrs. Yardley was much entertained by this tidbit of gossip, though appalled to think that a lord should have received such treatment under her roof. Along with most of her guests, she was avidly curious to find out what Lord Elverton had wanted from Helena Marshfield.

Helena did not hear about that until the following morning. After the incident she had endeavored to paste a pleasant smile on her face and pretend that she had not a care in the world. She had pinned up her dress and sought solace in performing her duties. Ignoring the whispers and stares, she had tried to show only her efficient, serene façade. Nobody watching could have suspected that her pulse was fluttering erratically in her throat and her hard-won confidence lay in shreds.

She had seen the Stafford men only for a moment when they left. As she stood behind the Yardleys, she had received a wink from Ned, and Sir Ivor had murmured quietly, "Pleased to be of service in that matter. Let me know if he troubles you again." This was followed by a quick bow, then he turned from her to address someone else. She was grateful for his help, but what a ninny he must think her, unable to deal with an importunate man at her age. After all, it was not as if she were a schoolroom miss. At four and twenty she should be able to deal with difficult situations with aplomb.

Fortunately Mrs. Yardley was so ecstatic about the success of the evening that she lost the opportunity to question Helena about Lord Elverton. Helena endured an hour of a lecture on all the smallest details Mrs. Yardley could recall, from listing the various attendees who had paid her compliments on the evening's enjoyment right down to the high quality of the mushroom patties and the fortuitous card-table seating. Helena smiled patiently and eventually managed to escape and drag herself upstairs to bed.

As she poked at the fire in her room, she brooded on the dent her reputation had just received. It was no use pretending that her argument with Lord Elverton was unimportant. Many people had overheard his comments.

It was starting all over again—the hushed whispers that culminated in disparaging glances. The past five years of carefully effacing herself in social situations had all been for nothing. She had swallowed jibes from those who were as equally in debt as her father had been, but who lived on tick or on expectations. To think she had endured grinding boredom in her chosen occupation and denigrating comments from Ariadne for it all to come to this. She had been so sure that she had finally left behind her those days of being the butt of gossipmongers.

Resolving to be sensible and set the matter aside, she spent a sleepless night worrying her problems like a dog with a bone. One moment she worried that the unsigned vowel hidden in her drawer applied to Lord Elverton; the next she worried that her wanton behavior in dancing in such an abandoned manner with Sir Ivor *twice* had been noted by all and sundry. Not that the cotillion when they had first paired together could be described as 'abandoned' precisely. But their waltz, although decorous, had, by its very nature, been…invigorating.

Instead of remembering all those hard-learned lessons she had slipped her leash well and truly with one waltz with *him*. Even now her body thrummed with the warmth and delight of giving herself up to the music and the shelter of his arms which said to her quite clearly "safe, you are safe now."

No, she was not safe. She rued her wayward nature which had whistled down the wind two boring but worthy suitors five years ago. Now that she was no longer on the marriage mart, she had found the man of her dreams—well, not exactly of her dreams—he was too arbitrary for that. But he could be kind when he chose. She preferred that to the too-easy manners of his brother. Ned was a pleasant man, but he did not challenge her.

And anyway, what was Sir Ivor Stafford about, dancing a cotillion and a waltz with a mere companion? She did not understand him.

Had she comported herself more like a companion and less like the favored daughter of the house, none of this would have happened. It was not that she had behaved with impropriety. It was just that for a short time she had forgotten what she had become.

And that was the crux of the matter. It seemed that even five years later she must still pay for her father's foolishness. Not for the first time, Helena wondered at her father. He had been a likeable man, self-indulgent and careless of responsibility. He had also been completely self-centered. How could he not have considered what would happen to his children after his suicide? Helena's greatest fear was that he had promised her hand in marriage to Lord Elverton. That promissory note she held was ambiguous and vague. But she remembered how her father had repeatedly requested her presence when Lord Elverton called on them, even though he knew Helena detested the man. Elverton's strange attitude toward her of a bizarre mix of indifference and avarice had made her cringe. Worst of all had been the cold, proprietary glint in his eyes every time he looked at her. That was the way he had looked at her this evening too.

At the time she had been presented to the Queen, a rumor was circulating that Lord Elverton had 'uplifted' the sixteen years old daughter of one of his friends and disappeared with her for several days. The marriage announcement was expected daily but somehow did not eventuate. Speculation ran rife because he was an undeniable catch. Some murmured that the young lady had prevailed upon her father to release her from any obligations. She had preferred perpetual banishment to life with Lord Elverton. Helena could understand that.

What had Sir Ivor said to Lord Elverton as he led him away? His face had been impassive as usual, and she could read nothing in it.

Wriggling beneath the bedclothes she sighed, exhausted but unable to sleep. It seemed as though she was now paying for cutting herself off from the world for the past five years. Yes, it had been a form of self-indulgence, but it had been for her protection too. Tonight she felt as if she had been stripped of several layers of skin.

The brightest star on her horizon was the Staffords' kind invitation to Robert. It would be wonderful to see Robert again. She desperately hoped his injuries would not prove to be too debilitating. She sighed as she rolled over, trying to still her restless mind in sleep. Alas, four o'clock in the morning was a friendless time.

Chapter Seven

Outside the city of Coimbra two horsemen, one Portuguese, one English, headed toward the French divisions commanded by Soult. As dusk drew in, they slowed their horses to a walk. At the point of the Mondego River where it curved so that the spires of the cathedral could be seen, they were intercepted by a French sentry accompanied by a French officer whose uniform was indistinguishable in the fading light. The Englishman dismounted and took from his saddlebag a sheaf of papers. Stepping directly up to the French officer he saluted and handed over the package.

****

When it came time to get up, Helena found it hard to face the day. She looked in the mirror as she tidied her hair and a wan, tired face stared back. Depressed and dreading the Yardleys' post-mortem on the evening's events she dragged herself downstairs with as much enthusiasm as the French nobility approached the tumbril.

First of all she had to approach Josh Yardley, and she knew he would not be happy about having his prize guest snatched away. Hopefully he was still thrilled about last evening's success.

"Mr. Yardley, would it be possible for me to visit my brother at Stafford House occasionally over the next few weeks? I promise not to neglect the girls in any way."

"Stafford House? I thought your brother would be coming here."

As she feared, he did not take the news well. He frowned and stared at her searchingly as if trying to read her mind, then suddenly he was all smiles. He changed tack. "Of course, m'dear. You must meet with your brother as often as you wish. And should you need an escort at any time, please let me know."

Aha! Mr. Yardley was hoping she would cement further friendliness between the Staffords and the Yardleys. She sighed inwardly but could not bring herself to condemn him. He was the father of two marriageable daughters, and his business dealings and political ambitions could be advanced with Sir Ivor as his patron. It didn't seem to occur to him that a mere companion would scarcely hold any influence over a family such as the Staffords. Mr. Yardley still saw Helena as Miss Marshfield of Marshfield Manor, Oxford. This was fortunate for Helena, but not practical in the eyes of the *ton*.

She murmured, "Thank you."

All during breakfast, Caroline received a constant stream of billets and posies, and though pleased to receive them, was unsure which particular young man had actually sent them. She confided to Helena, "The whole party is such a blur! I cannot recall anyone's names. Although I enjoyed my party—or I did toward the end of it—I would not want to go through all that too often."

Fortunately Ariadne had breakfasted in bed for she would have been excessively put out to see how popular her young sister had become overnight.

It seemed that Caroline had enjoyed herself as much as her sensitive temperament would allow, but unlike her sister and mother she had no bent for socializing tirelessly. Helena hoped that Caroline would not be forced into a mold more in keeping with Ariadne's temperament. That bright intelligence merited more than dances and rout parties and morning visits. She would make an excellent diplomat's wife or a wife for one of the more conscientious members of the House of Commons. A businessman such as one of the Indian nabobs recently come to town would find her intelligence and charm irresistible, but Helena knew that that was the very background from which Mr. Yardley was trying to elevate his daughters.

When Helena mentioned the kindness of the Staffords and how Robert would be staying at Stafford House, Caroline exclaimed, "Helena, how marvelous! That would be just the thing. May I visit Robert with you? It seems as though I almost know your brother through his letters."

Helena hesitated. She hoped Caroline was not seeing Robert as a hero from one of Mrs. Radcliffe's famous novels. Although pragmatic, she was of an impressionably romantic age. However, it was probable that faced with the reality of Robert crippled and unable to ride or dance, possibly in pain permanently, a damper would be cast on some of Caroline's more romantic notions. It would do her no harm to see what wounded heroes had to endure.

Helena mentally made a list of all the things she needed from the apothecary's which might be useful for Robert's recovery. Her hands clenched beneath the breakfast table as she gnawed at her problems. One thing was certain—as soon as Robert arrived, she would solicit the attentions of one of the better surgeons in the area. She would not be able to secure the services of someone like Sir William Fox of course, although she wished it were possible. The renowned gentleman was said to be a wizard, and it seemed as though only a wizard would be able to repair the damage done to Robert's leg and shoulder.

By good fortune, Ariadne bounced downstairs in a sunny mood. She interrupted Helena and Caroline's conversation without compunction. "Helena, why don't we go to the bazaar today? 'Tis always fun to shop for new ribbons and such. Do say we may go." Somehow she managed to project an order into her tone.

"What a good idea, Ariadne! I need to procure some trifles for my brother—"

But Ariadne was already starting back upstairs. She had not waited for an answer. She was not interested in the twitterings of her companion and had no hesitation in cutting short Helena's comments. Helena grimaced. She could not remonstrate with Ariadne because Ariadne's parents often did the same thing.

At the bazaar Ariadne darted straight to the ribbon sellers and Caroline meandered along in her wake. Keeping an eye on her charges from the next aisle, Helena sought out the medicines she might need. Having no clear notion of what would be required she purchased smelling salts, yards of bandage, basilicum powder, and lavender water. She would have to visit the apothecary's for laudanum drops. She had little experience of sickrooms, but that was of no account. This was her brother. She would do her best.

A couple of inappropriate prospective purchases by

her charges snapped her mind to attention. From habit she disparaged a tasteless knot of ribbons in a violent shade of purple chosen by Ariadne as "Charming, but definitely for a dowager, don't you agree?" and persuaded Caroline that "Darling you *know* the sweet pretty little kittens will only be suitable as rat-catchers. Your father will never allow them in the house."

Heavens, she would be glad when this day ended. As well as being on tenterhooks worrying about Robert, she was exhausted after her late night. It did not seem to have affected Ariadne at all, although Caroline was lackluster today.

Most of all, Helena longed to have some time to herself to examine her entirely unsuitable feelings about Sir Ivor. For in spite of telling herself hourly that she was causing herself grief, she was unable to stop her thoughts dwelling overlong on Ivor Stafford. And now it looked as though their paths would cross more often than she had anticipated, making it doubly difficult to see him only in the light of a mere acquaintance.

"You must nip this thing in the bud," she muttered to herself.

"What was that, Helena?"

Lord, had she spoken aloud? "Nothing, Caroline."

Nip it in the bud, indeed. It was already too late. Just because the man had shown her kindness and was disposed to flirt a little with her did not mean she should take his behavior seriously. He was a reformed rake who now had the responsibility of a family who depended upon him. She was sure that what he had in mind was a light-hearted dalliance, but it could end with her losing her heart to him. Then she snorted. Silly Helena. Too late. Usually a most reliable organ, her heart had been misbehaving oddly ever since that day at Hookham's Library.

Oh yes, she could enumerate all his faults, such as his arrogant desire to order the lives of all those around him, and his tendency to ride rough-shod over those he considered his dependents, but she knew all that and it didn't make a blind bit of difference. He was still the epitome of what she held most important in a man. It was easily seen that in spite of his past reputation he was a man of honor. If only she had met him five years ago…no. If she had met him then he would no doubt have on his sleeve an opera dancer or be carrying on a secret relationship with a society matron. Perhaps it was as well she had not met him in his salad days because she would have bored him witless. Anyway, her aunt would never have allowed her anywhere near him.

She blinked and forced her mind to dwell on something else—anything else than Ivor Stafford.

What if Robert decided to sell out? Would the proceeds, wisely invested, support them both? Probably not. It would not be a large sum. No, she needed to take herself to task and forget waltzes and impossible daydreams. It was just that she yearned for her own space—a place where privacy meant exactly that, not where she had always to keep her bedchamber door unlocked in case one of her charges needed her, and where she was at the beck and call of a group of people all *wanting* something from her.

The most frustrating thing of all was that she had no idea of the extent of Robert's injuries because that would determine what their futures might be. Anyway, under no circumstances could she expect Robert with all his physical problems to maintain her for the rest of her life. Whichever angle she looked at it from, she was left with the inescapable fact that she was destined to be a governess or companion forever.

For the slightest moment a vision slid through her mind of a tall, quiet man clasping her hand for the waltz. She was fathoms deep in longing. Then recalled to reality by the noise around her, she ruthlessly stamped on the yearning, relegating it to where all the other wistful dreams had gone. She lifted her chin and joined Ariadne and Caroline.

Her discomfiture and worry were complete when Mrs. Sowerby paid a morning visit the following day and managed by sly innuendoes to mention the Stafford men and Lord Elverton all in one breath whilst smiling archly at Helena.

"Why, Miss Marshfield, we did not realize that a governess would have such illustrious associations! My goodness, there you were, dancing several times with the Staffords and chatting with Lord Elverton. What a sociable young lady you are. I trust you had a pleasant evening, my dear?"

Gritting her teeth, and driven into a corner, Helena met the woman's eye. "Actually, they are all friends of my brother and father. I have not set eyes on Lord Elverton for several years and I have not met young Mr. Stafford before. However, they were all most kind."

Mrs. Yardley looked every bit as avid as her friend did, although her expression was tempered with a sort of ashamed pity.

Helena could not bear it. She would not be drawn further into any more post-mortems. She stood. "Excuse me. I must fetch a shawl for Ariadne. The fire is not drawing properly, and Ariadne is wearing a light dress. She must be cold." Before Ariadne could protest, Helena hurried to the door. Even then she was thrown upon the ropes by Mrs. Sowerby gushing slyly, "Dear Ariadne. Such a pretty dress! But what are you thinking of, Miss Marshfield? Surely Ariadne should be wearing a warmer garment at this time of year? Is there something on your mind, my dear, that you have not fulfilled your duties as conscientiously as usual?"

The barbs found their target. Struggling to maintain her countenance, Helena murmured her excuses and left the withdrawing-room. This was terrible. As if she had not agonized enough over her behavior at Caroline's party, she now had to suffer the coy innuendoes of the vulgar Mrs. Sowerby.

"You brought this upon yourself, Helena, so get over it." Common sense told her that her worry about Robert was contributing to the feeling that all her nerve endings were exposed. The harsh reality was that she would spend the rest of her life being patronized by people such as Mrs. Sowerby and Mrs. Yardley.

She couldn't bear it any longer. She would invent a task that took her far away from the household for an hour or two to give her time to compose herself. Leaving the room in such haste could only foment speculation. That had been a silly thing to do.

Sidestepping the withdrawing-room, she fetched Ariadne's shawl and passed it to Stalley to deliver. Mrs. Yardley had expressed a vague wish for some of the new sweet licorice sweetmeats from Prynnes the grocers, which she had seen on a handbill recently. Helena decided that was as good an excuse as any to escape the confines of the house, even though the rain was sleeting down outside. The girls would not want to go out in this weather so she would not be looked for.

With the weather being so inclement, she chose her heavy cloak and poke bonnet because at least they would protect her a little and best of all, they would dry in due course. She clattered in her pattens down the front step and on to the portico. One of the few advantages of being a companion was that at least one could use the front entrance on occasion. Stalley was ushering a visitor in but she did not look up. Keeping her eyes downcast, she scurried out into the wind and rain, hoping to escape to Hookham's for a peaceful hour alone.

It was not to be.

"Miss Marshfield!" exclaimed the voice which had kept her awake for the past few nights. "Just the lady I came to see."

Oh, God. Helena's heart sank. Much as she desired to see him, she did not relish meeting with Sir Ivor under the present circumstances.

"Is there somewhere my carriage could convey you on such a wet day?"

They were standing beneath the portico and the rain was blowing in on them, yet neither made a move to shift under shelter.

"No thank you, sir. It was just that…I mean…" She shrugged helplessly, keeping her head down so that he could not see her face. She hoped to Heaven that no one chose to look out of the withdrawing-room window at this moment. It would be just her luck that Mrs. Sowerby would call for her carriage to be brought around right now. Nervously her eyes darted around. Then she flinched as she found herself swept through the rain and up into the Stafford carriage.

Ivor Stafford sat down beside her, his coat speckled with raindrops. "Now, where was it you wanted to go?"

"Nowhere in particular, Sir Ivor." Dash it all. Her plans were all awry. She rearranged the damp folds of her cloak.

He raised his eyebrows, as well he might. "But the weather, Miss Marshfield! I know you are an indefatigable walker but really, this is not the day for a walk."

Hearing the laughter in his voice, she looked up unguardedly. "I have a small item to purchase for Mrs. Yardley. And I don't mind the rain—well, not much."

He laughed. "You must be a veritable Amazon if you don't mind this sort of rain! It has just begun to teem in torrents. I'm sure Mrs. Yardley is not so unkind as to expect you to go out in this weather?"

"No. Mrs. Yardley is all that is kind," Helena hastened to reply. She well knew that Mrs. Yardley would be horrified to see anybody stepping out in this weather. Dear Mrs. Yardley had a horror of the elements. She mistrusted dew, rain, sunshine, wind, cold, heat, snow, ice—anything at all really. And no doubt Sir Ivor suspected that.

"I just...*needed*...a walk, that's all."

"Has something happened to upset you?" Unlike his normal fashionably languid tone, his voice sounded kind and concerned. Her hands shook. It had been five years since anyone had expressed an interest in her feelings. Caroline was sweet but had no knowledge or understanding outside her protected sphere. She received trenchant sympathy from Miss Fichton, but Miss Fichton saw governessing as the most important vocation in the world. She did not understand that anyone *forced* into that occupation had anything to complain about.

This man may be planning to give her a slip on the shoulder, but he seemed to understand in a way that others did not, how difficult it was to change the whole style of one's life. For a fleeting moment she wondered what event had altered his life so much to change him from the dissolute rake she had heard about to the autocratic, self-contained man he was now. Was there more than the natural succession to his father's shoes responsible for the abrupt changes in his life?

She clenched her hands in her lap. She could think of nothing to say.

"Anyway, we may as well converse in my carriage as anywhere else," Sir Ivor said firmly. "I came to tell you that after some investigation, we have had word of your brother. So we have arranged for him to arrive in London tomorrow."

"Tomorrow? Dear Robert, I miss him so," she exclaimed.

"You do realize, Miss Marshfield, that Robert may be…well—"

"Oh no, I understand," she broke in. "I have been preparing my mind for a shock ever since I heard the news about the extent of his injuries. I must admit I am nervous about seeing his injuries for the first time, but I keep reminding myself that the sight of ugly wounds is nothing compared to the agony Robert has suffered. My main concern is to find a good surgeon to attend him. No doubt the army surgeons did their best but…" She shuddered, thinking of the butchering of limbs that was the main job of the army surgeons.

"Please do not worry. We have organized for Sir

William Fox to meet your brother two days after he arrives. We thought it best to let him settle in first before the surgeon sees him. Ned and I will send for you when Robert is ready to see you. You need have no fear of meeting him *in extremis*." He grimaced. "I fear this war is only just beginning, as the French have not been easily rompéed thus far. There will be many men returning in Robert's state. The appalling thing is that some Englishmen have no sense of nationality at all. Campaign secrets are being sold, and the smuggling in of French goods is rampant. Thoughtlessness and greed in England will not help our troops win battles on the Peninsula." Then he broke off and gave her an apologetic half-smile. "Forgive me. This is a hobby horse of mine."

She gazed at him in surprise. Most fine London gentlemen appeared to have no knowledge at all of war conditions on the Peninsula and cared even less. She had constantly been irritated at the frivolous yet hypercritical attitude toward the war, but she could not fault either Mr. Yardley or Sir Ivor. Admittedly, much of Mr. Yardley's interest lay in the decline in commerce between England and the continent, but she had also noted that he was patriotic and au fait with all the latest military maneuvers.

She ventured a query. "You seem to be of the same mind as Mr. Yardley on the matter, Sir Ivor."

He glanced at her. "Yes. He has a grasp of military maneuvers far beyond anything I have, but I fancy I have the best of him when it comes to the political reasoning behind many of our moves in Portugal and Spain thus far."

Helena hesitated. "Perhaps Robert may be able to

enlighten you with what he knows," she ventured.

"Possibly," Sir Ivor agreed, but she could see that he thought a captain acting as aide-de-camp in the field might have no especial knowledge of tactics. However, perhaps Robert could help in another way. Tentatively she broached the subject. "I have some letters, sir, which may interest you. They are from Robert about his brigade's escapades during the war thus far. Robert has it in mind to put them into diary form and perhaps publish them if he gains permission to do so from the Horse Guards."

He seemed greatly taken by this. "Excellent, Miss Marshfield!"

He saw her surprised look and said, "When Robert is fully recovered from his journey, I will explain precisely why I am so interested in his letters. It's rather complicated, but extremely important."

She had no idea what he was talking about, so she just smiled politely.

"Now that you know your brother is arriving tomorrow, is there anything in particular that you wish me to provide for his comfort?"

"You are very kind, sir," she said warmly, impulsively stretching out a gloved hand then drawing it back hastily. However he retrieved her hand and held it lightly, so that she might withdraw it at will. Her complexion heightened, she gazed down at her wet feet. "I shall wait until we have found out more about his injuries." In order to cover the fact that she was surreptitiously furling and unfurling her hand resting so snugly in his she changed the subject. "I-I fear it is too wet to go walking now."

"Miss Marshfield, it has been far too wet *all*

morning for walking," he said, in the amused tone he so often used with her.

She wouldn't call it *flirting* exactly, just dallying. No doubt there being no other suitable young ladies around he was amusing himself at her expense.

"I suggest you go back inside and keep warm. I must leave you now. Hopefully I shall see you late tomorrow, but if not, then the following day. I shall send a note. Is that acceptable?" He quirked an eyebrow, and his firmly chiseled lips held an upward curve, daring her to disagree.

"Er…yes. Of course." She could hardly say anything else. She was deeply in his debt, high-handed as he was. He assisted her down from the carriage and to her indignation she saw that his poor groom had been stoically sitting in the drizzle awaiting instructions. The indifference of him! How could he do that? Seem so kind one minute and yet be so insufferably uncaring of his employee's plight the next?

She cast a sympathetic glance at the groom who remained wooden-faced, staring straight ahead. "Your sympathy is wasted," said a voice in her ear. "He prefers waiting there like that. I suggested he wait in the Yardleys' kitchen but he said no. Something about Cook."

"Oh, yes. Poppy *hates* strangers in her kitchen and makes a lot of noise, stamping around and blowing through her nose until the person has gone. I understand why he prefers to sit in the rain." She giggled.

"Thank goodness I have a male chef." He quirked an eyebrow.

Helena refused to rise to the bait.

After a pause where it seemed he was waiting for

her to take him up on his comment, he continued, "Inside you go out of the rain. Till next time."

He then totally unnerved her by raising her hand to his lips and kissing it, after the fashion fast going out of style. A tremor went through her as his warm lips touched her gloved fingers. She could not of course actually *feel* the touch of his lips, but she could well *imagine* how they felt, and somehow that seemed more sensuous and breathtaking than had he actually touched her skin. And for a moment the look in his eyes as he straightened up took her remaining breath away. She gulped inelegantly. Whatever had made her think that gray eyes were cool? For a second she had glimpsed a silver conflagration that was swiftly masked.

Turning away he sprang up into his carriage. Helena, thoroughly discomposed, brushed past Stalley and hurried in through the door. Naturally Stalley had been standing beneath the portico, surreptitiously trying to overhear their conversation. She fled upstairs to her room and sat down on her bed to reflect.

But reflection brought little comfort. She was extremely puzzled by Sir Ivor's attitude toward her. One moment he seemed withdrawn; the next he was her self-appointed protector. At the same time he seemed to be lightly flirting with her. It was true that some gentlemen enjoyed flirting with governesses and companions, many of whom were highly born but unsuitable as marriage partners due to their lack of dowry or respectable family connections. Sometimes their reputations had suffered in some way. Helena wondered how many unhappy young women were taken in by the flirting and built false hopes based on nothing. She could well end up like that. She *must* take a firm hold of herself.

What did he want? A desperate little sob escaped. Why did her life suddenly seem so untenable? Her sense of humor had completely deserted her. She had managed up till now. Surely she could continue?

She was brought back to earth by drops of water dripping from her bonnet on to the rag rug at her feet. It was just as well she had proceeded no farther on her walk because even just stepping between the portico and Sir Ivor's carriage had dampened her cloak and bonnet considerably. She spread her things to dry in front of the small fire in her room. Betsy was kind about carrying lumps of coal all the way upstairs to Helena's bedroom. Helena had offered to do it herself, but Betsy was appalled. "That's not for you to do, miss. Leave it to me." She persisted in calling Helena "miss" as if Helena were one of the daughters of the house.

Since Helena had offered to teach her to read, Betsy had become Helena's champion. "You would make an excellent dresser," she had said to Betsy one day. "You are extremely talented in the care of ladies' dresses and such. I could teach you to read and write if you like. That way you could find work as a lady's maid."

"Is that right, miss? At home only my oldest brother had any schooling. All the rest of us went into service, praise be. For my father died when I was but a child, and Ma had her hands full with the rest of us. But my brother says that girls don't read."

"But I read, and so do Miss Ariadne and Miss Caroline."

However Betsy shrugged this off saying that she was only a maid and was not expected to learn to read.

Helena's response had been to place some picture books in Betsy's room, trusting that curiosity would one day get the better of her.

But Helena wondered now whether Betsy wasn't a lot happier in her ignorant state, just as Helena would have been had she never met Ivor Stafford.

Sometimes it was better not to know.

Chapter Eight

The weather remained uncertain, typical of early May. The Yardley daughters and their governess took a hack to Bond Street, to perambulate and be seen, hoping to meet some of their acquaintances and also to observe the fashions and behavior of those around them. They were peering in a shop front when they were hailed by Anna Morris. "Well met, Ariadne! I had hoped to see you. Do say you'll come to our place to have a chat about Caroline's party. You too, Miss Marshfield."

Like the Yardleys, the Misses Morris tended to treat Helena as one of the family. Helena reminded herself again how fortunate she was. She thanked Anna Morris and smiled. "But I know you young ladies will feel *much* happier without a chaperone to overhear your secrets."

They laughed, knowing she was teasing them, but relieved all the same that they could chat unguardedly. Helena felt almost a hundred years old, but she knew it was not their intention. She was just sensitive of late.

Having escorted all the young ladies to the Morris home in Chelsea Gardens, Helena returned to Russell Square to find a message awaiting her. It was brief and to the point. Obviously penned by Sir Ivor, she thought amusedly. "Your brother has arrived safely. He is pulled by his journey but is much better than we expected. Come when you wish."

How like Ivor Stafford! A strange mixture of commands and comfort. No waste of words. She examined the large black signature. It just seemed to be a large "S". She tucked the note away in her armoire.

Hurrying downstairs to find Mrs. Yardley, she was brought up short to see Mrs. Sowerby in full sail entering the small withdrawing-room. Helena waited quietly for a pause in the conversation and managed to attract her employer's attention. Under Mrs. Sowerby's avid gaze she explained where she was going, and that she would meet with Ariadne and Caroline later in the afternoon.

"Oh, my dear, *of course* you must go straight away to see Sir Robert! Take the carriage. I do hope he feels more the thing shortly. Please give him our kind regards, and I know you'll remember to thank Sir Ivor prettily. Of course you will," she added quickly, as Helena did her best to smother the outraged expression on her face.

Did Mrs. Yardley imagine she did not know her manners? If there was a lack of manners around here, it wasn't from her. Helena felt a hot flush rising beneath her skin.

Scrambling awkwardly to her feet, Mrs. Yardley demanded Stalley to ask Cook for any little tidbits which might tempt the appetite of an invalid. Cook of course declined to deal directly with Stalley, and Helena had to intercede. She chafed to be on her way. So near and yet so far, after all this time. Patience, she reminded herself, but Poppy must have seen the flash of exasperation in her eyes and was uncharacteristically cooperative, even going so far as to make suggestions for Robert's welfare.

Finally managing to extricate herself from Mrs. Yardley and Cook, Helena stepped into the Yardley carriage carrying a jar of restorative jelly in one hand and smelling salts in the other. Her reticule was stuffed full with her own recent medical purchases. Presuming that John Coachman knew the address in Eaton Square, she settled down in her seat feeling anxious and out of sorts. She knew Mrs. Yardley had meant nothing by requesting her to thank Sir Ivor. But it rankled that the Yardleys regarded the favor being done to Robert was being carried out for *their* sakes. Mrs. Yardley meant well but she had offended Helena so much that for the first time Helena had had to firmly close her lips tightly in order not to say something rude to her employer. Surely Mrs. Yardley knew that Helena would never be backward in every politeness to Sir Ivor. Good heavens! And the idea of upsetting Sir Ivor's chef by taking Robert tidbits as if he were a lapdog. Helena didn't know whether to laugh or cry.

She prayed desperately that Robert's injuries were not too debilitating. Most of all she hoped that when he had recovered sufficiently, they would be able to do as Sir Ivor suggested and embark on a future that would hold a few of the elegancies of life. Poor Robert was coming straight from five years of army life. He would probably not notice if they had to make do with cheerless accommodations, but Helena feared she had been spoiled by the Yardleys. She dreaded the further sacrifices she might be obliged to make to keep Robert optimistic when his illness had abated and decisions had to be made. How long could one put on a brave face and plaster on a smile whilst quietly dying inside?

Vonnie Hughes

"Don't be dramatic, Helena," she muttered and squared her shoulders. "You have done it before, and you will do it again." Just to be with Robert was more than she had expected.

The carriage slackened speed. She peeped out of the window, hoping to see the façade of Stafford House but it was raining again and she could see very little. Scarcely had the carriage lurched to a halt than the door was opened and steps placed beneath it. A gloved hand held an umbrella above her. A footman assisted her to descend, then guided her quickly through the pouring rain toward a doorway. She pulled up her skirts and paused for a moment beneath the portico, gazing about her at the imposing entrance and rain-drenched crocuses beside the walkway.

The Staffords' butler was a tall, reserved man with an air of calm authority rather similar to someone else she knew. Like master, like man.

She was ushered into a foyer which had not one, but two staircases leading upward. There was an air of light and grandeur about the place, but most of all there was a feeling of solidity. This house had the same ambiance as the home of her childhood. It felt as though several generations of Staffords had happily lived and died here. Even though this was not their principal place of residence, the Staffords obviously loved their townhouse. Tapestries were flung artfully over the upper balustrades, and the floors were polished to within an inch of their lives. Daffodils had been placed in brass urns at intervals up the staircases. Many London houses were only hired for the Season and as a result looked jaded and tired. This house was well loved.

"Has Miss Marshfield arrived yet, Timms?"

She turned and heard the butler and Sir Ivor conferring quietly. "There you are! Welcome to Stafford House." He smiled a wider smile than she had yet seen from him. Usually when he smiled it was just a glint which disappeared into the serious planes and angles of his face. But here in his own home he seemed much more relaxed. She bowed slightly and he held his hand outstretched so that she was obliged to place hers in it. As soon as politely possible she stepped back. For some unaccountable reason she again felt a rush of warmth spread all through her body. She raised her eyes to his and caught a strange expression on his face. It was as if he were unwillingly attracted to her.

She knew how that felt. She wrenched her mind away from the track it was rushing down. She could not afford for this to happen to her. If she was honest with herself, should this man offer her a carte blanche, she doubted she would have the strength to say no. So she must nip this thing in the bud. Feeling herself reddening, she shoved her thoughts aside and tried to concentrate on Robert. *She was here to help Robert.* Her life had already been completely upended by her father. She had no wish to inflict self-harm by ruining what remained of her reputation and future.

Her chin tilted, she said briskly, "Good day, Sir Ivor. I hope I am not inconveniencing anyone."

His welcoming smile disappeared. "My housekeeper, Mrs. Annerwith, will attend to you."

She was taken aback at his change of manner. Maybe she should not have been so brisk.

"Perhaps you would care to take a glass of ratafia with me, and then we shall go to see your brother."

Abruptly he strode from the foyer and left her standing alone at the bottom of the staircase.

Timms reappeared with a chubby, motherly looking woman dressed in the garb of a housekeeper. She bobbed a curtsy to Helena and steered her through to a powder room, chattering all the while. "Why, miss, what a terrible day for you to venture out. But naturally you were anxious to see young Sir Robert. Such a nice young man as he is too." She prattled on, and Helena understood that Mrs. Annerwith was already well disposed toward Robert. Good. They might have need of her for some time to come.

"Now, miss, sit here by the fire. We don't want you to contract a nasty head cold. The staff is ever so pleased to have such a nice young lady come to visit Stafford House." She put Helena's bonnet aside. "Such beautiful hair as miss has, too." She bobbed another curtsy. "No offense I'm sure, miss." The voluble woman had obviously recollected that she was speaking to a perfect stranger. Helena smiled warmly. "No offense taken, Mrs. Annerwith. How could there be? Now, tell me all about Robert."

They settled down to discuss the invalid upstairs. Time flew by, and they both jumped when there was a knock on the door. Helena stood. "Oh, I forgot. Sir Ivor suggested I join him for a glass of ratafia."

"*Ratafia*," Mrs. Annerwith whispered to herself, sounding amused. "She's just coming, Mr. Timms."

Sir Ivor awaited her in a small withdrawing-room. On a low table by the fire a silver tray was laden with glasses and pippin tarts. Helena was flattered by his kindness and ventured to say as much. "Sir, you are very extremely kind—" but got no further. He interrupted with an impatient wave of his wrist and gestured her to a comfortable wing chair. He seated himself on the opposite side of the fire.

"Your brother is resting at present, Miss Marshfield. We will go up to him in a little while. Do have a pippin tart. The pippins came from our orchards in Norfolk last autumn." The servants had left the room, and he seemed to be used to serving himself. Surprisingly he seemed rather nervous, as if he were making social chitchat for the sake of it. She hoped he did not have bad news about Robert that he was reluctant to tell her.

"This is a beautiful little room," she remarked, looking about her at the rosewood piano and carefully draped velvet curtains.

"Yes, 'tis my favorite. There is a larger reception room on this floor too, but I prefer this one. And my library, of course."

At the word 'library' she glanced up. "Yes, Miss Marshfield. I knew that would draw your attention. I heard from Mr. Yardley how you and Caroline are so fond of libraries. And I have seen the evidence with my own eyes."

This time she managed not to blush over that incident at Hookham's. "Indeed, sir. The prospect of owning one's own library must be the most wonderful thing in the world, I think." She pulled a face, her eyes laughing. "My father was not bookish unfortunately. But there. I know I am not in fashion with my love of books. Truly, sir, I *do* admire the Belgian tapestries hung over the balustrades in the foyer, and of course this early Georgian fluted silver tray is perfect. But I prefer the sound of your library, I must confess."

He laughed. "I understand. It is good to see your natural enthusiasm. When you assume the demure mien of a governess I confess to a certain irritation. But I understand the circumstances of your position, and for a while it must be so. Possibly when your brother recovers, things may be different."

She fastened on to the one thing that meant most to her. "You think Robert will recover then?"

"I have no medical knowledge, but he seems to be very tough physically. I do not think he will recover for some time, but I hope that with careful nursing he can be almost himself again. Just remember, Miss Marshfield, the key word is 'time.'" He turned aside. "I shall see if he is awake yet." He pulled the bell-rope, and Timms came to inquire their pleasure. He managed to convey the impression that he was extremely busy but would make an exception just this once. He left majestically and calmly to inquire after Robert, and Helena stifled a nervous giggle. Sir Ivor looked at her inquiringly, but she shook her head and fiddled with her reticule. Obviously he was used to Timms's mannerisms and saw nothing unusual. Timms returned saying, "Young Sir Robert can see you now." Helena was impressed at how Robert seemed to have the full approval and sympathy of the Stafford household.

When she paused on the threshold of Robert's room she saw why. Robert was not at all as she remembered him. He was dreadfully ill. He half reclined on several pillows on a huge bed on a dais in the middle of the room, but he was lost in its hugeness. His already thin frame had become even thinner, and on his white face sharp lines etched themselves from cheekbone to jawline. He was gazing anxiously toward the doorway, a lock of dark hair over his brow as always, but his body seemed to be screwed into an uncomfortable position, and his right arm and shoulder were in some sort of sling.

"Ellie," he murmured, and she flew to his side.

"Dear Robert," she exclaimed and attempted to kneel down beside the bed. A footstool was slid underneath her knees, and she turned gratefully, but Sir Ivor was already withdrawing from the room. "My poor, poor Robert." He held out his good hand, and she cradled it against her cheek. "I have waited so long for us to be together again, Robert, but not like this, not like this…" Her voice trailed away, suspended with tears.

Callused fingers weakly stroked her cheek. "I have to say, Ellie, that sometimes it was only the thought of you waiting here that kept me going. Particularly during the last few weeks," he added. He seemed glad and relieved to see her but was extremely listless. His innate good manners kept him from drifting back to sleep, but Helena sensed he was exhausted.

"Here Robert, take a little laudanum." She measured a few drops into the glass of water at his bedside and held it to his lips. "There. Now go back to sleep and get well. That's all I ask."

She stroked the lock of hair back off his forehead and propped herself against the bed. His eyes closed docilely but he kept hold of her hand, and Helena was obliged to perch uncomfortably on the edge of the bed, moving as little as possible. After a while she became cramped and shifted slightly, but even in his half-sleep Robert was aware of her movement and tightened his grip. Her eyes filled with tears as she gazed on the face she knew so well. So, this was what happened when young men went off full of dreams to fight for King and country.

Her mind drifted back to their idyllic childhood when the highlights of their lives had been to explore the neighboring Broads on their ponies or visit their grandmother in town. But Grandmother was dead now, and that carefree life had gone. Robert had gone to be a soldier and had come back wounded, and she was a governess.

She bent her head and prayed earnestly for Robert and also a little for herself as her tears fell on their clasped fingers. They only had each other now. Robert *must* recover. He had so much to offer the world. One-handed she groped for the handkerchief in her reticule to wipe away the telltale tears. She still did not want to release Robert's hand. Desperately scrubbing at her cheeks with her free hand she reminded herself that she was in someone else's house. This would not do. Unfortunately, lecturing herself on propriety did not seem to be working very well. The tears came harder. She heard the door open and kept her head bent. Mrs. Annerwith's skirts rustled toward her.

"Poor lamb," she said, pushing a fragrant square of cambric into Helena's hand. "I thought you'd have need of a handkerchief or two, my dear. I don't know what the young man looked like before of course, but I can see he's sadly pulled and in great pain. No wonder you're upset. Sir Ivor sent me to make sure all was well."

It was fortunate Sir Ivor had had the forethought not to come himself. There was nothing more calculated to horrify a man than a weeping woman, so her father had always said. And this would make the second time she had succumbed when he was around. But surely he would understand. With the Staffords' great kindness, she wished to look well in their eyes. It irked her that she was unable to repay their hospitality, but she would find a way to do so, she vowed. Breathing in a shuddery sigh, she composed herself. "Mrs. Annerwith, I brought with me some restorative jelly and some laudanum should there be any need for—" She broke off, realizing she knew nothing about the seriousness of Robert's injuries yet.

"Bless you, dear. We can provide anything that's needed for the poor boy." Mrs. Annerwith carefully unlatched Robert's fingers and moved Helena away from the bed. "Now then, when are you coming to see us again? Tomorrow?"

Helena was quickly reminded of her other responsibilities. She gasped. "Oh! I must be off to Chelsea Gardens to collect my young ladies. Is it very late?"

"'Tis only four o'clock, Miss Marshfield. Don't fret. Timms will arrange for the carriage to take you to the Gardens."

Helena dabbed at her face and attempted to pull on her gloves at the same time. Mrs. Annerwith hustled her downstairs to fetch her cloak and bonnet. Timms and the housekeeper kindly overrode her protestations that she could walk to Chelsea Gardens, and the butler disappeared into the nether regions to order the carriage to be put to. Helena bit her lip. She was being an infernal nuisance to the Stafford servants.

At that moment Sir Ivor ambled downstairs to find his butler ordering his town carriage and his housekeeper engaged in tying the strings of Helena's bonnet. "Here, let me, miss. The dratted things have knotted."

Helena felt quite embarrassed at the cheerful way with which the Stafford servants overrode all her protests and sailed ahead doing what they thought was best. *Very* like their master. She spotted him on the stairs.

"Sir Ivor…" she began, but he smiled down at her and she found herself floundering to formulate a simple sentence.

"Tell me, Miss Marshfield, how did you find your brother?"

"Oh, Sir Ivor, thank you so much for all of this." She swept her hand graphically around the foyer to where Timms was giving orders to the groom, and Mrs. Annerwith was explaining to a housemaid that 'young Sir Robert' must not be disturbed for a while. Helena swallowed. "I really don't know what to say—"

"Then don't say a word," retorted her abrupt benefactor.

He certainly did not like being thanked.

"What do you think about your brother's health?"

"Passable, I think, considering his long coach journey." Then she recollected that that journey had been undertaken in her benefactor's luxurious traveling coach and blushed. "He is weak and exhausted, but there is no sign of a fever, and that is the main thing," she added hastily.

"Yes," he agreed, "And Sir William Fox comes tomorrow."

"Sir Ivor, *please*. We already stand too much in your debt. I agree that Sir William is the very surgeon I would have engaged had I the funds, but I decided that Dr. Tibbert would have to do and..."

He waited until she had run out of breath. "I am sure you wish to do the very best you can for your brother. Therefore, I engaged Sir William. Let there be no more argument about it."

Helena set her teeth. Her even white teeth which were, at this moment, engaged in grinding against each other. *Never* had she known such an arbitrary, over-confident, generous, irritating man. How were they ever to repay him?

Then she caught herself up short. Weren't the characteristics of generosity, over-confidence, and arbitrariness the same ones that she had had to stamp out of herself since working for a living? Yet in Sir Ivor these characteristics, though trying, were the ones she found intriguing. On the other side of the coin, however, the fact that she had had to hide these self-same tendencies within herself pointed out the huge divide in their stations in life. Where once they might have been well suited, now they were far apart. She *would* get used to it. Just give her a century or so.

Depressed and locked into introspection she entered the carriage, not giving Sir Ivor more than a cursory "Thank you, sir."

****

Ivor Stafford stood staring after his carriage wondering if he would ever understand such a contrary creature. She fascinated him, sometimes annoyed him, and always he itched to take some of the responsibilities off her shoulders. He wanted to protect her. He had never felt protective of a woman before apart from his mother and sisters. He sighed. He had known the other day that he was getting in too deep. It was not fair to lead her on. He still had to drag their family fortunes out of the mire his father had left them in. Until some of his own pressing responsibilities were lifted, he could do nothing further except keep a watching brief over Helena Marshfield.

Fortunately, one of his responsibilities in the shape of the older of his two sisters was being lifted. Nerida was shortly to be married. But that meant settlements. Nerida and George had requested a small, convivial wedding to speed them on their way back to the Dower House on the Chisholm estate which abutted Ryewolds. Neither Nerida nor George were particularly enamored of the Season and had decided that three or four weeks of it would suffice this year. This was Nerida's second Season and George had been a man about town for almost as long as Ivor. Like her mother, Nerida preferred the countryside.

But their youngest sibling would cost him a pretty penny next year when she came out. It had been an almighty struggle to maintain Ryewolds and Stafford House for the past four years, as well as pay for Nerida's coming-out and Ned's fees at Magdalen. But now that Ned had put forward the proposition that 'he did not intend to batten' on Ivor for all of his days but would seek an occupation, things were definitely looking up. Thank God none of them took after their father. Their mother was the shining example they had all followed. A pity their father had not valued her as he ought.

Ivor gazed at the gloomy prospect outside the window. Miss Marshfield and his mother would deal well together. They were of similar temperament—

conscientious, ethical, and with a bone deep quality that overrode adverse circumstances. He sighed. All that aside, he still needed at least another six months till he was out of the woods. One more harvest, the sale of some livestock, and another six month's rent from the tenants would do it. Those minor investments in the Far East Investment Company were due to come to fruition shortly and would help considerably, provided circumstances continued as they were.

As he did not employ a bailiff, nobody had noticed that over the past few years farm workers on the Stafford estate who had retired or moved away had not been replaced. Likewise, a few staff from Stafford House had not been replaced once they had left. However, very few workers left his employ. They seemed to like it. He had even tentatively suggested that some of the housemaids and kitchen maids from Ryewolds could double up on their duties at the townhouse, as the family was only in London for a small part of the year. Instead of handing in their notice, they had beamed enthusiastically at the added responsibilities with all the assiduity of evangelists. He grimaced. He must be a very lax employer. No, he knew he wasn't. He simply preferred a dignified but happy atmosphere in his houses. Unlike a few of his contemporaries he did not want people to serve him from fear; respect perhaps, but not fear.

But he yearned to be free of the yoke of debt that had been his since his father died. Although he was naturally a reticent man, the necessity for extreme secrecy irked him. In an ideal society he would receive the sympathy of friends and be able to discuss varying methods of saving on expenses with those in a similar predicament. To have a friend in adversity lightened the load.

But this was not an ideal society. The Stafford family would be a source of gossip and even amusement if the *ton* knew how he struggled to maintain their lifestyle. And if it *was* discovered how close to the wind his father had been sailing, Ivor would have been encouraged to marry an heiress or something of that ilk. But it was not in his nature to use another individual to rescue him. He could not live with himself if he had to rely on some young heiress's trustees to loosen the purse strings. Anyway, just calling to mind a couple of last Season's heiresses was enough to put him off that idea. Over the years he had known several heiresses who had been married for their fortunes. He had never considered those alliances to be happy ones. He himself had an intense dislike of the idea of money as the only valid currency. He would hate to be married solely for what he could provide in material goods, even though it was the way of the world.

Some of the last couple of years' débutantes could not be called 'innocent' either. They had been tutored by their mamas to go for the jugular—a title or money. Some of those matchmaking mamas were little better than abbesses. They showed no mercy at all, neither to their quarry nor their daughters. Why else would they team their untried, helpless offspring with doddering, drunk roués or raw and uncouth moneyed merchants?

He had been pursued now for ten years by women who wanted him only for what they could get out of him. He despised the irrational secret hidden deep inside which nagged that he wanted to be married to a woman who could not live without him—in short, a woman who loved him, only him. The current vogue for young married women to have lovers was a pitfall for one of his nature. He did not relish sharing the affections of his wife with a slavering acquaintance who had been waiting for years to get back at him for some imagined slight, a not uncommon occurrence.

Yet he did number among his contemporaries several very happy marriages. On the whole those couples stayed well away from town and spent most of their time on their estates.

He had known since he was a child that as the older son it was his responsibility to carry on the lineage. His baronetcy was not important in the great scheme of things. It was not as if he were a viscount or an earl, but his was an old family name, much older than many of the titles which had been dished out haphazardly during the last two generations. And he owed it to previous generations of Staffords to pass on the estates unencumbered to his sons.

Thinking of sons brought him right back to Miss Helena Marshfield for some reason. Now there was a young woman who would make an admirable Lady Stafford, no doubt about it. She would be a partner in every sense of the word. He had offered to house her brother in order to keep in her good graces. For some reason he just wanted to please her, to change those uncertain smiles to open happiness. Oh, damn it all. He was falling fast for the lady. It had crept up on him. How had that happened? After all his years on the town and all those matchmaking mamas, he had been snared by a pair of violet eyes glancing back at him in Hookham's Library of all places.

It tore him in two to see her unhappy, but the best

thing he could do was to stand back from her. Through her brother he could be her friend if she allowed it. 'Friend.' Now there was a euphemism. After the alluring glimpse of Helena's luscious breasts as they danced together, 'friend' did not begin to encompass his feelings for Helena Marshfield. She did not display herself with arrogant abandon as did some women. As a result he practically panted every time she cast him a look, or he caught a fleeting glimpse of a slender ankle. He drew in a deep breath. The smooth, creamy breasts he had unexpectedly glimpsed during their waltz had put him in such a lather that he'd thought for one dreadful moment she had guessed his discomfort.

Lord, he wished he were free to court her *now* in the time-honored way, but he wasn't. If only he did not have this load sitting on his shoulders. He would like nothing more than to approach Helena right this minute and tell her of his feelings. In the past he had been able to extricate himself gracefully if he felt he was getting in too deep and raising false hope. But with Helena 'too deep' wasn't nearly deep enough. He wanted to hold her close and protect her from people like Elverton— and what had all that been about? —and from people who treated her as if she were a lackey.

He especially wanted to take his lady away from that little vixen Ariadne Yardley. He wondered at Josh Yardley; he really did. Helena was forced to take any number of undeserved set-downs from that young woman, and it was unfair. Certainly, she didn't show much emotion when Ariadne treated her unkindly, but the hurt was there, behind the beautiful violet eyes. He had noticed that her chin tilted just a little higher when she was upset. She became crisper and pretended a self-confidence she clearly did not feel. But he could not interfere in the Yardley household. It wasn't done to tell another man how to handle his family, but he could see trouble looming there. Miss Ariadne Yardley was damnably hot at hand and although Helena could advise, she could not control. How he wished he could step in and take her away from her life of genteel servitude.

Ivor gazed unseeingly out at the rain and thought that responsibility was one thing, but years of anxiety and tightrope walking was another. His father had always been a fool. He had deserved no filial respect and had been given none. Ivor, Ned, and the girls had been enraged at the way their mother was treated, left for months alone at Ryewolds whilst his father gambled and drank away their heritage. Their mother had been so happy when he had been at home, however, that they'd never made any comment to her. She had loved Theo Stafford deeply and agonized over his dissolute ways, blaming herself for some inexplicable reason. When he had fallen ill she had nursed him devotedly, and when the doctor had pointed out that a life spent in such a self-indulgent manner could only lead to an early demise, she had angrily ordered the doctor from the house.

When their father eventually died their mother had been racked with grief, and there was no way Ivor could have mentioned that the estate was not in order and that the debt collectors had already sent in their first demands. Had the bank not been accommodating when they realized he was in earnest about recouping the losses incurred by his father, both Ryewolds and Stafford House would have been sold. Damn his father to the pit.

At least the Committee gave him an outlet for his pent-up energy, gave him a chance to use his brain on something apart from how to wring the last groat from his estates whilst maintaining the land and buildings to a reasonable standard.

Ten minutes later he was still staring out at the rain, wondering how he was going to survive the next few months.

Chapter Nine

The gentleman garbed in dark colors lounged back in his chair in the gaming hell at Lincolns Inn Fields, observing the play. He was sitting out this hand, not being one to throw his blunt away. His saturnine face was closed and sour as if his inner thoughts were not pleasant, and his long white fingers tapped rhythmically on the arm of his chair.

"Damn you. Can't you stop that?" one of the players asked irritably.

The man's face altered subtly, but not for the good. "What is it, Berkley?" he sneered. "The cards not going your way again?"

"You should know," Berkley muttered.

"What do you mean by that?" The icy, threatening tone was enough to send chills down the stiffest spine.

****

The following day found Robert a little better. A good night's sleep seemed to have strengthened him and eased some of his pain. When Helena arrived at Stafford House, she watched him carefully from the doorway. The rain had stopped at last, and he was propped up in bed gazing out of the window, feasting his eyes on England's spring greenery.

She knocked gently, and he swiveled in the bed, smothering an exclamation of pain as he turned. Stretching out his hand to her he murmured, "How often I longed to see England on such a morning as this."

"Was it all so very dreadful Robert?" she inquired hesitantly.

"Oh no, Helena. Not all of it. The men in my company are the best of fellows, loyal to their division and to each other. We are rather like a big, mismatched family with a few squabbles now and again. Of course there are one or two who er—" he sought for a description which would not offend Helena's ears and she smiled covertly in appreciation "—are not so trustworthy, and of course we had our share of drunkards and deserters, but on the whole we could depend on one another."

After which he lapsed into a brown study.

When Helena quizzed him about the countryside in Portugal, he became lyrical. "Don't I wish you could see it, Ellie! I know you would love the massive cork trees and the fertile soil in the river valleys. And the cities and small towns with such romantic names." He trembled and lay back on his pillows, exhausted.

Helena saw how much he longed to be back there and was stunned. Somehow she had imagined that, after the rigors of war in a foreign country, he would be relieved to return to England. However, when necessity had dictated army life as his calling it had obviously done him a great favor. After a few minutes he added, "Of course the forced marches over dried up plains, and mile upon mile of devastation where Boney's army had been before us was ghastly. Naturally the country folk were hostile and treacherous. For the foot soldiers it was hell, just putting one foot in front of the other, mile after mile. It was fine for me with two mounts to choose from." He frowned, looking back in his mind's eye. "The retreat from Corunna was appalling. Endless tracks of blood-sodden snow—never mind," he finished as he seemed to recall who he was talking to. Then he added, "I've let my brigade down, getting injured like this and leaving them behind to regroup."

Helena realized that this was at the heart of his depression. She did not know how to contend with such a thing.

He moved restlessly in the bed, and she raised him up on his pillows to make him more comfortable.

"Robert," she asked hesitantly. "Would you go back?"

"I don't know, Ellie. I don't know. More needs to be done at this end, in England, by way of preparation. I've already heard talk back here in the hospital that Sir John Moore 'failed', but I think the 'failure' started back here. Not enough preparation was done, and most of us felt that the French knew what our plans were. Boney definitely has some good spies in England."

As she eased back on to her chair, Helena stared at him, startled. "I had not thought of that! Mr. Yardley mentioned something of that sort."

"Yes. Stafford has already mentioned Yardley's ideas to me. It seems Sir Ivor and Mr. Yardley are in the minority though."

Helena was unsure what he meant and remained silent.

For a while Robert lapsed into a daydream but roused himself to exclaim that he had not even asked her how she went on. He was the most thoughtless of brothers!

She soothed him because he seemed to be easily

agitated. "My position with the Yardleys is all that could be desired, Robert. They have been very kind to me. And my future looks secure. It is possible that when either Ariadne or Caroline marries, I shall go with them. So you may be settled in your mind about me. I say, wasn't it kind of the Staffords to organize your convalescence? No doubt you will be seeing both Ned and Tally Wishart in the next few days."

She sidetracked him and prattled on until she had soothed him into a restless slumber. She sat quietly by as he slept, holding his hand. He must never suspect that she was unhappy with her lot in life. He was not well enough to cope emotionally or physically with his own future, and it would be cruel to hint at her own despair.

Her arm was beginning to ache from holding it extended on the coverlet and she was wriggling about on her chair when there was a gentle tap on the door and Sir Ivor and Mrs. Annerwith entered, followed by an elderly, dapper man with a spiked gray beard.

"Miss Marshfield." Sir Ivor spoke softly. "I have brought Sir William Fox to see you both." Helena disentangled her fingers and rose. Robert did not even stir.

They adjourned to the landing where Sir William made her acquaintance and asked her how she thought Robert was doing.

"Sir William, I agree with Sir Ivor that Robert is quite pulled from his journey from the hospital at Portsmouth. But he has always been strong physically. He is not in good heart, however. He feels he has let his men down by being shipped home. Unfortunately I know very little about his injuries so I cannot be of much help to you." Sir William nodded shrewdly, watching her all the while from underneath his jutting eyebrows.

"You sound like a sensible woman," he said gruffly. "Your brother will take no harm with you. Now I have to wake him up." Nodding dismissively, he entered the bedroom and closed the door.

Helena remained on the landing, worriedly twisting her hands this way and that while Mrs. Annerwith and Sir Ivor communicated in low whispers.

"Come, Miss Marshfield." Mrs. Annerwith gestured to Helena to follow her downstairs.

"No, no. I must wait to hear Sir William's opinion," Helena protested.

Sir Ivor took her arm and urged her toward the staircase. "Sir William and I will be with you directly," he promised.

The man seemed to enjoy ordering her about, and she drew herself up ready to take back the reins. "I know," he said. "It's difficult when one is an autocrat to meet another such."

"*I*, an autocrat?" She bridled, then realized he was trying to divert her from her worry. She smiled wanly.

"But of course, Miss Marshfield. I know you are an autocrat and a martinet," he said, guiding her down the staircase. "I have it on the best of authority from Miss Yardley."

Helena snorted indelicately. "Not nearly as autocratic as I should like to be with Ariadne," she said unguardedly, and he laughed delightedly, throwing his head back.

"Yes, I can well imagine that your task there is extremely difficult. A high-spirited young woman to say the least. Take a seat in the library, and Mrs. Annerwith will fetch you some coffee. As soon as I can, I shall bring Sir William to you." Again, she found herself out-maneuvered, but with kind intent. She was amused at his description of Ariadne as 'high-spirited'. He must have a deep regard for Ariadne if he thought her wildness could be termed 'high-spirited'. Spoilt more like, she thought gloomily. It seemed as if Sir Ivor had joined the throng of Ariadne's admirers. He knew she was difficult but did not regard it as important. On the contrary, it amused him. Possibly her fortune was enough to gild the lily. Well, he was certainly autocratic enough to control Ariadne, should a marriage take place.

Helena sighed and moodily surveyed the excellent library. Mrs. Annerwith was engaged in pouring Helena a cup of coffee from an ornate silver urn. A silver dish beside it was piled with macaroons. Helena accepted the coffee and selected a macaroon but was unable to sit still and instead wandered aimlessly among the tall bookshelves in the magnificent room. Spying a beautifully bound copy of *Hours of Idleness* she wandered over to the bay window with it, gazing sightlessly out over the crocuses and boxthorn hedge. For weeks she and Caroline had searched for a copy of Byron's much maligned novel, but now she had it in her hand she was too worried about Robert to even open the cover. It was also hard to admit to herself that she was disappointed at the prospect of seeing Sir Ivor in Ariadne Yardley's clutches. Reason dictated the unsuitability of the match. But the man had been positively *avuncular* when calling Ariadne 'high-spirited'.

Mrs. Annerwith's voice interrupted her lowering thoughts. "...you'll see, Miss Marshfield." She had no idea what Mrs. Annerwith had been saying but the dear lady was obviously trying to be consolatory. Helena was ashamed of herself. This entire household had put itself out for her brother, from the owner down to the lowliest footman and scullery maid. The advent of both Helena and Robert into their settled routines must have caused everybody considerable upheaval. Helena made an effort to collect herself.

"Mrs. Annerwith, would you please be so kind as to convey to the household how grateful I am for your kindnesses. Make sure everybody knows that Robert and I understand what extra duties we are causing. You have all been marvelous."

"Why, we have loved the bustle! Cook is busy inventing recipes that will tempt young Sir Robert's appetite, and with her ladyship at Ryewolds until next week, I am thoroughly enjoying having another lady to see to."

Helena stared at her. "Oh no, Mrs. Annerwith. You are mistaken. I am just...a governess." There, she had got the words out and nothing terrible had happened. The sky had not fallen in or anything like that.

Mrs. Annerwith was not aghast. She just chuckled. "Howsoever that may be at the moment, my dear, you are a lady born and bred. We all know that."

Helena wondered what on earth Sir Ivor had said to his staff to foster this idea. The library door opened, and she took a few steps in the direction of the doorway till Sir Ivor said, "Do sit down, Miss Marshfield. Has she been wandering around like this all the time, Mrs. Annerwith?"

Mrs. Annerwith just smiled and murmured something of which the main words seemed to be 'worry' and 'poor lamb'.

Sir William burst into the room behind Sir Ivor sniffing the air and saying, "Ha! Coffee!" He was offered something stronger but declined as he still had another patient to visit. "Well, Miss Marshfield. Do you wish to discuss your brother alone, or would you rather have somebody with you?" he began ominously. Helena's Sèvres cup clattered in its saucer, and she hastily placed them on a table.

Sir Ivor moved to her side. "That's enough, Fox. She's nearly done in. Can't you see that?"

"Very well, m'dear." Sir William carefully selected a macaroon and settled comfortably into a wing-backed chair. "Young Captain Marshfield's shoulder which is giving him so much pain, is not, strangely enough, his main problem. When the swelling and bruising have subsided, I will put him on a regimen of exercises to strengthen those muscles again. So…for the shoulder, further bedrest, arnica rubs twice a day, then in about ten days or a fortnight when I expect the healing to have taken place, the recuperative phase can proceed."

The first macaroon disappeared, and Sir William reached for another. "At that stage I will acquaint you with various useful exercises which will complete the healing. But for the next two weeks at least he will need more rest, some good food, plenty of arnica to rub on the muscles, and possibly a little laudanum to help him through the pain. Now…the leg. That, I'm afraid, will take longer. I am annoyed that the surgeons at Portsmouth Hospital overlooked the fact that your brother has had a badly shattered shin-bone since

Corunna. It is understandable that a field hospital could have missed it. They sometimes do. With hardy soldiers who won't admit to pain it is often difficult to diagnose such a complex fracture in midst of all the tumult of war with hundreds of serious casualties. However, the naval hospital should have known better. I am writing a Report," he finished portentously.

"But what—?" Helena began.

Sir William held up a hand. He was enjoying the limelight. "Young lady, I have just re-set the leg, much to your poor brother's discomfort. I did the best I could considering that it has now been at least four weeks since it was broken. I also had to dig out a few bone splinters. The bone had not yet begun to mend. Indeed, there was no way for it to mend as it had nothing to attach itself to, the break being so severe."

Helena felt sick. Poor, poor Robert.

Sir William quaffed a mouthful of coffee and looked at Helena over the top of his cup. "My big fear is infection. He has been amazingly fortunate so far. He *must* be kept scrupulously clean. The bandages keeping the splint in place must be replaced every day. I do not anticipate the leg even *beginning* to heal for another four or five weeks. During that time he should be kept as immobile as possible. Now Sir Ivor has suggested that your brother might be better off at Ryewolds in the country rather than here in the city. But I cannot entertain the idea of the poor fellow being jogged around anymore for several weeks. After that we shall see. In the meantime I shall leave it up to you to keep him entertained. In about a week you will be at your wit's end, I'll be bound," he finished, laughing.

"Don't worry," Sir Ivor said. "We will all take

turns at keeping him entertained." He smiled at Helena. "There now, not so bad after all, was it?"

She smiled back weakly. "Sir William, what about the future?"

"We can only wait and see. I suspect the shoulder will always be a trifle weak as shoulder dislocations often recur. However, that should only be a minor inconvenience provided he is careful in the future. But the leg—well, he may limp a lot, or just a little. It will depend on how the leg mends. It is possible he may one day sit astride a horse again. Let us wait and see."

Helena sat back in her chair like a limp doll. Her mind was a blank.

"I-I cannot begin to thank you all…"

"Then don't," Sir Ivor cut in incisively. "Thank you, Sir William. We are very much obliged to you. When will you come to see Robert again?"

"One week from today, unless you should contact me earlier." Sir William regretfully eyed the remaining macaroons. However, Sir Ivor was obviously hustling him on his way so good manners dictated that he finish his coffee and leave. After reminding Helena to keep an eye out for infection and melancholia in his patient, he left.

When the door shut behind Sir William, the silence was deafening.

"What a noisy, restless person he is," Sir Ivor murmured, "but with an excellent bedside manner. He had Robert chatting about his fears and ambitions in no time at all. I suspect he succeeded much better than a kind, sympathetic doctor would have done."

She smiled tremulously. "I had best leave now, sir. Thank you—"

"Enough, Miss Marshfield! Don't thank me again, *please*."

Mrs. Annerwith bustled in and began to collect the crockery so Helena subsided.

"Now we know that Robert will be here for a few weeks, I propose to meet with your employer to see if he may spare you from your duties for some of that time. Obviously it would be best if you stayed here at Stafford House so you can be with Robert as much as possible. He will need you during his convalescence."

"Oh! I don't think I could. Caroline has only just come out, and of course there's the household. Mrs. Yardley would find it extremely difficult to manage."

"So you *do* order the household! I thought as much. Tell me, what does Mrs. Yardley *do* exactly?" Then he waved his hand in negation. "Sorry, that's none of my business. I was surprised on the evening of Caroline's coming-out party to see you had an inordinate number of tasks, but I didn't fully realize that all the household organization fell on your shoulders. Does Josh Yardley agree with this?"

"Oh yes. I do small commissions for him, too, from time to time."

He stood looking at her for a moment, and she wondered what he was thinking.

"I'm sorry, Miss Marshfield, but I will have to impress upon the Yardleys that you need to be here. It is true that I have a large household who all seem to be devoted to your brother already." This was said with a wry grin. "But naturally the best nurse for him is his own sister. That goes without saying. If you are worried about the proprieties, there is Mrs. Annerwith as chaperone of course. My suggestion would be that you ask Miss Yardley to stay here too to keep you company until such time as my mother and sisters arrive. I realize my company will be but a poor substitute for a more congenial female one."

Helena stared at him. "You have been very gracious, Sir Ivor, but I would not wish to take up any more of your time. It's not that I prefer female company but…" She trailed off, seeing pitfalls ahead.

His smile glinted. "But you prefer my library to myself, is that it?"

Oh dear. Whichever way she answered, she would be in trouble. "Not really. That is to say…" She was lost in a welter of words and gesticulated helplessly. One thing she did see was that he appeared to want Ariadne in his house. She was forced therefore to put forward that young lady as an appropriate companion. "Very well. I will ask Miss Yardley…"

"As you wish. Though I would have thought Miss Caroline was a more kindred spirit."

"Yes."

He threw back his head and laughed again, and she stared bemusedly up at him. "I adore your unqualified statements, Miss Marshfield. Pound dealing for you! If it does not interfere with her social obligations, please ask Caroline if she would care to come and join you here for a week or so. I will make all well with her parents."

Helena didn't know how to interpret that. She presumed she had disappointed him by preferring Caroline's company to Ariadne's, but he did not seem to be put out. In fact he had laughed. But then, she wasn't sure *what* he thought.

Or even what she thought.

Chapter Ten

In his study, Josh Yardley faced his daughter and her governess over the expanse of his desk. He frowned and steepled his fingers together as he considered the faces in front of him. On his desk was a note from Sir Ivor Stafford which was cryptic in the extreme. Josh had always considered himself to be up with the play, but this time he was damned if he knew what Stafford was playing at.

It was a highly unusual situation. And Stafford was a complex man. What lay beneath his oh-so-polite invitation to both ladies to stay for a week at Stafford House 'to assist in the recovery of Miss Marshfield's brother'? Had it been anyone else he would have assumed that Stafford was lusting after either Caroline or Miss Marshfield. Yet Stafford was an honorable man. Josh knew that from experience. He knew that if Ivor Stafford had wanted to pay his addresses to either young woman, he would have followed formal procedures.

But this was the second week of Caroline's coming-out. Surely Stafford realized Caroline's social calendar was full to the brim at the moment?

As far as Helena Marshfield went…now that her brother had returned, officially she was young Sir Robert's responsibility. But Josh rather wanted to keep his trump card. He smiled to himself. How horrified

Miss Marshfield would be if she knew how he had scored over his business associates and friends just having her as his daughters' companion. She was a lady of quality through and through, and no amount of misfortune could hide that. It wasn't just his daughters who had learned from her. He, too, had found some of her gentle advice invaluable. And he fully intended that she would remain under his aegis as long as possible. It wasn't that he wanted to rub noses with the *ton*, exactly—well, not much. But he wouldn't mind a knighthood for services to the business world. That wouldn't go amiss. The Marshfields and Sir Ivor Stafford could help there.

Also, there was the other thing, the worrying one of national importance in which he was involved. He had not set out to work for the Committee with the aim of doing anything more than to assist with the centralization of the control of the Army, lending a layman's opinion here and there. But when treason reared its ugly head, he'd felt he had no option but to continue with a more wide-ranging portfolio. So as the French marched inexorably over Europe he had found himself assisting in more and more complex investigations. At that stage he'd given no thought to his political aspirations, but now perhaps…

He shook himself out of his reverie, realizing that the two faces on the other side of his desk had grown anxious.

"Caroline, my dear, this is most irregular. I believe there are many invitation cards awaiting your consent. Do you really wish to accompany Miss Marshfield to Stafford House? If you do not wish it, we can make other arrangements."

"Papa, I would *far* rather accompany Helena than attend parties. I'm sorry to disappoint you, but I don't like…well…" Caroline trailed off helplessly.

"You haven't disappointed me, my dear, and I don't suppose you ever will. But I require a note from you every day to let me know how you are going on. Perhaps I shall come to see you if Sir Ivor permits."

Caroline and Helena were aware that the person who would suffer most from their abandonment would be Mrs. Yardley. She would have to bestir herself to accompany Ariadne on her many social outings, whilst at the same time endeavor to control the worst of Ariadne's tantrums. Also, she would have to reassume responsibility for the ordering of the household, something she had not done since Helena's advent.

"Poor Mama," Caroline said feelingly.

"Yes. I feel bad about this," Helena responded. "I only hope that some of Ariadne's social engagements do not need a chaperone so that your mama gets some time to rest."

But Robert came first with Helena and always would.

When they talked to Mrs. Yardley, they found her husband had already apprised her of their plans. She seemed to be resigned to her fate.

"Oh, my dears, I will miss you so. Won't Ariadne be mad as fire when she finds out where you're both going though? Oh dear."

But Ariadne was not angry. She was smugly preoccupied. She had made a new conquest. She would not discuss it with Caroline or Helena and was so secretive that Helena became worried, aware that Mrs. Yardley may not have the inclination to urge Ariadne to toe the line should an eligible *parti* be on the horizon.

"Ariadne, *please* behave circumspectly whilst I am not by," Helena begged her. "Remember how important it is to your matrimonial chances to preserve an unexceptional demeanor. Promise me?"

Ariadne just nodded casually. "Don't worry, Helena. I can say nothing to Mama or Papa yet, but I think a certain person means to approach Papa shortly. Just wait, Caroline, till you see who wishes to marry *me*!" And off she flitted, not caring at all that her sister and her companion were going away. She had obviously given no thought as to who her chaperone would be. Helena prayed that Mrs. Yardley was able to cope.

Resolutely she cast Ariadne from her mind and directed Caroline and Betsy with the packing. "It seems strange to be packing a bandbox to go such a short distance away, doesn't it?" Caroline said.

Stolid old John Coachman agreed. "Don't seem right you young ladies leaving us. But I'm sure you'll soon have Sir Robert hale and hearty again, Miss Marshfield."

"Thank you, John." Somehow servants always knew every detail of their employers' movements.

When the carriage drew up in Eaton Square, John Coachman had little to do. Helpers materialized from everywhere. A groom held the horses' heads. Timms placed a footstool on the cobblestones and assisted the ladies from the carriage. Two footmen bustled to extricate the bandboxes and carpet bags from the carriage. Mrs. Annerwith awaited them in the foyer and showed them to their rooms. Caroline was most impressed. Helena was amused. How did Caroline think a large home was run? It would do Caroline no harm at all to be at Stafford House where the influence of quality rather than quantity was the order of the day. It may possibly give her some ideas as to how to run her own household one day.

Of course, the lowering thought was that *this* might well be Caroline's household one day, or even the household of her sister. But Helena pushed away any gloomy thoughts. She was happy to be with Robert again and happy to be staying here. This house had an agreeable atmosphere. She loved its architecture and wall hangings. It was pleasant to find that the household servants in this establishment were happy, anxious to please and very efficient. She marveled that by the time she had got back from exploring Caroline's bedroom and had helped her shake out her dresses, her own clothing was neatly disposed of in various drawers and a large nosegay of flowers had mysteriously appeared by her bedside.

For the first time in years, Helena felt at home. She felt welcome. She was not paid to be of use to someone as she was in the Yardley household; she was a guest here. It was such a relief not to have to act as arbiter between Stalley and Cook or to hide Ariadne's indiscretions from Betsy and Katy. She smiled to herself, remembering that Marshfield Manor had had just the same well-run, peaceful ambiance. Nobody could possibly accuse the Yardley household of being peaceful!

A brass can of water stood on the water stand, and as well as the flowers on her bedside table, a small silver filigree bowl sitting on the mantelpiece over the fireplace contained marzipan fruits. Helena wandered over to the window and saw she had been given a room that looked out over a small flower garden. Most town houses had very little in the way of gardens, yet some of these older established homes in Eaton Square were renowned for their larger allotments which had enough room for small gardens and gazebos.

Mrs. Annerwith tapped on the door. "Is there anything I can get for you, Miss Marshfield?"

Helena straightened up from examining a patch on her best dress. "How kind of you, Mrs. Annerwith. I shall see my brother and let him know that Miss Caroline would like to meet him. I had best forewarn him in case he doesn't want to meet strangers at the moment."

Helena peeped around Robert's half-open door and saw that Sir Ivor and Robert were chatting seriously. They had a map spread over the bedcover and Robert seemed to be showing Sir Ivor various details on it. They both looked up as she tapped on the door, and Sir Ivor stood.

"Good day, Miss Marshfield. You will want to be with your brother. I shall leave you both now." He turned to Robert. "Perhaps we can continue our talk later this afternoon?"

To Helena's surprise, he seemed anxious to leave the room. She gained the impression that he found her presence chafing, that she annoyed him in some way. Perhaps she had interrupted something important? Well, he had invited her here! She raised her chin.

"Caroline is with Mrs. Annerwith. I'm sure you would like to greet her," she said.

Ivor Stafford's eyebrows rose. He was unused to being chastised in his own house, or anywhere else for that matter. What had got into Helena? She was frowning at him. She almost sounded as if she were throwing young Caroline at his feet. He certainly hoped not. He very much wanted a certain woman, but it wasn't little Caroline Yardley. His taste ran to a stronger female with an annoying habit of self-abnegation.

Perhaps Helena was jealous of the rapport between himself and Robert. He and Robert Marshfield had quickly established a friendship and were happily conversing on all manner of subjects. But he wouldn't have thought Helena Marshfield was that petty.

In his salad days Ivor had rather prided himself on being able to understand most women, but of course he hadn't met Helena Marshfield then. He was never quite sure how she was going to react in any given circumstance. The real Helena was hidden under a number of layers, and it all depended on which layer you unpeeled as to which facet of her personality was revealed. She was an enigma. Sometimes she appeared to challenge him as she did now. Whoever became leg-shackled to her was in for an interesting time. He grinned reflectively. He had better go and welcome Caroline Yardley as he had been ordered to do. There was no doubt that 'Miss Marshfield the autocratic governess' was the part of Helena's personality which was to the fore today. But he admired her for not mincing matters. With the exception of his family, most women he knew would have swallowed such a lapse of manners on his part and cloaked it with a smile. Then they'd make him pay, possibly financially, a little game understood by both sides. Helena Marshfield did not play games.

But Helena had eyes only for her brother. She hurried to Robert's side, and Ivor knew she had already forgotten him.

Helena smiled at Robert, pleased to see that he looked much more alert today. "My dear, how are you this morning? You are looking so much better."

"Yes, that surgeon might not be a gentleman's idea of a sympathetic doctor, but for someone straight out of the army he is a breath of fresh air. Told me exactly what to expect. I feel certain of recovery now."

"Mmm, he's certainly bluff, isn't he?"

Robert grinned. "Is that what you call it?"

Helena laughed. "He's quite the actor. But yes, he engenders confidence. Now, what can I do to make you more comfortable?" But Sir Ivor's staff had already seen that Robert was made as comfortable as possible, and Helena found that her main task was simply to entertain him.

When Caroline was introduced to Robert, she blushed and lowered her eyes as he took her hand in his. Helena noted that a tinge of color stole into her brother's pale face as he stared intently at Caroline. In only a few minutes the two of them were chattering away happily, making Helena feel quite *de trop*.

For the rest of the week, Caroline opted to spend hours at Robert's bedside, listening to carefully censored stories of his travels with the army, playing backgammon with him, and unraveling acrostics. He seemed to prefer her awkward ministrations to those of his sister, and Helena began to worry, much to Ivor Stafford's amusement. He advised her to wait and see before she got upset.

"But sir, only think! Mr. Yardley will be very

annoyed if an attachment should spring up between the two of them. What shall I do?" she asked as they stood in the window embrasure in Robert's room.

"I don't think you should do anything. If the attraction does not run its course and becomes permanent, there is nothing for you to do. And should a temporary flirtation assist with Robert's convalescence, then that is good. Why do you think Josh Yardley will be angry?"

"You know very well that he is hoping for his daughters to make good marriages. Although Robert is the best of brothers, I hardly think Mr. Yardley would be likely to see his suit as favorable. Not when the Yardleys have their sights set on the nobility for their daughters."

"Robert *is* the nobility. So are you, Miss Marshfield. I wish you would stop this ridiculous modesty. As soon as I am able, because there are several other people to be taken into consideration here, I wish to put a proposition to Robert which I hope will ensure his future. But I cannot at this stage—"

"What are you two whispering about?" Robert demanded. "Look, Helena, Caroline has just beaten me at backgammon for the third time. It is too bad of her, don't you think?"

Smiling, Helena turned, wondering what Sir Ivor had been going to say.

It was nearly two years since she had last spent time with Robert, and in those years he had seen atrocities of war and had had the comradeship of people from all over the world. He had grown away from her to a certain degree. So she trod carefully.

Sir Ivor suggested to Caroline that she might like a

walk in the garden, leaving Robert and Helena alone at last. Robert wasted no time in asking her if she did not find Caroline a delightful companion.

Helena grabbed the opening. "Yes, she is a darling. Such a lovely nature. Her parents have high hopes for her."

"Do they look for an ambitious marriage for her?" he asked bluntly.

She hesitated. "I suspect they are looking for a title at least. I am not sure how high they are looking. But you will meet Mr. Yardley tomorrow, I believe. Perhaps you will be able to elicit further information from him."

He grasped her arm. "Stay with me, Ellie. Ned and Tally are calling this afternoon, and I want to see you alone for a little while." He hesitated. "Are you not happy that Caroline and I deal so famously together? Sometimes I see you frown."

"Oh Robert…I don't know. It's just that Caroline is the first young woman you've met since returning to England. She is helping you to recuperate and under such circumstances perhaps you make too much of…" She trailed away helplessly.

His jaw set in the way she knew so well from childhood.

"Ellie, it may not have occurred to you, but since being on the town and in the army, I have met literally scores of young women, some of whom I've…well, formed quite close relationships with. And of all the young women I've known, Caroline is…" He shrugged, unable to express himself. "If her father should warn me off, of course I'll toe the line, but if he should show willing, then I plan to press my suit. There. What do you say?"

"I say that it is all very sudden but if it should be acceptable to the Yardleys, I would be thrilled! I know you will not declare yourself to Caroline without her father's consent, but I do so hope that you will not have to face—"

"So do I. It doesn't bear thinking of. In the meantime, I shall just treat her as another sister."

Helena smiled; her fingers surreptitiously crossed in her lap.

That afternoon when Tally Wishart and Ned Stafford called on him, Robert spent a roisterous afternoon considering he was still very much an invalid. Caroline and Helena were invited to share the goings-on. The ladies giggled at some of the tales of university exploits which they were sure had been embroidered for their benefit.

"Do you remember the spider race in the Square when the dean came over and asked us what was going on?" Tally reminisced.

"*Spider race*?" Helena asked.

"Yes. You get some spiders and tickle them along with pens when they slacken off. It's fun!"

"Ugh." Caroline grimaced.

"Oh, it's not so bad. Better than cockroach racing anyhow."

"Oh!" Both ladies were horrified.

"I made a lot of money from that," Robert said.

"Robert, you didn't *bet* on the races, did you?"

"Of course we did, Ellie. Nothing much else to do in our spare time. I had a brilliant spider. Kept him in a box. Called him Nor'east because he'd only run in one direction. Unfortunately, after the main race the dean trod on him and killed him. Poor old Nor'east."

Helena looked speakingly at Caroline, and they both shuddered.

Helena reflected that it had done Caroline a lot of good to spend time with an undemanding group of young men such as this, far more so than the rout-parties and dances that were on her social agenda. If she had had a couple of brothers her initial stiffness would not have been apparent, but Tally and Ned were the kindest of young men and soon had Caroline fascinated by their tales of derring-do. And if Robert gave the impression of a dog guarding a bone, well…Helena had to admit that Caroline evinced no opposition to his attitude; indeed, she rewarded him from time to time with shy smiles.

Helena secretly wished that Ivor Stafford would look at her the way Robert did when Caroline entered the room. But for the past few days Sir Ivor seemed to have withdrawn into a shell. He treated Caroline as a favorite sister, was friendly with Robert, but with Helena he kept his distance. She came to the unpalatable conclusion that either she had offended him in some way, or else he was no longer interested in pursuing a flirtation with her. Perhaps he had other fish to fry.

On their second morning at Stafford House, he had provided her with a delightful little mount, a sorrel mare that was kept in London for his sisters when they visited. Mrs. Annerwith had unearthed Miss Stafford's riding-dress for her, and she had accompanied Sir Ivor on a gentle ride through Hyde Park. She was thrilled to be on horseback once more, even though the stately trot down Rotten Row could scarcely be called a challenge.

She caught the passing glances given them by other riders and pedestrians and realized that no one seemed particularly interested in them.

However, on the third morning, a couple of Sir Ivor's friends accosted them and requested to be introduced to Helena. It was from then on that he had behaved toward her with a polite, distant air. She realized he was embarrassed to be seen in public with a governess, the daughter of a man who had disgraced his family so publicly. She was mortified that his kindness should have caused him embarrassment.

"Sir Ivor, could you spare me a moment?" she asked him nervously later that day.

"Of course, Miss Marshfield. Come into the library." He smiled down at her and without thinking she responded with a shy smile. Then she hastily brought herself up short and took a deep breath, praying that this would come out right. "Sir Ivor, I am much obliged to you for your many kindnesses to Robert and myself. However—"

"Haven't we already covered this topic?" he inquired in a bored voice.

"*However*," she persisted, "you do not need to spend your spare time accompanying me on...well, accompanying me anywhere. I must not take up any more of your time. But thank you." She stood, trembling, hoping her pride would see her as far as the door at least.

"I see." His voice was cold, uninterested. In some way she had offended him. But there was nothing further to be done. There. Honor was satisfied.

From then on, she saw very little of him. Josh Yardley came to visit and expressed himself well pleased that Caroline was enjoying herself at Stafford House. Under the circumstances, Sir Ivor was left with no option but to extend his invitations to both Caroline and Helena.

A smug little smile played about Mr. Yardley's mouth as he said, "Well, that is up to Caroline and Miss Marshfield. Should you like to stay for a few more days, my dear?" he asked his daughter.

Caroline nodded, and her sweet smile sparkled.

Mr. Yardley was then introduced to Robert, a meeting from which Sir Ivor absented himself as several other gentlemen had arrived to see him. The Yardleys and Marshfields were getting on famously when Timms requested Josh Yardley's attendance in the library. Standing beside the bed, Yardley held out his hand to Robert.

"Well, Sir Robert, I'm pleased to have met you at last. It's possible that the Committee meeting being convened downstairs may adjourn to your bedside. We have some questions to ask you about your experiences on the Peninsula. Your comments may be useful in our planning for next year."

Robert seemed to understand what Mr. Yardley was referring to. "Anything I can do to help, I will," he assured Josh Yardley.

When Yardley had left and Caroline had gone to pen a note to her mother, Robert said to Helena. "Yardley is a good sort of a man. He certainly has a strong grasp on the difficulties of provisioning an army waging war far beyond its own shores. Many civilians do not understand how impossible it is to have a wagon train strung out for miles, while the main army waits days for the commissariat to arrive. Things like horseshoes and nails can hold up the advance for weeks."

"I suspect his business background has helped him there. But he is quick to pick up new ideas too."

"Yes. I can understand why he is on the Special Advisory Committee."

"What Special Committee?"

He looked puzzled. "I thought you had guessed that he and Sir Ivor and another couple of fellows have been making inquiries at this end regarding the preparedness of troops for the Peninsula War. Apparently the other two Committee members are from the Horse Guards and the War Office. But this is very hush-hush, Helena. Please don't repeat it."

"As if I would!"

"No, under normal circumstances you would not. But the very walls have ears, and the problem is that Boney has many spies right here in England, and so far some of them have been successful. The Prince Regent has requested that any English-born spies be winkled out. He is especially sensitive since one of his lady friends was accused of passing information to the enemy. Although he himself was cleared of any wrongdoing, apparently it brought home to him how important it is that we stop this languid attitude with regard to the war. The citizens must understand that information carelessly passed on here can be responsible for the deaths of hundreds of soldiers over there."

"Are they asking you to join this Committee?"

"They have."

"Robert, I'm so proud of you! A Special Committee reporting to the Prince of Wales! And you have only just returned to England."

He grinned at her exuberance. "Until the Regent talks to me, I'm afraid the position is an unpaid one. But he has said he wishes to see me. The Horse Guards will make arrangements for me to sell out. But we must wait and see. In the meantime, I am awaiting delivery from the War Office of some questions from Arthur Wellesley who is apparently going to the Peninsula next month to take over from Cradock."

None of this made much sense to Helena who knew only vaguely where the Horse Guards were and had never heard of Cradock, although she had heard of Wellesley's excellent service record in India. Being a loving sister, she smiled at Robert's enthusiasm and hoped passionately that this would set Robert on the road to a speedy recovery and a rewarding career.

A tap on the door interrupted them. "Excuse me, Miss Marshfield, tea and cake is being set up in the small withdrawing-room for you." Helena was puzzled. She saw no reason why Timms should not deliver the tea things to Robert's room as usual, but this was not her house to order about, so she rose and followed the butler. She was joined by Caroline who was puzzled and a little indignant at being herded out of the library. She looked at Helena, her eyebrows raised.

"Do you think Sir Ivor's servants have been complaining about running up and down stairs with refreshments for us?" she asked Helena.

"My dear, I don't know. I feel distinctly like a naughty child being kept out of the way. Did you finish your note to your mama?"

"Yes. I told her we will go to see her tomorrow, if that is fine with you?"

"Yes, and perhaps I could escort Ariadne somewhere to give you some time alone with your mama. She must be quite er...fatigued with all Ariadne's social jobations by now."

Caroline laughed. "Poor Mama!"

Helena held up her hand. "Hush. What is that?" There was the thud of several pairs of booted feet climbing the staircase outside the withdrawing-room.

"It must be Papa's meeting. They are all going upstairs."

"I think they are going up to meet with Robert. How exciting!"

Caroline was surprised and confused. "Why do they wish to meet Robert?"

And it was brought home to Helena just how easy it was to betray your country. A careless word at the wrong time could lead to appalling repercussions. She made a hasty recovery. "I mean it will be exciting for Robert to be able to discuss business for a change. He must be getting bored with our company by now. He was greatly taken with your papa."

"I'm so glad. It is extremely important that Robert and Papa deal well together," Caroline said earnestly, then blushed hotly.

Helena took Caroline's hand, praying she would say the right thing. "Caroline, I have been meaning to talk to you about this. Do you realize that Robert has no means of supporting a wife? Your parents are determined you shall make a good marriage. I would not be doing my duty if I didn't warn you that they might not look kindly on Robert's suit. As a friend, I beg you not to set yourself up for a dreadful disappointment."

"Papa would not be so cruel!"

"My dear, many fathers would order you to keep away from Robert or make it impossible for you to meet him again. You and I have been fortunate to have indulgent fathers who have not set harsh parameters on our choices. Forgive me for such plain speaking, but I cannot let you go further without warning you. It is difficult for me because I love my brother and cannot conceive how any father cannot see his true worth. But I am not a man with a marriageable daughter so I have no notion what may happen."

Caroline was silent for a while as she sipped her tea. Then she said, "Papa is very astute. I am sure he will see Robert's true worth. And Robert has already set about selling his company since he cannot return to fight."

It was true that a purchaser would be easy to find as there were many young men determined to show their mettle on the Peninsula. With the prospect of this war lasting some considerable time, a man stood a good chance of promotion and advancement up through the ranks.

They could hear much laughing and calling out on the floor above them which gradually quieted down to a steady rumble of masculine voices.

When the ladies had finished their tea, Helena moved toward the door saying jestingly, "Now that we have had our tea, I presume Timms will allow us to go about our business." But she was stunned to find when she turned the doorknob, that the door had been locked from outside. They were locked in!

Chapter Eleven

The only sound in the room was the rustle of papers turning. The Accused sat, head bowed, his hands between his knees. This was the end of the road for him. It wasn't that he had been careless; he had had no idea that there was an organization set up to combat the leakage of information. Obviously they had suspected him for some time. The capture had been swift and efficient, timed to accost him when he had a great deal of incriminating evidence on his person. Fleetingly he wondered if his blackmailer knew about the organization. It mattered not. He was done for, and he was glad of it. Glad of it! At last he was free of that devil who had turned him against his own country. His accuser glanced up and met his eye. "We shall not be asking you any more questions. We know most of it. I am sorry for you." He stood. "I shall leave this dueler here on the table. It is fully loaded. You know what to do."

****

"Whatever is happening?" Helena exclaimed. At the same time the noise they had heard previously began again, as several pairs of booted feet trod downstairs. Caroline and Helena stared at each other, amazed and confused. There seemed to be a discussion going on in the foyer and then they heard the sound of farewells and the crunch of carriage wheels on gravel.

Suddenly a key turned in the lock. Helena and Caroline stood back from the door. Timms entered. He bowed, then moved to clear away the tea things.

Helena gathered her courage. "Timms, why was the door locked?"

"Ah…Miss Marshfield, I was requested to lock the door. We have had a *very* important visitor here today who did not wish to be recognized."

"I see."

Caroline looked askance at Helena who shrugged and smiled. Fortunately Caroline was more concerned to find out what her father and Robert had discussed and went upstairs to find out. Helena lingered and said to Timms, "The Prince of Wales, Timms?"

"Lord Sidmouth from the Home Office has been here, miss, but as to the other influential gentleman, my lips are sealed. I must say you are close to the mark."

Amused, Helena followed Caroline to Robert's room where she found a celebration taking place.

"Ellie, congratulate us! Ivor and I are to be rewarded for services rendered. And I have been appointed permanently to the Committee. There is a stipend that goes with the position."

Helena sighed a deep, thankful sigh. "Wonderful!" Then to everyone's surprise—especially her own—she burst into tears of relief. Embarrassed, she fled the room. She had been under such a mountain of worry lately that it seemed she could not comprehend the lifting of the big load off her shoulders. Her brother was safe. He had an occupation which he would enjoy doing. And Sir Ivor, too, had been rewarded in some way. She wondered if Mr. Yardley would receive anything. He certainly deserved it because she had a strong suspicion that a lot of funds from Mr. Yardley's businesses had been diverted to the Special Advisory Committee. Who were the other two mysterious members of the Committee who were based at the Horse Guards and the War Office?

She sat on her bed feeling thankful and lethargic. Their futures had taken a turn for the best, but she was exhausted, unable to bring herself to understand their good luck.

Caroline peeped around the door. "Dear Helena, are you better? Such a surprise as it was when you cried. Sir Ivor says that it was not to be wondered at, as you had been under a strain since first hearing of Robert's injuries."

Helena smiled mistily through her tears. "Yes, I suppose he is right."

Caroline pushed open the door and practically bounced into the room.

"Helena, what is even better is that Robert has been promised a small estate by the Prince Regent! Something to do with services to the Crown. I don't precisely understand. Apparently the occupation he is to undertake is something to do with what Papa and Sir Ivor have meetings about. Perhaps you may understand more than I do."

"Not really, Caroline. But I am very thankful; especially about the small estate, since some of Prinny's stipends are often delayed."

"Oh?" Caroline's brow wrinkled.

"Did they give any indication where the estate might be?" Helena was dying to know. It could make a great difference to all of them if it was a viable estate.

Caroline sat on the bed beside Helena. "Sir Ivor

seems to know all about that," she said. "Helena, do you think Robert should speak to Papa now?"

Helena sighed. Caroline was concerned only with one thing. "I don't know, Caroline. It's not for me to say. It seems such a short time that you have known one another but…"

Caroline smiled and patted her hand. "All will be well, Helena."

Helena felt that Caroline had moved beyond her, that she had matured considerably in the past week and left her erstwhile governess far behind. It was as if their roles had been reversed.

She kissed Helena lightly on the cheek then got up off the bed. "I must go to Robert to glean all the information I can. Perhaps he will speak to Papa today."

Helena sat, gazing out the window at the spring sunshine. Her world was changing fast. She was not sure what ramifications Robert's appointment would have for her. Restlessly she rose and paced the room. She wished things were more settled so that she knew whether she was to continue working for the Yardleys or not. Should Caroline and Robert gain permission to marry, would they really want her living with them? Newlyweds would surely require a certain amount of privacy at first. Oh, heavens! She didn't know whether to laugh or cry. She could end up just being Ariadne's companion. How ghastly! Time would tell.

But a major problem still remained. The promissory note hidden in her reticule preyed on her mind. It would be the last straw if Robert were to lose his newfound security over that wretched vowel. She had brought it with her to Stafford House. For some reason, a sense of impending doom hung over her whenever she looked at that awful vowel.

She must discuss it with Robert as soon as possible, now that he was much improved. He had probably long since forgotten about it. He would most likely think her fears were far-fetched.

But when she returned to Robert's room, she intruded upon a scene where she had no place.

Josh Yardley held Caroline's hand in one of his own and had placed his free hand on Robert's good shoulder. "I couldn't have asked for a better bargain for my girl," he was saying emotionally.

Helena began to creep quietly away, but he noticed and turned to her. "Come in, Helena. I have just received the grandest news! Did you know about this?"

"Er...yes, I suspected."

"Now we are all one family. And of course, Robert and I will be doing a little work together won't we?" He waxed lyrical in his excitement. Robert grinned good-naturedly. Helena could tell that he would deal well with his future father-in-law.

"I must make haste to go and tell your mama," he said to Caroline. "I had no hesitation in not consulting her on this matter because we are of the same mind. Even though she has not met him, I know she will be as pleased as I to welcome Robert into our family. After all, we have known about Sir Robert for some considerable while. Congratulations to you both." He nodded to Robert. "I shall speak to you further on this." After a swift pinch on Caroline's chin he was off, in his usual ebullient fashion.

Robert pulled a face. "When he speaks to me further, I hope my dismal prospects do not make him change his mind."

"No!" Caroline was most indignant.

Robert grinned and tightened his clasp on Caroline's hand. Helena realized that his years in the army had bolstered his confidence considerably. He was a long way from the frightened, lonely youth who had set out for army headquarters with his commission in his pocket and most of his worldly goods in a valise.

Lucky Robert. Caroline was a young woman who wouldn't care that he couldn't ride or dance well. He had been her *beau idéal* ever since she had read his war correspondence. She would be a helpmate in good times and in bad. They deserved each other.

But where did that leave Helena? In the middle of all the excitement she had been forgotten. She wouldn't have it any other way of course. She loved them both dearly. No doubt within the next few days Robert would make known his plans for the future, and she would find out if they included her. If they did not, well…there was always Miss Fichton's seminary. Not a thrilling prospect, but a secure one, and a lot easier than being a companion to Ariadne. She would get used to boredom once more.

Unfortunately, if that was to be her fate, she would not see Robert and Caroline above once or twice a year.

And she might never see Sir Ivor again. No doubt he would marry within the next few years. He would need an heir. Helena would hear about it from Robert and Caroline in due course. She sighed heavily. Well, she had plenty of experience at putting on a brave face so she would manage. Nobody would ever suspect that she'd fallen head over heels for someone so far above her touch.

But now she must draw Robert's attention to that promissory note so that any remaining debt could be paid out prior to his marriage. It was possible he had cleared the debt without her knowledge.

When Caroline left Robert's room to prepare for dinner, Helena showed the vowel to Robert. "Robert, do you remember this?"

"What is it? Oh, I vaguely remember that we found that just before I joined up."

"Yes. Nobody has come to collect."

"Frankly, it looks to me like the sort of thing men write when they're in their cups. It probably doesn't mean anything."

"It's just that I have a strange feeling about it."

Robert shouted with laughter, then winced at the pain in his shoulder. "Dear Helena, if I had a penny for every time a female had a 'strange feeling' I would be a rich man!"

Helena pulled a face at him. "Thank you. You know I'm not given to fancies. No, what I dread is that this scrawled letter might be an 'E'".

"If it is, so what? It could stand for Edgecumbe, Evesleigh, Elverton, or—"

"That is what frightens me, Robert. That it might stand for Elverton."

"Look here, Helena. We paid that sour-faced clutch-fist every last groat he said he was owed. I know Father was friendly with him, but you and I never trusted him. That's why I made sure I paid him out in full. What else could we possibly owe him?"

Helena's cold hands twisted in her lap. "I have a terrible feeling that Papa may have been trying to arrange a marriage between us. Do you remember how

Elverton always acted as if I were a chattel of his?"

"But Ellie, they would not use a vowel for such a serious transaction. All they had to do was arrange it formally between them. Surely you don't believe Father would stoop so low as to use you as a *gambling chip*? Don't be ridiculous!" Robert was becoming angry.

"You have no idea how often I was brought into the room when Elverton called," she said quietly. "At first you were at Magdalen. Sometimes you were away in town. At other times you were tooling about the countryside with friends, so you never saw his attitude toward me. Last month at Caroline's dress-party, he tried to force me to dance with him by saying we still owed him something. If it weren't for Sir Ivor, he would have told everybody there what the stake was. I couldn't bear it."

Robert stared into space, saying nothing for a moment. "It must be several years since you saw him. Do you think he lost track of you, didn't know where you were?"

"Yes. I have been careful not to frequent any place he might go."

"Oh, Ellie. You shouldn't have kept this to yourself. Why didn't you tell me? I would have arranged for Ned or Tally to make sure you were safe."

"That was what I wanted to avoid. If our father was so lost to decency as to promise me to Elverton in a card-game, I didn't want the world to know. We have had enough to live down. I did not want your prospects soured."

Robert twisted restlessly in the bed. "I know one thing. Yardley and Stafford are both suspicious about Elverton's activities, but I don't know what it is they suspect. It just came about in general conversation."

"Then why did Mr. Yardley invite him to Caroline's dress-party?" She stared at her brother. "I presumed that Mr. Yardley was toad-eating him, wanting it known that he hobnobbed with an earl. Maybe I was wrong. Maybe he had another reason for inviting Elverton."

Robert shrugged. "I should say so. I see my future father-in-law as a very shrewd man. I doubt he'd let his social ambitious override his common sense. Why don't we leave it up to Ivor and Josh? And that vowel may have nothing to do with him. It's probably meaningless now. Why don't you burn it?"

"You don't know how often I've wanted to! Now that you've suggested it, I shall do so. Right now," she said with decision.

Light-hearted with relief, she hurried to her room and poked the screwed-up paper into the grate. When the maid came to light the fire that evening, it would be gone forever. For so long it had hung over her shoulders, and she was well aware that she had become embittered with its threat to derail her life. Lord, what a relief to think that Robert did not consider it to be of any import.

Chapter Twelve

That evening as they sat down to dinner in a festive mood, there was the sound of an arrival in the foyer. Sir Ivor threw down his napkin and rose to his feet just as Timms formally announced at the doorway, "Lady Stafford and the Misses Stafford, sir."

A slender gray-haired lady glided in, removing her bonnet with one hand. "Ivor, my dear! I begged Timms not to be so formal, but you know how much he likes to do the right thing." She kissed her son, holding one of his hands clasped in her own. "And who are these charming ladies? Just fancy. I come to town to find you dining with not one, but *two* delightful young ladies!"

Ivor cast his eyes up, looking embarrassed as his mother twitted him. "This is Miss Marshfield and Miss Caroline Yardley, Mama. Ladies, this is my mother, Lady Anthea Stafford, and if I'm not mistaken, my two sisters are not far behind."

There was a lot of giggling, and two young women rushed into the room. He attempted to formally introduce them, but the younger one would have none of that. Whilst the older of his sisters went to her bedchamber to put off cloak and bonnet, the younger one protested, "Ivor, I'm simply *famished*. Timms, please take my cloak. I shall sit down at the table right now."

She was a charming, bouncy young woman of

about sixteen, and Helena saw that Lady Stafford put out a restraining hand to contain her enthusiasm.

"Let us all introduce ourselves properly first. Miss Marshfield and Miss Yardley, this is my younger daughter, Erica. As you can see, she has not touched a morsel of food since the beginning of our journey yesterday." She said in an aside to Helena, "As a matter of fact we stopped for quite an hour on the road for Erica to consume a large repast at midday. She ate an apple not more than an hour ago." Lady Stafford sighed and laughed. "It is to be hoped she will not resemble a butterball on her coming-out."

"And when is her coming-out out to be, ma'am?" Helena inquired politely.

"Not for three Seasons yet if I have my way," Lady Stafford said darkly.

"No, Mama! Ivor promised that I would come out next year. You know he did, and you agreed."

"That was before you ate us out of house and home, my child."

"But I'm *hungry*, Mama."

"Then please drink your soup which has been in front of you for some time, darling."

"Oh!" Erica attacked her meal with zest.

Caroline had been watching quietly from the sidelines as was her wont, and Sir Ivor commented to Erica that Caroline was just 'out' this Season.

"Are you being presented?" Erica demanded, her dark ringlets bouncing as she swiveled to face Caroline.

"No. I'm not…er…"

"Neither am I," Erica said unexpectedly. "Nerida didn't bother either, did she Mama?"

"No. If you don't wish to be presented to the

Queen, that is acceptable. I have no quarrel with that. Quite a few young ladies nowadays are just having coming-out balls," Lady Stafford commented.

Nerida, the older daughter, joined them at the table and agreed with her sister. "Indeed. I have no wish to wear an old-fashioned train and feathers and to meet people I shall never see again," she said.

Caroline's eyes met Helena's across the table, and they smiled.

"Ah, I gather that you were formally presented, Miss Marshfield," Lady Stafford said.

"Yes. I told Caroline about my adventures with my train, whilst trying to back out of the Queen's presence."

"How ghastly! Did you trip over?" Erica asked, laughing.

"No, but nearly. The worst part was that my feathers were slowly sliding down the back of my neck, and that distracted me. Very unnerving."

Erica hooted with laughter until remonstrated with. "That is the sort of thing that would happen to me. That is why I shall not bother."

Ivor Stafford watched the woman he loved interact easily with his mother and sisters and thought how right it all looked. Until four weeks ago he would have dismissed such a thought. Now he knew without a doubt that Helena Marshfield was exactly where he wanted her to be—in his house, amongst his family. He felt his mother glancing at him and hastily averted his gaze. His mother knew him too well. She was not the sort of person who would make an adverse comment about his choice of life's partner, but he did not wish her to assume that he had already made a formal offer to Helena and treat it as a fait accompli. He desperately needed to speak to Helena alone. Now that his mother and sisters had arrived, that looked like being difficult.

"By the by, Ivor," Nerida said, selecting a spoonful of collop of beef. "You didn't tell us you had guests. I went to the blue room as usual, and a charming young man was sitting up in bed, eating his dinner from a tray. Then Mrs. Annerwith came clucking around and, before I could introduce myself, she escorted me to the room at the end of the corridor. Who is he?"

"Well, if you had arrived earlier, instead of lingering on the road, and had then had time for introductions..." her brother baited her, "then you would know all about it."

Helena leaned forward. "I am sorry if my brother has your usual room, Miss Stafford. He was injured on the Peninsula and is unable to negotiate any long corridors or stairs for some weeks. That is why he is not at the dinner table."

Nerida glanced up quickly. "Oh, I was not complaining. Yes, of course." She laid her head on one side and examined Helena's face. "I should have seen the resemblance. It is just that Ivor is extremely uncommunicative. And where is Ned? I thought he would be here to welcome us."

"So he would be if you had given us notice of your precise movements," Ivor retaliated. "All we knew is that you were expected sometime this week." He seemed to be able to hold his own amongst his womenfolk. Indeed, he gave a considerable license to his sisters, which would have been unthinkable in some more formal households. Helena was enchanted. They were such a friendly, unaffected group of ladies. Just the sort of people one would like to have as friends. She brought herself up short—if one was not merely a companion, of course.

"And are you and Miss Yardley enjoying your Season so far, Miss Marshfield?" Lady Stafford inquired, under cover of the general conversation.

Helena drew a breath. "I am just here to assist with my brother's nursing, Lady Stafford. Caroline is my friend. At least…I was her governess."

There was a general lull in the conversation at this point, and several heads turned toward her. Nerida was the first to speak. "Why, what a coincidence Miss Marshfield! We have a governess in *our* family, don't we Ivor?"

"Yes. I thought Miss Marshfield and Mama would deal well together."

Helena swallowed hard and slowly turned and looked at him. She was sure her jaw was dropping. But now the mystery as to why he had befriended a mere governess was solved.

"Miss Marshfield, if you could but see yourself! Your eyes are as round as saucers. I keep telling you that governessing is an honorable profession, but for some reason you seem to be ashamed of it." Ivor Stafford then had the infernal cheek to go on calmly eating his dinner.

"N-not ashamed of it. It's just that—"

"It's just that one is neither of the family, nor of the servants, isn't that so, Miss Marshfield?" Lady Stafford's hand covered Helena's where it lay on the table. "Well do I remember that feeling. I was only employed in one household where Theo—my husband you know—was the older son. It was not an easy thing for him to marry me, because his parents were high sticklers. Although they professed to like me, they were not prepared to admit me to their family at first. However, it took but a few weeks and things gradually resolved themselves. I think when faced with the choice of his marrying me, or marrying the scandalous daughter of one of their aristocratic friends as planned, they decided I was slightly more acceptable. Besides which, the young lady was quite clear about her disinclination to marry anyone at all. And you, Miss Marshfield…how long have you been a governess?"

"She is our companion now," Caroline broke in.

"Ah, of course. You are 'out' now, aren't you Miss Yardley? May I call you Caroline? Do you have sisters?"

"An older sister, ma'am."

"And is she as pretty as you?"

"Oh, *much* prettier, ma'am."

"You are very pretty, Miss Yardley, so your sister must be exceptional!" Nerida exclaimed. Sir Ivor's sister was a rather plain young woman with a lovely smile, and she obviously had beautiful manners. Caroline blushed, and Helena smiled warmly at Nerida. Sir Ivor unexpectedly joined the conversation. "I think you would find that Caroline is the more prettily behaved of the two sisters. Ariadne bears a marked resemblance to our Erica here," he said, laughing at his younger sister. Erica indignantly repudiated any suggestions that her behavior was less than exemplary, and everyone ended up laughing.

Under these conditions Helena slowly relaxed. This was not a judgmental family, nor were they interested in character assassination as was so often the case nowadays when groups of people socialized. On the contrary, they were open and sympathetic.

"It has been an eventful day here," Sir Ivor remarked to his mother. "Caroline has become engaged to marry Helena's brother, and Robert and myself have received gifts from the Prince of Wales."

"How wonderful, Miss Yardley!"

Caroline smiled shyly, and Lady Stafford turned back to her son. "What do you mean—'gifts?'"

"Prinny's usual thank-yous. He certainly has his aides do plenty of research before bestowing estates. Robert's has yet to be decided, but he presented old Fickling's land to me."

"Ah, a prime piece of land. A pity poor old Hugh Fickling was the last of his line. And it is so close to us."

"Yes. It will be jolly useful not to have to travel too far." He turned to Helena. "The land we are referring to lies just beyond Nerida's future home. So I shall see you and George nearly every day, Nerida."

"Still keeping an eye on me?" Nerida asked cheerfully.

"Hardly. That is George's job now."

"And he does it very well too."

Helena couldn't help laughing.

"Nerida!" Lady Stafford remonstrated feebly. But Nerida, dreamy-eyed, just smiled at her mother. Helena reflected that between Nerida and Caroline, any unattached young woman was likely to feel quite left out of things.

After dinner everybody traipsed upstairs to meet Robert, and his bedroom became a drawing-room. Robert and Erica settled down to play checkers, watched by the others.

"Come, my dear. Tell me all about your career." Lady Stafford drew Helena to one side so they could sit in the window embrasure.

Ivor fervently hoped that his dear mother was only discussing governessing, not anything too personal. Since the Prince Regent had called today, he had seen his way clear to finally getting what he most wanted out of life. He had been trying to quench a bubble of anticipation all evening, hoping desperately that what he wanted might soon be his.

When Robert stifled a yawn, Lady Stafford stood. "Come away now. This poor young man is an invalid and needs to rest." Ignoring Robert's polite protests, she firmly shepherded the little party out of his room. They repaired downstairs to await the tea tray. Erica was sent to bed protesting that she could easily have beaten Robert had they played but one more game. Neither Nerida nor Lady Stafford stayed long after the tea tray was removed, both saying they had had a tiring day.

Helena prepared to follow them upstairs, but Ivor stopped her.

"Miss Marshfield, may I have a word with you in my study?"

Lady Stafford glanced back from her position at the top of the staircase with her brows raised in surprise. Quickly she swept Caroline and Nerida along in front of her.

Helena followed Ivor to his study, wondering what he wanted. Heavens! What had she done?

Increasing her trepidation, he closed the study door and walked across the room to stand in front of the fire. "Take a seat, Miss Marshfield."

She chose a seat far away from the fire. Had she offended him in some way? Was it to do with his family? Oh God, please don't let him invite her to be his mistress. He was not precisely averse to her, she was sure, but nor had he shown any inclination of late to spend time with her. She would have said that he had been avoiding her.

Then common sense asserted itself. With her brother and his mother under his roof, was it likely he would give her a slip on the shoulder? No. of course not. This was about something else.

She flicked a quick glance at him from beneath her lashes. He shrugged his shoulders as if his coat was too tight and looked down at his feet. He seemed to be having difficulty with what he wanted to say. She sighed inwardly. He was more handsome than any man had a right to be, and he was playing havoc with her heart.

Then he dragged his gaze up to meet hers. "Miss Marshfield, I brought you here to…that is to say, you must be aware of my regard for you. It has not in the past been in my power to do as I wish, but now it seems as though the way has been cleared for me to…in short, Miss Marshfield, may I have the honor of your hand in marriage?"

Helena stared at him in confusion. She had not at first understood what he was talking about. Her mind would not clear itself. Then when he had said 'may I have the honor' her heart had wanted to bolt from her chest. Just out of reach was the thing she desired most in the whole world, but it was not hers to take. Struggling for composure she embarked on a disjointed, sad little speech of which the words 'sensible of the great honor you do me', 'unfortunately unable to…' and 'hope we shall remain friends' were the only audible words.

****

What the hell? Ivor swallowed hard. His heart sat like a stone in his chest. He had plotted and scrimped and saved to keep his family estates intact, had done the right thing. Of late he had had to deny himself the one thing above all else that he desired. Then today the Prince Regent had taken him to one side and pressed into his hand the deed of the Fickling estate in Norfolk, some fifteen miles distant from Ryewolds, and his heart had leapt, knowing that *now* he could ask her. He didn't have to wait any longer. He wasn't a coxcomb, didn't necessarily expect her to fall into his lap like a ripe plum, but he didn't understand why she had so quickly rebuffed him. She had scarcely even looked at him. Lord, he wanted so much just to touch her.

"Helena darling, *please…*" He moved toward her, but she stood up quickly, spreading her hands in denial. He stopped. "Would you at least give me some idea why you do not wish to be my wife?"

"'Wish' does not come into it, sir. I…I—my station in life does not equal yours. It would not be right, and even if that were not a consideration, I suspect that you have offered for me because the real object of your affections is now promised to another." Heavens, she sounded like one of Mrs. Radcliffe's romances! But she was so full of anguish she could not think straight.

"What are you talking about?" Disappointment was making him angry.

"Caroline."

"Caroline is a child! A nice child, but still a child. I have no designs on Caroline, and never had. I need a woman, not a child. I love you, Helena. Surely that must be obvious to you. Your brother suspects it. My housekeeper knows it. Even my young brother who is not renowned for his acuity has dropped heavy hints to me. And now my mother is slyly watching me when she sees me looking at you."

She shook her head despairingly.

"Dammit, Helena. What must I do to prove it to you?"

"Sir," she whispered, "if you had a regard for me, because we have been together so much of late, surely you would have mentioned this before? Before Robert and Caroline became engaged?"

"No, Helena. I couldn't." He didn't blame her for feeling skeptical. Curse his father. He assembled his words carefully. He felt as if he were fighting for his life. Now he began to see how she saw things, the reasonableness of her understanding, and he had a sinking feeling that he had made a strategic error in not declaring himself sooner.

"Helena, I could not ask you before. There is a family problem which I had to solve." She looked up at him wonderingly. "Unfortunately I cannot divulge the details because it involves many other members of my family."

****

Helena sat up straighter. She felt a slow burn beginning deep inside her. Did he think she was a fool? Was he saying that she was good enough to propose marriage to, but not good enough to entrust with his family's secrets? Some marriage that would turn out to be!

She couldn't understand why he had approached her *today*. She was certain it had something to do with Caroline. Perhaps he felt that as Caroline and Robert were engaged that Helena would need protection in the future? Did he actually feel *sorry* for her? Something was not right about him delaying his declaration until today of all days.

"I see," she said in a chilly voice, not seeing anything at all.

"Helena, *please*, listen to me, you cannot possibly think that—"

"Sir Ivor, I think we had best finish this fruitless discussion." She had to get out of here before she cried. He was breaking her heart. If only the words he was using were sincere, she would be the happiest woman on earth. He had probably only said he loved her because he thought that was acceptable form when proposing. She would far rather he had proposed an honest marriage of convenience. At least she would know where she stood.

The knots in her stomach pulled tighter. She had had an eventful day. Her brother had accepted a role working for the government; he had also become engaged to be married to her best friend and had advised her to burn that horrendous vowel. Now she had declined an offer of marriage from the one man whose heart she most wished to own. All she needed now was an earth-shattering event such as a tidal wave and her day would be complete. She yearned to burrow under the bedclothes and not emerge for at least a month.

First, however, she had to leave the room in a

dignified manner. She stood up, and such was her confusion and distress that she found her legs shook and would not hold her up.

He moved toward her instantly and took her in his arms. "My dear, I *cannot* believe this has come as a shock to you. You must know how I feel!"

She felt his gaze searching her face and lowered her eyes. She had never in her life been held this close by any man, not even during the scandalous waltz. None of her previous suitors had ever ventured beyond a chaste, brushing kiss on the hand. She felt the warmth of his body protecting hers and without thinking adjusted her curves to his hardness in an attempt to fold even farther into his body. He felt so good! Her face was pressed against the bottom of his cravat, and she felt the slip and slide of his sateen waistcoat. Where her legs pressed against his she felt every sinew and muscle. And every bulge. His clasp strengthened, and he bent his head. With a murmur of surprise, she raised hers and he brushed his lips tentatively against her mouth.

She jerked as if burnt and backed away. "P-Please don't. I am so sorry...so sorry." Her mind a seething cauldron of want and sorrow, she hesitated at the study door, knowing she was confusing him with her behavior.

And then the stupid man actually took her at her word! Instead of coming to her and reassuring her of his sincerity; instead of telling her the truth about why he'd hesitated to propose to her before this, he strode to the other side of the room and stood for a moment in the shadows. Then he said nothing further but bowed correctly. In other words, he accepted her decision. It was over.

Stumbling, she left the room and scrambled up the stairs to her bedchamber.

****

Ivor Stafford was left bereft, puzzled, and shattered, wondering how to put back together the pieces of his life. This had not turned out the way he had envisaged at all. He knew there might well be a stumbling block if Helena thought it was not suitable for him to marry a governess. He realized that she thought of herself as no longer eligible to marry anyone of rank or from the landed gentry. But he had assumed that introducing his mother was the way out of that.

However he had no idea how to disabuse her of the strange notion she had taken into her head that she was to be some sort of substitute for Caroline Yardley in his affections. Evidently the life she had led for the past five years must have affected her self-confidence so strongly that she could not even receive an offer of marriage without deeming it to be meant for someone else. She had always given the impression of owning a quiet self-confidence, particularly when dealing with her charges, but that must be an assumed manner, not really how she felt at all. The poor darling must have suffered mightily at the hands of some of the catty tabbies around town when the Marshfield fortunes took a turn for the worst.

But maybe her excuses cloaked another reason altogether and there was some secret he did not understand. Perhaps he could ask Robert. God, what a conundrum.

He paced urgently up and back, up and back. Whether he liked it or not, he would have to tell her about the Stafford family problems. He was a fool not to have explained his background. Instead of alienating her he should have asked for her support. It would be willingly given, he knew. She was hardworking and well used to responsibility. She would be happy to take some of the responsibilities of the running of Ryewolds and Stafford House off his hands. Aside from the fact that he loved her, she was an ideal helpmate. She was talented, lovely...He found himself becoming maudlin.

And look how similar her family's problems were to his! Surely, she *must* understand. No, in the morning he would approach her again. One thing was certain, she damned well *would* marry him, even if he had to solicit the aid of her brother. He leant his arm along the mantelpiece thinking that if the Regent's generous gift of a small estate in Norfolk caused this much trouble and frustration, he would rather that Prinny kept his gifts to himself.

****

Upstairs, Helena forced herself to share Caroline's enthusiasm about her future with Robert. "Well of course I think he is a wonderful man, Caroline! He is my brother. An odd creature I should be if I did not agree with you." and "Yes, was it not fortunate that army headquarters has offered him a position?"

She could not bring herself to dampen Caroline's unusual verve and spirit, nor could she be jealous of the soft light in Caroline's eyes when she spoke of Robert. No, the people she loved most in the world were well matched, and she could be easy now that Mr. Yardley had lent his approval.

But when Caroline had left her, she sank her head in her hands, wondering what had possessed her to decline Ivor's offer. Over a period of time, would not people eventually forget that she had been a governess, although it was interesting that his mother preferred Ryewolds to being in town. Maybe some people had not forgotten her origins. Normally it was the way of the world to forget old scandals provided another scandal did not bring them to light. Usually, a fresh *on dit* took its place.

And even if Caroline *were* Ivor's real love, could she not be satisfied with half a loaf?

No! She was not made like that. If she could not be first in his affections, it was better not to know a life with him. *Half a loaf is better than none?* No. Never. She knew enough to understand that her dissatisfaction with being a poor second would lead to an arid, unhappy marriage. In the last ten years it had become much more common to enter into marriages born of love, mutual affection, and respect. In the past, many titled families had been forced to accept as their own the illegitimate offspring of their unhappy wives. Gradually, as times changed, people looked for a love match. She knew herself well enough to know that she could never be satisfied with less. Truly, she did not think that Ivor loved Caroline. She believed what he said about seeing Caroline as a child.

But there was definitely *something* about Caroline and Robert's announcement that had prompted him to offer for her—she was sure of it. The whole thing was just too coincidental. And if he had offered for her out of pity, seeing her as being alone in the world once Robert moved on with his life, how could she live with that? Lord, who on earth wanted to be married out of *pity*? With his manners being as polished as they were, how would she ever know if he truly loved her or not? He was experienced in the art of dalliance, and she was not. She didn't know if that kiss she had pulled away from had affected him as it had her. Lord, she had been positively singed with the heat emanating from them both. Oh yes. She had felt his touch from her hair to the tips of her toes. How could she withstand such an onslaught?

Too bad. She must. That was all there was to it. It was bad for her to be vulnerable to any pressure he might bring to bear. She would steel herself to stand firm. He was not for the likes of her. But God, how she longed to be back in his arms again. For the first time in her life, everything had fallen into place. She had felt safe and cherished. Yes…cherished.

She had better not get used to that idea. It was over before it had begun.

In spite of what Robert thought, what if the owner of that vowel should turn out to be Lord Elverton? She could not visit that disgrace upon Sir Ivor, if it turned out that her father had valued her so lightly that he had lost all sense of decency and sold his daughter.

And this 'family problem' Ivor was not prepared to tell her about. Did that not prove she was not first in his affections? His family came first.

No, it was best to finish it.

On that noble resolve, she went to bed and lay miserably awake until dawn.

Chapter Thirteen

At the Horse Guards two gentlemen pored over a map. Beside the map lay a thick document entitled 'Summer Campaign.' One of the gentlemen dipped a pen in the ink and began copying portions of the map on to a fresh sheet of vellum. His penmanship was superb, and the finished product looked very similar to the original. There were, however, a few deviations from the original; the route of a few walking tracks had been altered and in particular he had interchanged three place-names.

His partner leaned over the new map. "Excellent," he proclaimed. "That should do it. Close enough to be probable, and devious enough to throw them right off the track."

****

Helena arose early the next morning and peered into the unforgiving mirror. Heavens! She looked as though she had spent six months in a dark room with no hope of escaping into the light. Even her hair looked lackluster. Unable to face anyone over the breakfast table she sipped coffee in her room then paced restlessly back and forth waiting until the hour was respectable enough for her to go downstairs.

She paused in Robert's doorway.

"Good morning, Robert. I shall be back to see you shortly. Just going for a walk." And without further ado she sped downstairs. She *had* to get away and a long, hard walk was called for. Hopefully she could escape without Caroline noticing. The last thing she wanted was company of any sort.

She hesitated until Timms had finished talking to one of the housemaids in the foyer then slipped quietly out of the front door, which was ajar. As she pulled on her kid gloves under the portal of Stafford House, a housemaid called out, "Miss! If you be going for a walk, I need to come with you. Master says!"

Stiffening, Helena pretended she had not heard and hurried past the boxthorn hedge onto the flagstones of the Square. How dare he? Now he was setting the housemaids to keep watch over her! What next? If she wished to walk alone, she *would* walk alone. As a governess she did not need an escort and even as 'Miss Marshfield' she had frequently walked and ridden about the countryside near Marshfield Manor unescorted. "Stuff and nonsense," she muttered as she stepped out briskly.

She was not quite so enthusiastic when she realized that yet again it had been raining. A closed carriage passed by her, splashing water from last night's rain puddles over her kid half boots. So lost in thought was she that when the carriage stopped a few yards in front of her she did not take any notice. The door of the carriage swung open, and its owner descended and stood stock still, right in front of her.

"Lord Elverton!"

"Yes, Miss Marshfield. Well met," he said pleasantly, and then without warning grabbed her around her waist and hoisted her up into his carriage.

"Put me down! Please…" She trailed off as he

climbed in beside her and slammed the door. With his cane he banged on the roof, and his carriage started off, trotting at a brisk pace out of Eaton Square.

"What do you think you are doing?" Helena tried to make her tone haughty and demanding but failed miserably. Her voice came out frightened and querulous. "I demand to be set down at once!"

"Oh you *demand* do you? Be quiet, woman. You will do as I bid you from now on. You could not have pleased me more," he added sarcastically. "There was I racking my brains as to how I could extricate myself from my present predicament, and along came Helena Marshfield. Just the woman to help me."

"I…help you?" Helena stuttered. "How?"

"Yes, you will help me." His voice had changed to a silky soft threat. "You have no choice in the matter. But first I shall take you to a place where we may have a sensible discussion."

Helena stayed in the corner of the carriage where he had flung her. Her thoughts scrambled about in her head. Her deepest fears had been realized. Of all people to meet twice in a month when she had so assiduously avoided him for five years! And she had no idea what he was talking about, but she knew it boded no good for her.

Then he made a comment under his breath and leaned across her to pull the curtains together. As he did so, his arm brushed hers. Involuntarily she pulled away and his eyes narrowed. "By tomorrow you will not be so missish, I promise you, *Helena*."

He emphasized her name in a contemptuous manner and, trying to regain her courage, she snapped, "I did not give you leave to use my name, sir."

He laughed shortly. "By the time I am finished with you, I will not need permission to use either your name or your person." He had been leaning over her, but on these words, he flung himself backward into the far corner and propped his booted feet on the seat beside her.

Petrified, she knew that to show fear to this man was tantamount to handing him a weapon with which to abuse her. She must gain command of herself and show him a bland face, not give him the satisfaction of knowing how desperately ill equipped she was to deal with one such as he. This man had been her worst nightmare since the days when he had brushed against her, seemingly by accident, on the staircases and garden paths of her father's house. She had known him then for the unprincipled villain that he was. That was what frightened her most. It was no consolation to discover that her assessment of him had been right, and her father's had been wrong.

Worst of all, nobody knew where she was, thanks to her own foolishness in avoiding Sir Ivor's housemaid so she could be alone. She might not be missed for at least another two hours, then probably Robert and Caroline would begin to wonder where she was. How stupid she had been to rush off in a pet, to nurse her wounds on her own. Stricken, she wondered if she really knew herself at all. During the past five years she had lost her confidence and self-assurance and replaced it with the mien of a starchy governess. She had allowed herself to lose all sense of proportion. So she had had to become a governess? So what? Many young women were faced with the same fate. Lady Stafford had done so. She had survived.

And many poor young women were faced with a lot worse than becoming a governess. She could have ended up on the streets. Much good her pride would have done her then.

Stricken with self-loathing she huddled in the corner of Lord Elverton's carriage, struggling with her own epiphany. She might well have wasted the most wonderful opportunity life would give her. She had thrown away the love of a wonderful man and if she read Elverton correctly, she might also have thrown away her liberty. Even if she could escape him, after spending time in his company unchaperoned, her reputation would be such that it was unlikely she would ever again attain a situation with a respectable family. And Elverton would undoubtedly see to it that everyone got to hear about his conquest.

Not only would Sir Ivor withdraw his offer—as a man of good family he would have no alternative—but she would never again be considered a suitable wife for *anyone*. Of course, she didn't want just anyone, she wanted Ivor Stafford. Really, Helena? Now was a fine time to discover that. Her secret hope that Sir Ivor would renew his addresses today receded into oblivion.

As time passed, she began to feel less sorry for herself and more determined to escape as soon as she had a chance to do so. Some time ago the rhythm of the coach-wheels had changed. There was no longer any noise of voices or horses' hooves outside the coach, and it was clear that they were leaving London behind. Locked into her own misery she had not taken note of the direction the coach was traveling in. In short, she had no idea at all of where they were.

She began to plan a campaign. Somehow, she

would get through this. Even if Elverton ruined her, she could still rely on Robert. Elverton probably didn't know or care that Robert was back in London. She wished she knew why the Special Advisory Committee was interested in Lord Elverton. After all, the Committee was concerned primarily with the war on the Peninsula, rather than the questionable behavior of various members of the aristocracy.

Elverton suddenly spoke. "I've waited a long while to get you to myself, Helena Marshfield. How fortuitous that I happened to notice you in the Square. You have a very distinctive walk you know," he said conversationally, as if he were prepared to pass the time of day. "Your walk is brisk as though you are on an important mission, and you hold your head up high as if you were a member of the *ton*." Then he snorted derisively. "An actor like your father was. He pretended to be a gentleman. But of course, when things became difficult, he could not act any longer. He chose the easy way out."

Helena, intending to say nothing to him, was unable to remain silent. "*Easy way out!*" she stormed. "Do you think choosing death is easy?"

"Of course it is. It takes courage to live."

Unexpectedly, Helena realized that she agreed with him. He was correct. If she did not have Robert to turn to after Elverton was finished with her, she did not know whether she would have the courage to kill herself. Without Robert, it might have been the only option. She would not be the only young woman who chose that road. She nodded her head slowly.

"Come, Helena! We are agreed on something at last," he said in an amused tone. He had behaved in this whimsical manner sometimes when he had visited Marshfield Manor. No doubt he thought he was being charming. With her father he had at first been all friendly politeness, but later his manner had changed to a thinly veiled contempt. He had had hardly anything to do with Robert. But with Helena he had always maintained a watchful amusement, rather like a cat with a mouse.

Her disquiet returned, and she hunched a shoulder away from him and settled her clothes about her. It was best to feign sleep.

To her surprise she must have actually fallen asleep. After rejecting Ivor's suit, she had slept little the night before, and the rhythm of the wheels lulled her into a light doze. She awoke some time later when the pace of the carriage slackened as it turned a corner. Then it proceeded down what appeared to be a well-used carriageway and slowed even more. When the carriage turned sharply into a driveway, Helena was thrown along the length of the seat. A hard arm shot out to grip her about the wrist. Without ceremony Elverton shoved her back on to the seat. "We don't want the goods damaged just yet, do we?" he said, and all Helena's fear came rushing back. "By the way, what were you doing in Eaton Square so early in the morning?" he asked suddenly. "I couldn't believe my eyes when I saw you there. Just the person to strengthen my hand."

She didn't answer. The coach had stopped, and after a quick look at his face Helena stayed where she was. His persona had rapidly undergone a change. She had seen this before. The harsh, saturnine look had returned, and with it his customary viciousness.

Grabbing her by the arm he hustled her in front of him and kicked down the steps at the carriage door. Helena glanced around for help but there was only a groom in attendance and there was no help from that quarter. The young man was standing, wooden-faced, at the horses' heads and purported not to have noticed Helena at all.

Foxhyth propelled her in front of him up a narrow path to what looked like the back door of a large home. Overhead the sun shone brightly, and Helena estimated that it was now well past noon, possibly as much as two o'clock. She was prodded through a kitchen where nothing was cooking and no kitchen maids were working, into a small empty room that looked like a disused stillroom.

"There, Miss Marshfield. This will be your home for some while. You will have to remain here while I tie up some loose ends, and then you and I will have a little talk about this and that. We need to discuss your future, don't we?"

Helena stared up at him, her face and hands as cold as ice. He turned toward the door, then retraced his steps. "Here's a little something to be going on with, my dear." To her shock he bent and kissed her full on the lips. His lips were hard and bruising. It was a travesty of a kiss, a punishment. Before he pulled away, he savagely bit her bottom lip. She recoiled and brushed her glove across her mouth. He laughed. "Let me give you something to *really* complain about, my little Puritan." He tugged her toward him, belly to belly. Cringing backward she desperately struggled to escape. Grinning, her held her tightly with one arm while the other stroked down her body, lingering at her breast. Then he tweaked her nipple—hard. So hard that a streak of pain bolted through her body.

Gasping, she felt tears come to her eyes. He laughed again and headed for the doorway. At the door he turned and blew a kiss. Then he slammed the door shut, and she heard a key turn in the lock. Helena struggled to swallow a whimper.

His footsteps receded across the kitchen and out along the pathway. Within a few minutes she heard the carriage moving out along the driveway again. She was alone, which was at least preferable to his company.

She slithered down the wall and sat on the floor, rubbing her breast. The room was empty; there was not even a stool. Taking her handkerchief out of her reticule, she dabbed at her lip again. It was bleeding badly, but that was of little consequence. By tomorrow she would be his mistress and she would have more injuries than just a sore lip. If he could hurt her by barely touching her, what would he do to her when he had her at his mercy? Maybe he would simply use her and discard her, but she did not think so. This was a man who liked to make people pay and pay and pay. He enjoyed witnessing the pain of others, and she suspected he also enjoyed inflicting pain.

It was all very well to sit in his carriage and try to make a plan to deal with this. Left on her own in a strange place with no chance of assistance to hand, she had no idea how she was going to save herself. And she would have to save herself. Nobody else could do so because they had no idea where she was. Even if Robert did, by some miracle, find out where she was, he was bedfast and unable to come to her aid. Sir Ivor had no doubt washed his hands of her by now, and anyway, like Robert, would have no idea where she was. It was just possible that the housemaid who had wanted to accompany her might have seen her scooped up into Lord Elverton's carriage, but she could not pin her hopes on that. It was not likely. A large tear of self-pity trickled slowly down Helena's cheek, and she brushed it away angrily. Now was not the time to cry.

She tossed aside her reticule and took off her gloves. The room had no windows at all. There was only the door through which she could escape. She knelt down and peered through the keyhole, hoping against hope that the key had been left in the other side. She knew a trick with keys which Robert had taught her years ago. She hoped to push it out of the lock on to the ground, then, if possible, use a handkerchief to pull it toward herself under the door provided the gap was big enough.

But Lord Elverton knew all about keys too. He was no doubt experienced when it came to locking people up. Helena was certainly not the first prisoner he had held. He had taken the key with him.

She took off her bonnet and pelisse and set about checking all the wall panels, in case one was loose. Then she checked the flagstones. Impossible. There was simply no means of escape. As a last resort she snapped a piece off the Spanish comb in her hair and tried to insert it in the lock. The lock was a big, old-fashioned, rusty one, and the tines of the comb had no effect on it at all. She smiled crookedly at the beautiful Spanish comb Robert had brought her.

What now? A hero such as the one in Mrs. Radcliffe's latest romance would be welcome. But she should not look for someone else to rescue her. This horrible dilemma was all her own doing. And she had two choices.

She could succumb to Lord Elverton's power, or she could fight him. She had no delusions about her ability to oppose him for long.

She might be disappointed in herself at the moment, but one thing she did have confidence in was her ability to work her way through a problem. And this was the worst problem she had ever had to surmount. On the face of it there was no solution to this one. All she could do was await his return and see what he had in store for her.

The room had obviously not been opened up for some time, and the air was stale. At first it was stuffy and hot but as hours went by the room cooled. Helena began to feel faint from lack of fresh air and the fact that she had had only a cup of coffee all day. By now it must surely be the end of the afternoon.

Half in a swoon she was slumped in a corner of the room when she heard carriage wheels again. She sat up and straightened her clothes. Several pairs of footsteps approached the room, and the door was unlocked. Still sitting on the floor, Helena gulped in lungsful of the fresh cold air that swirled into the room.

A cup of water was thrust into her face. She glanced up through the mist in front of her eyes and saw a rough, swarthy face in front of her. The man must be a servant of Lord Elverton's. She took the cup and drank gratefully. As her head cleared, she became conscious that there was quite a commotion outside the room. The door which had stood half-open was suddenly thrust wide. "Greetings, my dear," said a hateful voice. "I have brought you a companion," and to her dismay, Ariadne was pushed willy-nilly through the doorway and the manservant left, slamming the door shut on his way out. Stumbling drunkenly, Ariadne lurched to a stop in front of Helena. She was tousled and red-faced.

"What are *you* doing here?" she demanded. Then she turned toward the door and called, "Lord Elverton! What are you doing? What is this place?"

"Have patience, my dear," he called through the door, "and all will be revealed."

Helena was aghast. What on earth did Ariadne have to do with Elverton? The only possible solution was that Elverton had gotten wind of Josh Yardley's opinion that he was involved in some havey-cavey business. Even so, that would hardly explain the necessity for Elverton to kidnap both her and Ariadne. He certainly believed in holding the whip hand.

At least, it *looked* as though Ariadne had been kidnapped, but Helena was not sure about that. Ariadne, though puzzled, did not appear to be worried. On the contrary, she seemed her usual petulant self. Unable to stand properly with her head swimming with faintness, Helena propped herself up against the wall. What use was she to Lord Elverton if he had Ariadne? His attitude to Ariadne was vastly different to the way he treated her. He sounded unctuous, if he could ever be said to sound anything but vicious or sarcastic.

"We are to be married, you know," Ariadne announced chattily. "This is the man I told you about before you and Caroline went away. Is he not the most famous of men? Of course we kept it quiet for a time. After all," she said knowledgeably, "there is a disparity in our ages. But I am to be m'Lady Elverton. Won't Caroline and the Morris girls be envious! This will make Papa stare. He was *so* pleased yesterday with Caroline when she became affianced to your brother, Helena. But I have gone one better. M'lord has vast estates and huge wealth. He is not a mere baronet like your brother." She giggled inanely, setting Helena's teeth on edge. "What? Have you nothing to say?"

In truth, Helena did *not* have anything to say. She saw how clever Elverton was. He had achieved his aim very neatly. Mr. Yardley and Robert would not move against him whilst he held herself and Ariadne. Of course, he might not know that Robert was returned from the Peninsula. Ariadne, being so self-centered, may not have mentioned her sister's engagement. If that was so, Helena stood in even greater peril because it meant he had kidnapped her for his own ends only, wanting power over her and to satisfy his unhealthy desire for her. She would be a useless pawn, expendable and ruined. And eventually discarded if she survived.

On the other hand, if he knew Robert had returned, she could be considered a bargaining chip so that Robert would keep quiet about Foxhyth's dubious dealings. How could she find out exactly what the Committee suspected him of? She propped her aching head on her arm. Lord, what a predicament.

Ariadne was tired of being ignored. She was not used to it. "Well? I asked you what you were doing here."

"Ask Lord Elverton. He brought me here. I have no idea what he wants of me."

"Perhaps he thought I needed a chaperone? But I do not care for that. If we are to be married shortly, it is of no account that there is someone to accompany me.

The silly man!" She gave a little trill of laughter.

The smug expression on her face revolted Helena. "You have no idea what Lord Elverton is capable of. I have known him for years, Ariadne. I would not recommend him as husband material."

"Faugh! You are jealous. You are left sitting on the shelf whilst I have made the catch of the Season." She laughed again.

"It is not marriage that Lord Elverton has in mind for you."

"What? How dare you!"

"You will see shortly. I think he wishes to hold you captive so that your father falls in with his wishes."

"My father? What has he to do with this?"

"He seems to know something about Lord Elverton which is dangerous. I am not sure what it is all about, but I know that your father meets with important people in the government, and they are interested in Lord Elverton's business dealings. That is all I know. But be careful, Ariadne."

Ariadne eyed her uncertainly. "I don't believe you. If I knock on this door, I am sure he will let me out."

"Perhaps. He certainly won't let me out."

Ariadne marched smartly to the door and rapped on it. "Let us out at once, m'lord!"

"In good time, *ma belle*, all in good time." The unctuous tones set Helena's teeth on edge. She would rather he was an honest villain, passionate about a cause or stealing to live. But this man did not want money; he wanted power, and if it was not forthcoming, he took it. How she hated him.

The door opened, and a fat servant woman waddled in. She set a tray down on the floor and jerked a head at

Helena. "Come with me."

Lord Elverton stood in the doorway, waiting.

Helena's pulse thrummed so that it almost crammed her throat. What now?

"Water closet," was all the woman said, and she jerked at Helena's arm. Helena wasn't sure if it was a trap to get her into Elverton's clutches without upsetting Ariadne, but she went anyway, because those words were the sweetest she'd heard all day. The fat woman spent some time tying a piece of string around Helena's wrist, and she then attached the other end to her own wrist. There was no chance of undoing those knots as they were the tightest, biggest knots Helena had ever seen. However, she was relieved to find the surly, dirty woman would not be accompanying her right into the water closet.

When she came out, Elverton was nowhere to be seen. The woman produced a sharp knife with which she simply cut the string, not bothering to unknot it. Before she could step back Helena pushed into her, trying to wrest the knife from her. It was like pushing into a large suet pudding. Taken by surprise, the fat woman stumbled, her great weight carrying her backward with Helena pressed close to her like a lover. Triumphantly Helena grabbed the knife and the blade sliced into her hand. She winced. It hurt but it wasn't serious. She hitched up her skirts and ran toward the kitchen door but as she got there, she heard a shrill cry from the next room. "Stop it! What do you think you are doing, sir? Helena, help me!"

Ariadne. Helena skidded to a halt. If she had only herself to consider she could have escaped. But technically Ariadne was still in her charge, and anyway, how could she leave anyone at Elverton's mercy? It sounded as though Ariadne was already learning that her 'fiancé' was not what she had supposed.

Unwillingly Helena tiptoed quietly back into the stillroom. Elverton was standing with his back to the door. He held Ariadne tight in his arms. She was struggling and panting in her effort to break free. He laughed. "You didn't really think we would be married, do you? A little chit from the manufactories? And here I thought you were up to every rack and row! I thought you knew exactly what I wanted from you, and I'm sure you were willing. You can't change the rules now, my sweet."

Helena hesitated. She had never harmed anything or anyone in her life. Could she attack this odious creature? She would have to strike deep in order to wound him. The pocket knife in her hand was a very small one.

The decision was taken away from her as the fat woman waddled up behind her calling out, "'Ware sir! She's free!"

Elverton swung around still holding Ariadne with one hand, and with the other he smote Helena hard across her face. She dropped the knife as her hands went instinctively to her face, and her head rang. Stumbling against the door frame she slid to the ground.

"Helena! Don't hurt me, Foxhyth!" Ariadne shrieked at Elverton as she dropped to her knees in front of Helena.

Through stinging lips Helena snarled, "You devil. Leave her alone."

"That's right, my dear. Sport your canvas! You are worth two of this sniveling child here. How I look forward to schooling you! We will have such sport together. In the meantime, I suggest you both cool down. I hold all the cards." He pushed them both to the far side of the room and slammed the door shut.

Ariadne began to cry in loud, gulping sobs.

Helena sagged against the wall, closing her eyes while she tried to gather herself together. Her whole face burned with pain. Her lip must have split again because she felt the warmth of blood on her chin.

She had known it would come to this but had not allowed for Ariadne's presence. All those years ago she had sensed that Elverton had it in him to do this sort of thing; that was why, without any just cause, she had mistrusted him. It stunned her that Papa had been impervious to this man's nature, but more to the point, *had her father been well aware of it yet still called him 'friend'*? That was what Helena could not stomach; that the father who had given them such a privileged childhood should have sunk to the depravity of gambling their livelihood away with a monster like this. How had Papa allowed himself to sink so far as to disregard his children's futures? She had no respect left for him. If he had used her as a gambling chip with Elverton, then he was no better than the revolting Elverton himself.

It stung deeply. From an early age she had been encouraged by her father to run his household. She was his darling Ellie. Although he occasionally checked her when her high spirits went beyond what was acceptable, he was proud of her accomplishments. He had had no patience with the current vogue for feminine megrims and die-away airs and had discouraged her from 'simpering' as he had called it.

And yet in the end, he had sold her as if she were a commodity he was tired of.

When she had said no to Sir Ivor's offer, it was because she knew herself to be unfit to marry into his family. Not because she was a governess. Well, not much. Not because she thought he was fonder of Caroline than he was of her. No. Those were excuses she'd used for a smokescreen. It was because she would not bring disrepute upon the Stafford family when it became known how low her father had sunk. It was all very well saying that an *on dit* faded with time, that other scandals took their place. If she married Ivor, and if the full extent of her father's depravity became known, the Stafford name would also be dragged through the mud. Elverton would make sure that everyone knew her secret. He would revel in her downfall.

She would not do it to the Staffords. Sir Ivor's mother and sisters were wonderful people, and Ned was a darling. As for Ivor, well…he was everything that was good and honorable. She could not help but love him. Look how he'd helped Robert and herself. Look at his attitude toward his siblings and his mama. They were a truly estimable family, and she would not bring them down by association with her. One did not do that to the people one loved.

Noisily Ariadne wept into her handkerchief. "What shall we do, Helena? What shall we do? I shall be ruined. Papa will be furious. I should not have gone out to meet him."

Helena was amazed. For the first time ever, Ariadne had actually admitted a fault. The girl must be very frightened indeed. Helena put her arms around the young woman and cradled her until she stopped crying.

"There now. We will just have to wait and see what happens. Dry your eyes."

Helena eyed the tray on the floor. She was exceedingly hungry. She selected a piece of bread and stoically chewed her way through it, dipping it into the cold soup. She did not expect to come out of this situation with her honor intact, but she was damned if she was going to lie around weakly succumbing the way her father had. She chewed thoughtfully. Even if she was ruined, if she came out of this alive, she knew that Robert would do his best to provide for her. She glanced sideways at Ariadne, dabbing at the tears on her cheeks with a minuscule handkerchief. Compared to another year of being that damsel's chaperone, a life of ruin looked almost tolerable.

"Now let us think, Ariadne. There must be a way out of this."

"Think?"

"Sorry," Helena rejoined acidly. "I forgot that thinking was not one of the things you do best. But if you continue to snivel, you will play right into Lord Elverton's hands. Try for a little courage. Pull yourself together and have some food. We may need our strength later."

"Ugh! I could not possibly eat…"

"Suit yourself. Just give your mouth a rest, would you? Let me think."

Ariadne gasped. "How dare you speak to me like that!"

"Good. I thought it wouldn't be long before your normal nature asserted itself. Now listen. I think it probable that Foxhyth wants to keep me, not you. I don't mean any disrespect, but I think he only captured you as insurance. I must pay for a long-standing dispute between my father and Lord Elverton. So if there comes the slightest chance that you might escape, I want you to do so speedily. Do not look back or worry about me. I will try to divert him." Helena smiled wryly as she reflected that it was highly unlikely Ariadne would worry overmuch about her. However, she wasn't entirely sure. The girl was still shaken and might want to cling to Helena, since she had always been shielded from unpleasantness. *Unpleasantness?* That was a polite term for what was going to happen to Helena. She had a mental vision of Elverton ripping off her clothes till she stood before him naked, cold, and terrified. *Oh God.*

She swallowed. "Tell me, Ariadne, did your father or mother or even Betsy or Katy have any idea where you were going?"

"Not Mama or Papa. Of course not! But I left a note, and I had to get Katy to pack my valise. Oh…where is it?" Ariadne began looking about her as if her valise would suddenly appear.

"Never mind where it is. We don't have time to worry about it. That is the least of our concerns. Now do you know exactly where this house is? I have no idea where we are, you see."

"Oh! Well, Foxhyth said this was one of his estates on the Weald. He said that after we had broken our journey here, we were to go on to The Priory at Elverton village and he would send a message to my father. We were eloping of course." She gave a watery giggle that made Helena's teeth itch.

"But why would you need to elope? I'm sure your

father would be delighted to have you marry Lord Elverton."

"I don't precisely understand. He said something about 'forcing Papa's hand.'" Ariadne shrugged negligently. Details never interested her. So long as things went her way, details were for other people to sort out.

"Do you not realize that Elverton never had any intention of marrying you?"

Ariadne was recovering fast. "Of course he did! Anyway, just because he is disagreeable to you does not mean he dislikes me."

"So why did he not apply for your hand in the normal way? And what was the scream I heard from you before all about?"

Ariadne began to pout.

"Ariadne, we are in a dangerous position. There seems to be some conflict between your papa and Lord Elverton. I think you have played right into his hands, meeting him secretly. Anyway, how did you meet him?"

Ariadne rolled her eyes. "Betsy went with me to Bond Street several weeks ago. I dropped my reticule while I was looking in one of the shop windows and he was walking by. He kindly picked it up for me, and we met often after that…" She shrugged.

Helena ground her teeth. Any other well-bred young woman would not have continued an association with such a casually met acquaintance. A well-behaved young woman would simply thank him prettily and move on with her maid. But nobody could ever accuse Ariadne of being well-behaved. No doubt Lord Elverton had selected his quarry carefully. He had probably done the groundwork at Caroline's coming-out. He must have been watching the Yardley family for some time. Yes, that was it. He would have watched Ariadne and planned the best way to scrape an acquaintance with her. Susceptible to flattery as she was, she was an easy target. Even now her self-importance would not allow her to admit she had been duped.

"We must find a way home. If we are here after nightfall, we are both ruined," Helena said. "It does not matter for me so much, but your papa has faith in me to protect you. I cannot do this alone, Ariadne. Please help me. Stop worrying about what might-have-been and try to remember which roads you took on your journey here."

"I saw the signpost to Folkestone," Ariadne muttered resentfully.

"Folkestone! Why, that is not so far from London at all."

"No, but I don't think we are actually at Folkestone yet. I saw no sign of a town. But I have never been to Folkestone so I would not know."

"Nor I. Do you have any money? If we are able to escape, we might have to hire a carriage to get back to London. I have no idea if the stage comes through this part of the world."

"I have money. He asked me to bring some clothes and jewelry and whatever money I could find. I was not to return home till we were safely wed."

"Ariadne, I think you know that he was not going to wed you."

"He might." Ariadne tilted her chin.

"Ariadne, I must be cruel to be kind. You have no

value for him except as the object of blackmail. He is very dangerous, and you would do well to fear him."

Ariadne seemed confused and did not look convinced. However, all doubts fled when the door opened again and Lord Elverton stood on the threshold.

"Ah…my blushing bride from the stews." He saluted Ariadne with an exaggerated bow. "So easily duped. Did you seriously think that a Foxhyth would ally himself with a little nobody whose father dabbles in national secrets best dealt with by the nobility?" He laughed jeeringly. "The daughter of a trader! No, I think not."

Helena saw that he had left the door open this time. She edged unobtrusively toward it while his attention was on Ariadne.

He spun around suddenly. "But you, my little Miss Marshfield, now *you* are a prize I've long awaited. Your father promised you to me you know," he said conversationally.

Fearing the worst, she was still devastated to be confirmed in her suspicions.

"No."

"I had a vowel from your father. He *promised*." His words ended rather like a little boy's, whose treat had been denied him. "But I have you now, my dear Helena. I have you now. And I shall keep you."

Swallowing hard, Helena glanced at Ariadne. She jerked her head toward the open door, encouraging her to escape. But from outside there came the sound of voices raised in altercation. The three of them stood still like chess figures on a board, straining to hear what was happening. Elverton swung around abruptly and left the room, pulling the door closed behind him.

"Do you think someone has come to rescue us?" Ariadne asked hopefully.

"Unlikely." Helena scurried toward the door. If she stood here, she might have a chance to escape when Elverton returned and swung open the door. Could she slip out behind him? But whatever she planned would be hampered by Ariadne. She could not leave the girl behind. Yes, she knew deep down that if Ariadne and she were in reversed positions, Ariadne would have no hesitation in deserting her. But that was beside the point.

There seemed to be a tremendous amount of noise outside now—shouting and stamping. Then it grew quiet again.

Then unexpectedly the door was flung back, and a circumstance Helena had not allowed for occurred. As the door swung it hit her full on her bruised face and she cried out.

"Helena!" Ivor Stafford exclaimed. He pulled her out from behind the door and to Helena's eternal shame she flung herself bodily into his arms. "Sir Ivor, Sir Ivor…" she stammered and buried her sore face in his driving cape. Shaking helplessly, she clung to him. The shock of seeing him when she had thought all was lost was too much to bear. "Safe, safe," her silly heart chanted. His arms folded around her and for the first time on this appalling day she wondered if there might be a way out of this dreadful maze. Leaning gratefully into him, sinking deeper into his embrace, she absorbed the faint aroma of freshly laundered shirt and the warm-skin smell that was uniquely Ivor. Safe. She was safe.

Then as she felt his arms tighten around her and his lips on her hair she was suddenly recalled to her senses.

Horrified at having thrown herself into his arms—what option did the poor man have but to catch her—she tried to draw back.

"Too late, Athena. After that welcome, don't imagine I could let you go. Ever. I have you now." He chuckled, sounding more relieved than amused.

His words unconsciously echoed Lord Elverton's and Helena shivered, but Ivor murmured "Ssh" as he stroked loose tendrils of hair away from her sore face.

God, the sheer relief and comfort of having him with her.

Gradually she became aware of where she was and what she was doing. What *had* she done? Embarrassed, she hung her head.

He moved her back in order to examine her face. In a totally different tone, he said sharply, "Helena, surely I did not do all that to your face? Did this happen before we got here?"

She nodded.

"What a pity I knocked him senseless straight away. There was no time to play with him, because although there are three of us, we didn't know what opposition we would find. Never mind, when he comes to, I am sure I can continue with the treatment before we hand him over to the Runners."

"How-how did you know…?"

"Where to find you? We didn't. But when I sent one of the housemaids to find you, she said you were not at home. To my surprise, Mary said she had seen you in the Square being taken into a carriage with a crest on the panel. Naturally I asked her what the crest looked like and, as soon as she told me, I went straight to your brother to see what we should do."

"Robert?"

"Yes. Now that he is on the same Committee as I am, I thought it best to hold a council of war. The other two gentlemen I brought with me are from the Horse Guards, and one of them is on our Committee."

"But what have they to do with Elverton?"

"We have been after Elverton for at least a twelve-month. In that time, he has done irreparable harm to England. But he has friends in high places, and we have been unable to touch him until now."

Helena's eyes grew round. "I don't understand." Then she shrugged helplessly. "How did you find us here?"

"We sent the militia to all his known land-holdings. We presumed this one was the most likely, it being near the coast, so my colleagues and I chose to come here first. Thank God we did."

"Sir Ivor!" a peremptory voice interrupted. They had completely forgotten Ariadne. She was *not* happy about that. "I wish to leave this place and return home *immediately.*"

Still holding Helena within the protection of his arm, Sir Ivor told Ariadne, "I'm afraid that's not possible at the moment, Miss Yardley. We have many things to do before we can return you to your relatives. Be assured that your father knows what has transpired."

"I don't *care*! I just want to go home." Her voice rose to a wail.

"Miss Yardley, your distress is understandable. But you must wait. While we question Lord Elverton, perhaps you could tend to Miss Marshfield. She has need of help." Ivor's voice had turned contemptuous. He held Helena's face to the light flowing in through the open doorway and tucked some wayward strands of hair behind her ears. "This will take some time, Helena. Ignore any noises you hear, and make yourselves as comfortable as you can. 'Tis still light outside. Perhaps you should get some air after being locked in here."

He threaded Helena's arm through his and led her away from the back part of the house toward the front door. The whole house had a closed-up, musty smell. Cobwebs draped every corner and, as they moved forward, the cobwebs' inhabitants scurried out of the way. Though normally terrified of spiders, Helena was past caring. She did not even squeak when a large black specimen trundled over her foot and tried to hitch a ride on her skirts.

Ivor dragged open the heavy oak front door and settled her in an old cane chair, the only furniture he could find, where she could look out into the dying rays of the setting sun.

He took off his driving cape and wrapped it around her. "Darling Helena, you *must* stay here. Do not come to the back of the house no matter what you hear. You are safe now. No further harm will come to you at Elverton's hands. Where is that wretched girl?"

From the back of the house, Ariadne's voice could be heard calling peremptorily, "Helena, come here at once! Where are you?"

Even in her exhaustion, Helena could not help feeling a catty satisfaction that he regarded Ariadne as a liability, nothing more. He returned to fetch the girl, and their progress toward Helena was punctuated by Ariadne's shrieks as she passed the festooned cobwebs.

"What a tiresome young woman you are," he commented as he left them.

Helena could not agree more, but she was too lethargic to object when Ariadne demanded that Helena give up the chair to her. Helena sank to the floor and cuddled into Ivor's driving cape. It was still warm from his body.

Dusk was setting in, and it was growing chilly. Huge oak trees were etched against the darkening sky. A blackbird sang its evening song, and under other circumstances it would have been pleasant and peaceful, gazing out on to the sleeping, overgrown garden.

But Ariadne prattled ceaselessly. "I would never have thought Lord Elverton would behave so ill. Are you sure we could not talk to him and discover why he has acted thus? And goodness me, Helena! Was it not unseemly that Sir Ivor held you in his arms as he did?"

Helena made no response but snuggled farther into the cape.

When she could see no reply was forthcoming, Ariadne started off again. "I'm so cold. I should like that cape."

"No."

There was a startled silence from Ariadne, but she did not press the issue.

Just as well. The comfort Helena was deriving from Ivor's coat was worth any amount of griping from Ariadne.

"When do you think we may return home?"

Eventually Helena, goaded beyond what was proper snapped, "All in good time. You silly girl. I did my best to get us out of this coil, and you did not help at all—not one bit. Thank goodness for the Committee. I still don't understand what Elverton has got to do with this Committee, but I am extremely thankful Sir Ivor was able to find us." She did not say "in time", but even Ariadne understood that. Ariadne sniffed and did not deign to reply. No doubt she was storing up a multitude of complaints to present to her parents.

The stars were beginning to peer through the clouds when there came the crunch of carriage wheels on gravel and Sir Ivor's carriage was driven around to the front entrance where it stopped. The groom jumped down and approached Helena.

"Miss, Sir Ivor asks if you would care to step into the carriage? It will be a squeeze, but we know you wish to get home as soon as possible."

When he assisted them into the carriage, they saw what he meant. On the bench seat facing them Lord Elverton sat, flanked on one side by Sir Ivor and on his other side by a gentleman they had not met. He was wearing a heavy greatcoat, and the Regent's insignia was engraved on the buttons. Sir Ivor did not introduce him, and most of the long trip back to town was undertaken in silence. Elverton looked the worse for wear. His shirt was in tatters and his coat had disappeared. He sported a large bruise on one cheekbone and his nose was hugely swollen and occasionally droplets of blood from it dripped on to the carriage floor. Yet he retained his haughty, supercilious air, as if he had divorced himself entirely from the proceedings. He spoke only once, and that was to address Helena. "Your father *promised* you to me. You know he did. You should have come willingly. The rest is nothing. It was good sport, and you would have been useful."

Helena felt sick. Everyone in the carriage now

knew that her father had sold her like a commodity to this evil creature. She could feel the heat of scalding shame flushing her face and neck and kept her eyes down.

Surprisingly, Elverton leaned forward again. "And then he reneged. Your father reneged on the deal! He acted like the veriest peasant." Elverton sibilantly spat out the words in contempt.

Sickened, Miss Marshfield glanced away and noticed that the knuckles of Sir Ivor's hands were considerably grazed. He followed her glance and smiled ruefully at her. She smiled back wanly and then looked directly at Elverton for the first time. "I am glad my father would not keep to the deal. I have hoped for years that he did not sink that low. Now you have confirmed that we have nothing to be ashamed about. I can respect his memory again. Thank you."

Elverton snorted with contempt and vouchsafed no answer.

Slowly Helena became conscious of a sense of relief, of freedom from that appalling sense of hurt she had felt for five years. Knowing that her father had loved her enough to say no to Elverton was an immense satisfaction. No doubt her sense of self-worth would take some time to heal. But hearing from Elverton himself that John Marshfield had drawn back from that iniquitous arrangement restored her love and respect for her father as nothing else ever could. Thankful, she eased back on the seat and closed her eyes.

No further conversation took place for the remainder of the journey. After showing revulsion at the steady dripping of blood on to the carriage floor, Ariadne fell asleep, but Helena remained upright in her corner of the carriage, holding on to the strap as the well-sprung carriage swayed along in the dark. All three men stayed alert, jailers and prisoner alike. It was apparent that Sir Ivor and the unknown Committee member considered it imperative to keep a sharp eye and a firm hand on their prisoner. Elverton's alert demeanor no doubt kept them on their toes, knowing he would take advantage of any slackening of their concentration.

Finally the pace slowed as they entered the city environs, and Helena roused Ariadne. "Are we to be put down in Eaton Square or Russell Square?" she asked Sir Ivor.

"At Stafford House," he answered. "Mr. Yardley and Robert are waiting for you."

"Papa?" Ariadne asked. She blinked nervously, as well she might. Obviously, the thought of her father waiting for her, well-armed with the truth and impervious to her cajoling, unnerved her.

Ivor said to Helena, "I'm sorry I cannot hand you down from the carriage. James will attend to you. I shall probably not return home tonight, but we shall talk in the morning." He smiled encouragingly at her, and she nodded her understanding as the carriage drew to a halt in Eaton Square. She handed his greatcoat to him saying simply, "Thank you."

As Helena and Ariadne gratefully descended from the carriage, at Sir Ivor's gesture, one of his footmen exchanged places with them. The captors were taking no chances that their prisoner might escape.

Helena and Ariadne hurried into the house where Timms and Mrs. Annerwith waited anxiously in the foyer.

"Miss Marshfield, we have all been so worried about you," Timms said. He stared hard at her face. Mrs. Annerwith bustled forward, her skirts rustling, and in the background, even at this late hour, several servants hovered.

"Oh, my dear, your poor face! We are so relieved to see you. And who is this young lady?"

"This is Miss Yardley, Miss Caroline's sister. She is tired and upset, Mrs. Annerwith. Would you please take her to her sister? And perhaps some tea and bread and butter might make her feel better."

Mrs. Annerwith bobbed a curtsey and Ariadne, for the first time in her life known as "Miss Caroline's sister", meekly followed her upstairs.

Helena had a fence to mend, however, before she could retire to her room. "Timms, if Mary is still awake, would you be so kind as to fetch her for me? I think she saw me go out this morning, and her information helped Sir Ivor find us."

"She is here, waiting for you, Miss Marshfield."

Helena held out her hand to the little maid who was hovering, trying to hide herself behind Timms' bulk. "If I had turned back when you called me this morning, Mary, I should not have got myself into the fix that I did. I have you to thank, I believe, for noticing the crest on the coach panel?"

Mary bobbed a curtsey and wrung the corners of her apron. She seemed unsure about taking Helena's hand. "Oh, ma'am. I were that worried." She took a deep breath. "When I saw you taken up into that coach, I didn't know what to do. I couldn't quite see what the whole crest was, but I told sir and he understood."

Yes, he would, if he had been trying to catch

Elverton out for some time. He would definitely know the Elverton crest. "All's well that ends well, Mary. Thank you very much."

Mary bobbed again and raised trustful eyes to Helena. "I am right glad to be of help, miss."

Feeling dreadful about eliciting such loyalty from someone she had virtually swatted to one side, Helena smiled wearily and dragged herself upstairs to her room. She would tidy herself up before meeting Robert. He must be beside himself by now, although hopefully the efficient Mrs. Annerwith had apprised him of her arrival. She washed her face and hands, trying not to gaze too long into the mirror. Flinching, she saw that her face had swollen considerably and looked lopsided. But her worst wound was her cut hand. It stung every time she moved her fingers.

She had changed her clothes, dropping them in a pile on the floor—for she never wished to wear those clothes again—when there came a tapping on the door and Caroline flew in. She embraced Helena with tears in her eyes. "Helena, your poor face! Whatever happened to you? We were all so worried. Sir Ivor and Robert would not tell me anything. Then Papa arrived. Then two other men came, and they all began..." She finally ran out of breath.

Helena gave her a one-armed hug, trying not to nudge her hand.

"I am so sorry to have given all this trouble. But even if I had taken Mary with me, I doubt that would have stopped Elverton. He would simply have kidnapped Mary too."

"I don't understand about Elverton. I saw at my party how you feared him, but why?"

"He was a crony of my father's, and I've always feared him. His attitude toward me was such that…that…oh I can't explain it, but he acted as if it was his right to have control over me. However, it seems that Sir Ivor and your papa have been suspicious of Elverton for some other reason. I do not know precisely *why*, but I suspect."

Caroline's eyes grew round. "Lady Stafford and Erica and Nerida kept asking me questions all day, and I didn't know what to say. Now Ariadne is in my room storming about and complaining that you have 'spoiled everything.' Poor Mrs. Annerwith is horrified."

"Just one minute and I shall try to pacify Ariadne. There, is my hair better?"

"Your hair is as neat as a pin, Helena, apart from a streak of bl-blood over one ear."

"Drat it." Helena swiped at the blood and made matters worse.

"Let me see that." Caroline took Helena's hand and examined it. She searched quickly through the big armoire in the corner of the room and came up with a scarf. "Here, this will do. I shall bind it up to stop the bleeding." She glanced up with a half-smile. "I'm getting used to doing this since Robert persists in moving his injured leg about instead of lying still. There now. That should stay in place. Helena, you must rest. You look exhausted."

"Thank you, my dear. Our roles are reversed. Here you are ministering to me."

"Of course. I am your friend."

Helena surveyed Caroline mistily. "You are the best friend anyone could have, Caroline. I thought of you when I was left alone in that house for hours and wondered if you had missed me."

"Of course I missed you! I shall not tease you now, but you must tell me all about it tomorrow. I think Nerida and Erica have gone to bed, but Lady Stafford is waiting up for you. And you had best see Ariadne and Robert as soon as possible."

Helena grimaced, and Caroline giggled. "I asked Mrs. Annerwith to organize some tea for Ariadne but she said she didn't want it. She wished only to go home. But Papa is here and will take her home."

Papa was indeed there. He was not impressed with his older daughter and did not mince his words. His wife was prostrate, having found Ariadne's carelessly penned note informing her parents of her elopement with Lord Elverton. As Helena approached Caroline's room, she heard Ariadne's angry weeping and Mr. Yardley's measured tones. "We are deeply disappointed in you, Ariadne. I have decided that you will go to my sister in the country for a few months. Perhaps she may succeed where we have not."

"Aunt Warren? No!"

Mr. Yardley was unmoved. "Miss Marshfield endeavored to school you both in the ways of gentlefolk, and with Caroline she succeeded admirably. But you have come to believe yourself perfect because of your prettiness. Your mother and I are partly to blame because we have much indulged you. Your Aunt Warren may not be able to divest you of your sense of self-importance, but at least she will keep you away from London temptations for the time being."

Approving heartily of that speech Helena began to tiptoe away, but he had caught a glimpse of her. "Miss Marshfield...Helena! We are so pleased to have you back, safe and sound. But your face looks very sore indeed. My dear, I shall speak to you tomorrow. Just at this present your brother is anxious to see you. It has been a long, terrible day for us all." He pressed her hand speakingly, and she flinched as the cut from the knife wound began to bleed afresh.

She brushed his apology aside. "Thank goodness for your Committee, Mr. Yardley. No doubt Robert will tell me exactly what all this is about, but I am pleased Ariadne has come to no harm."

"For which I thank you. But if she had not been so silly, she would not have been put in that position in the first place. No," he said shaking his head, "we do not blame you, Helena. You are an excellent governess and companion. But some of the fault lies with us. We indulged our girls too much, and this is the result." He seemed to be rather despondent, so Helena mentioned how pleased she was to be getting Caroline for a sister-in-law and he brightened up considerably.

"Yes indeed. You two ladies have always dealt well together. But I must take this young woman back to her mother now," he said, indicating Ariadne. "Sir Robert will explain to you all about the work of the Committee."

Helena peeked around Robert's door, wondering if he had given up waiting for her and fallen asleep. After all, he was not yet recovered from his severe injuries, and it was now well past midnight. But as soon as he saw her, he called out, "Ellie, at last! I have been so anxious." As she approached his bed he stared and exclaimed, "Your face! What happened?"

She settled down to tell him about the day's adventures. Then she queried, "Robert, why is the

Special Advisory Committee investigating Lord Elverton?"

"Ellie, I think you've guessed. He was supplying information regarding army maneuvers to the enemy."

"I thought so. How long has it been going on?"

"We are uncertain, but we think he has been doing it ever since Bonaparte's invasion of the Low Countries. I wonder how many men have died because of him," Robert ended bitterly.

They both sat silent, reflecting on the appalling damage done by a traitor such as Elverton, how many lives had been lost.

"Apparently Ivor and Joshua and the others have been suspicious of him for almost a year but were unable to find out how he was operating. And they had to be very sure, because he is an influential person. Then there was a death at the Horse Guards and unexpectedly the fellow left a letter. It seems that Elverton's modus operandi was to blackmail people into joining his smuggling ring. He winkled out their secrets then left them with no alternative but to work for him, else he would inform on them. He only smuggled information, never goods. Apparently that would have been too tame for him. He would have been just another smuggler. You were quite right about him, Ellie, and I apologize for not taking you seriously when you said you feared him."

"It is not your fault, Robert. I spent much more time with him than you did, not that I had any idea he was a traitor. But somehow, I could not trust him. He seemed to revel in other people's difficulties. Several times when he visited Marshfield Manor, he commented upon men getting into gambling difficulties or some such, and it seemed to me that he was amused."

"Yes, I think our father was one of those he especially pursued to ruin. But I don't think he tried to turn Father into a traitor, because Father had no political leverage nor much of an interest in politics. I suppose he simply enjoyed having power over him."

"Exactly. I hope that now he is caught, other people he has forced into that way of life can be free."

"They, too, might be taken up as traitors, Helena, if they are found."

"How unfair!"

"Perhaps there may be mitigating factors, but the laws on treason are harsh. And rightly so."

Helena knew that on this matter she and her brother would never see eye to eye. She deplored treason but could not help but sympathize with anyone caught in Lord Elverton's coils. She roused herself. "And how are *you*, Robert? How is the shoulder?"

"My dear, it's just like you to worry about me. Apart from the frustration and boredom of lingering in bed, all is well with me. I can help the Advisory Committee a little from my sickbed because I have more time than the other members have. While they are out making inquiries, I am mulling over maps, assessing the proposed military plans for next season. At least that way I am contributing to the cause." He grinned. "And of course I have Caroline who asks me every few minutes if my shoulder or my leg pains me." He was a happy man, and Helena envied him.

She herself had come too close to evil today to feel free just yet. Exhausted, she stood. "Robert, I must go to bed. It must be nigh on two o'clock."

"Later than that I should think." He looked searchingly at her. "Poor Ellie. You will have a very bruised face tomorrow. And I heard from one of the footmen that Ivor contributed to it. How I shall chafe him about it! I shall pretend to be indignant that he treated you so, and that all that bruising is solely his doing. I shall demand an explanation."

She forced a smile which pained her swollen lip. "He will come about, I assure you. He has the confidence not to mind being teased."

"Do you like him, Helena? He seems to be very taken with you."

"He is a good man," she responded quietly with her head bent and would say no more. She was away to her bedroom before he could question her further.

Lady Stafford was lying in wait. She had heard from Timms and Mrs. Annerwith about the state of Helena's face and was waiting to see for herself how Helena did.

"Here, my dear." She held out an ointment jar. "Use this arnica on your face straight away. When you wake in the morning you must apply some more. It will work wonders."

Helena nodded and smiled mistily. Everyone was so kind.

Lady Stafford unclasped Helena's dress and, when she attempted to undress herself, told her to simply stand there and she would do it all. "For I can see that you are totally exhausted. 'Tis a nervous reaction. Now here is your night-rail which Mrs. Annerwith has warmed by the fire. You shall shortly have some tea and bread and butter, but while we are waiting for it, I will brush your hair. There, that feels better, doesn't it?"

Helena relaxed thankfully and submitted to her ministrations. This must be what it was like to have a mother. She had never known her own but had seldom felt the need of one. Her father and governess had seen to her every need. But lately she had felt the need of a loving companionship such as the Morris girls had with their mother.

Lady Stafford's voice held only kindness and concern. She was not curious, just anxious to see that Helena was made comfortable. Helena reveled in the feeling and let the lady's conversation flow over her like soothing syrup.

"My goodness, Ivor was beside himself this morning. When Mary told him you had been dragged up into a carriage, he went so white I didn't know what to do. Then later on when he and the other gentleman set out to bring you back, he said to me, 'Don't worry, Mama. I shall bring her back safe or I won't be back,' and my son is not given to dramatics, let me tell you."

Helena wondered just how much Lady Stafford knew. Probably most of it. "He was wonderful, Lady Stafford. If it weren't for him, I'd be…I'd be—"

"Hush! Don't think about it anymore. Ah! Thank you, Mary. Here's your tea, my dear. I shall cut the bread and butter into tiny pieces so you will find it easier to chew. Your mouth looks very sore."

How kind everyone was. Ivor made her feel cherished. He had subjugated his anxiety and had searched intelligently for her so that he had found her in time. Caroline had been dreadfully worried about her. Her brother had been half out of his mind with worry.

And now here was Lady Stafford, determined to

ensure that she was put safely to bed. When she could eat and drink no more, Lady Stafford tucked Helena into bed as if she were a child. Exhausted, Helena fell asleep before she could thank her.

Chapter Fourteen

The morning dawned still and clear. It would have been an excellent day for a ride, but Helena had no wish to show her battered face in public. She lay in bed relishing the comfort and peace of being free at last of the apprehension which had dogged her for so long.

But she had one insurmountable problem. How on earth she was going to meet Sir Ivor without embarrassment? Having tossed herself into his arms with such abandon, how was she to face him today? Hopefully he would put it down to her sheer relief at being rescued. On the other hand, he had promised he would not let her go. That was the sort of thing the heroes in ladies' novels said. She did not think Ivor would be thrilled to be compared to one of Mrs. Radcliffe's Byronic heroes. Anyway, he might just have said that in the heat of the moment. Perhaps he had been humoring her, trying to make light of their difficulties.

No, no, no. She hoped he had meant more than that—a lot more. According to Lady Stafford he had been 'beside himself.' Surely that meant he loved her? Surely?

Sighing, she propped her chin in her hand. If only. Yesterday she had taken a good look at herself. She saw a young woman who had become unnecessarily embittered over her lot in life. The fact that she had chosen the life of a governess over one of genteel poverty living as Robert's pensioner in the first place showed her strength of character. Why then had that strength of character deserted her of late? Honesty compelled her to confess that she was unhappy because she had seen what might have been; what she could have had if her father had not made it impossible for her to pursue a relationship with Sir Ivor Stafford or any other gentleman of his caliber. She would like nothing more in this world than to be Ivor Stafford's wife. She had loved him virtually since the day she had met him, although her realization of that had only come recently. Lord, he was just so…so loveable. Those shoulders, that quirk of his mouth when—she was becoming maudlin.

But until yesterday she had had her suspicions about her father's motives in 'selling' her to Lord Elverton. Thank goodness he had changed his mind about doing so, and she need have no fear that the taint of his relationship with Elverton would have repercussions for either Robert or herself. Now that she had heard from Elverton himself that her father had not cooperated in his schemes, she was profoundly thankful. Perhaps Papa had unearthed proof of Elverton's treasonous activities? That might well have been the catalyst that caused John Marshfield to confront Elverton and renege on the arrangement to marry Helena to him. But she hoped passionately that it was simply the love of a father for his daughter that no matter how far he had sunk, he could not use his daughter as a pawn.

She must speak to Robert straight away to find out his view of the situation.

And then if Sir Ivor asked her again…

Mrs. Annerwith tapped on her door, and Helena struggled up on to her pillows. "Miss Marshfield, how is your face today? Oh my!" she exclaimed, examining what Helena knew would be multi-colored bruises from her forehead to her chin. "Do you think a bath would be refreshing?"

"Oh *yes*. Just what I would most wish for."

Twenty minutes later Helena slowly and luxuriously lowered herself into a tubful of soft suds. "Hold your sore hand out of the water, ma'am." Mrs. Annerwith bustled about, thrilled to have somebody to mother. After Helena had had time to wallow peacefully and soak some of the stiffness out of her body, the housekeeper fetched Mary, and they thoroughly washed Helena's hair.

"Such lovely, lovely hair, ma'am. 'Twill take some time to dry though. If you sit next to the fire for a time it will dry faster. Now let me bandage that hand."

Smothered in loving care, Helena relaxed and let all the attention flow over her in a warm stream. When she was dressed, she peered into the big mirror and discovered that her injuries looked even worse than she had imagined. One side of her face was mottled with dark bruising, and her bottom lip bore a marked resemblance to a duck's bill. She licked it tentatively. It certainly *was* sore. She presented a very odd appearance indeed. Although dressed with neatness and propriety as became a companion, her bruising gave her a rakish look. She looked as if she had been carousing but sought to exonerate herself by trying to dress sedately to impress. Her damp, wayward hair refused as usual to comply with her wishes. What a mess she looked! She hoped fervently that Sir Ivor was busy at the Horse Guards today. And tomorrow. And the next day. She had no wish to see him before her face had begun to heal. Wounds always looked their worst on the two or three days following an accident, not of course that her injuries could be termed an accident precisely.

She hurried to Robert's room to find that Caroline was there already. Their heads were bent together, and Robert's hand lay over the top of Caroline's. *Helena, you are employed as a chaperone for Caroline, and you are not succeeding very well at your duties.* She coughed gently, and they looked up.

"Dearest Helena! Your face!" Caroline was stupefied at Helena's appearance.

Robert was more pragmatic. "Told you it would look worse today," he chortled. "You look as if you've fallen off a horse."

"Thank you, dear Robert."

Then Robert's face changed. "I hope that when they caught up with him yesterday, they made him pay for that."

"I don't think Sir Ivor was particularly gentle."

"No, he wouldn't be."

Helena looked askance.

"Don't be silly, Ellie. The two of you have been smelling of April and May since I arrived home. You know perfectly well what I mean."

Flushing, Helena glanced at Caroline. Caroline laughed and blew Helena a kiss. She got up to leave the room.

"I shall leave you two. Will you come downstairs to breakfast soon, Helena?"

"Yes. I cannot go riding in case I meet someone I

know. I shall keep to the house."

When Caroline had left, Helena asked Robert, "Have you given any further thought as to what Papa's relationship with Lord Elverton was?"

"I gather that Elverton introduced Father to the gaming tables. Then I think he sought to blackmail Father. It was his usual modus operandi once his unsuspecting victims were well and truly caught. But it looks as though his price was too high for Father. I think the price was you."

Helena looked down at her hands. "Yes, I've always suspected that. It has been a terrible burden to bear, knowing that I was indirectly the cause of Papa's death."

"*No*, Ellie. You were not the cause, indirect or otherwise, of Father's death. Father *chose* both his way of life and the method of his death. And remember that he had many, many debts besides Elverton's. But I think that after he defied Elverton and would not give you up, it was the beginning of the end for him, and he knew it. I imagine Elverton then began to work on him to turn him traitor, but that would never have happened. The Marshfields do not sell their daughters, nor are they traitors."

"Well said, Marshfield," Sir Ivor's voice murmured from the doorway. The brother and sister turned to face him. "Most of your suspicions are true. Elverton shows no remorse for his conduct and just cunningly divulges only that which we have already discovered. He must have known that once his contact at the Horse Guards died by his own hand, the death would be investigated. Instead, he cheekily attempted to suborn that man's replacement! It is a pity he did not put his courage to better use."

"It is also a pity he did not use that business-like brain for something other than blackmail," Robert cut in dryly.

"Certainly. The most despicable crime of all."

Sir Ivor looked tired. He had obviously spent all night at the Horse Guards assisting in the interrogation of Lord Elverton. He was dressed as neatly as usual, but he seemed a little frayed around the edges, as if some of his vitality was missing.

Helena desperately tried to avoid his eyes. She could feel herself blushing.

"And how are your wounds this morning, Miss Marshfield?"

"They are nothing," she disclaimed. "Just a little sore."

"Then perhaps you would care to join us for breakfast? Robert, it is a pity you must eat alone, but we shall come back upstairs directly."

Helena trod sedately beside Sir Ivor as they headed to the breakfast-room. At the door he stopped and reached out to take her hand. He looked at it reflectively as if he had never seen it before. He seemed to be in a strange mood.

"Helena, as soon as we have eaten I should like to speak with you. But we should keep Caroline company over breakfast. Mama and the girls have not yet come down." He said no more, but just looked down at her, still holding on to her hand.

She lowered her eyes, again feeling that rush of warm excitement which overwhelmed her whenever he was near. Was he going to renew his addresses, or was this was about Lord Elverton's conviction? He seemed to be in a determined mood about something, and after yesterday's ordeal she was not sure she was ready to face him. He released her hand, and she murmured a meek little "yes" looking at him from under her eyelashes. He smiled, and her stomach jolted.

Breakfast took forever. Caroline chattered happily whilst Ivor seemed to be preoccupied. Helena struggled to chew a sliver of roast beef from one of the chafing dishes on the sideboard. She was exceedingly hungry, but her stomach was in such a turmoil and her lip hurt so badly that she was unable to do justice to more than a few sips of lukewarm tea. Caroline was concerned.

"Helena dear, you missed all your meals yesterday. Surely you must be hungry by now."

"I am ravenous, Caroline, but it is too difficult to eat just now. Perhaps later I might be able to eat more." Helena enunciated her words in a slurred manner that she found hurt her lips less.

Sir Ivor broke open a soft scone and buttered it lavishly. "Try this," he suggested, passing it to her.

She smiled gratefully, albeit lopsidedly, and managed a couple of mouthfuls. Then she glanced up and saw Caroline watching them both, her head on one side.

Helena blushed and dipped her head. So much for imagining they were being discreet.

Ivor said nothing further as he worked his way through a huge platter of ham and eggs. He must be hungry, too, after being up all night. What would it be like to sit like this every morning after a ride through the park, discussing the day's news and working out which of their responsibilities should be attended to? Heaven, she decided. That's what it would be like.

Would he renew his offer? *Oh yes, please God.* But what if he merely wished to talk about where Robert's further convalescence was to take place or something of that nature? She sighed inwardly. Yes, that might be it. After all, a man did not look for rejection a second time.

Armed with this sensible delusion she followed him into his library. He closed the door behind them and turned the key in the lock.

Helena swallowed. Hard. She looked down at her house slippers.

He approached her slowly, giving her time to retreat if she should wish. She didn't wish. He slid an arm around her and raised her chin. "Look at me, Helena." He drew in his breath. "Your poor face, sweet girl. I compounded what that creature did to you. If I could take it back I would. But I was in such a hurry to see if you were all right after having been with him all day that I just..." He shrugged expressively.

"It's perfectly all right, sir. I understand. I would have done the same."

"You mean you would have crashed the door on to my face?" he asked, laughing.

"Not unless it was warranted."

"And under what circumstances would you consider it warranted?"

"Er—I don't know."

"Neither do I. My darling Helena, you know I would never hurt a hair of your head intentionally. But I was so worried—"

"I understand. No need to apologize, Sir Ivor." She toyed with the idea of pointing out that she had not given him leave either to call her by her given name, nor to call her 'darling.' Of course, considering she had tossed herself into his arms yesterday, it was a bit late to demur over niceties.

And anyway, she had no objection—none at all— even though it would be seemly to protest a little.

"Come and sit down, Helena. I want to make some explanations to you that I was unable to do before." He seated her comfortably on a settle and took up a stance in front of the fireplace. "Do you remember that I said the Staffords had a family secret I could not reveal? I didn't realize how insulting that was, close on the heels of my proposal."

She made a brushing motion with her hand to show him how unimportant that all was now.

"No," he persisted. "I must tell you."

He took a turn about the room, his hands clasped behind his back. "When I succeeded to my father's shoes, I made the unpleasant discovery that the family fortunes were exceedingly diminished. We were on the point of bankruptcy. On making inquiries with the family solicitor and our old bailiff, I was told that my father's way of life had been ruinous. He was often from home when I was a child, and as I got older, I noticed that he was at home less and less. Sometimes we would not see him for weeks on end. Like your father, he, too, was bitten by the gambling bug. He also drank to excess, though probably no more than any others among his cronies. But his gambling was out of control. My bailiff told me that Father would gamble on anything: a horse race, the turn of the dice, how many curtain calls Mrs. Siddons would take after a performance, how many foals and calves would be born on our estates during a season, or even the result of a race between two pigs or some such thing. As a result, when I took over the reins there was very little to take over. Fortunately Ryewolds was entailed so he couldn't raise funds on that property, but Stafford House had two mortgages over it, and I despaired of being able to retain it. The farms attached to Ryewolds had been run so badly they were producing only a fifth of what was possible. The bailiff had grown tired of making suggestions to my father for ways to improve the situation. Father just kept saying that he would 'see to it later.' And then of course there were my father's personal debts." He took a deep breath.

Helena put out her hand to stop him. "Sir, you have no need to tell me all this. It is none of my business."

He held on to her hand. "Of course it is your business, or I hope that it will be. Please, Helena. I need to explain how my hands have been tied. Anyway, I kept the true situation to myself and set about improving things as best I might. As you can imagine, this was a slow process. I tried to manage it so that the family lived in the same style to which they were accustomed. It was *my* responsibility, not theirs, to set things to rights."

Helena stared at him. She had the utmost sympathy for him but could not understand why he thought he was the only responsible person in this situation.

"But surely your mama and your brother and sisters would have helped if they knew?"

"I did not want them to know. I did not want them to be worried about their futures, and I am still of that mind."

She shook her head but said nothing further.

He sat down beside her. "I have managed slowly to

improve matters. The farms are now producing better yields, and several of my investments have borne fruit. As a result, my father's personal debts have been repaid. I have retired my bailiff and taken over his duties myself so that no secrets leak out. There is still a mortgage on this home, but there is scarcely a large house in London which is not mortgaged. Darling Helena, *now* do you understand why I wished desperately to ask you to share my life right from the first time I met you, but could not do so?"

"Oh Ivor, I could have helped. And I am far from being a spendthrift." Sympathetic she might be, but she was indignant that he thought of a wife as an expensive undertaking.

Raising her hand to his lips he said, "It would not have been fair, Helena. You are a special woman who deserves to be treated generously." He smiled at her mutinous expression. "But our circumstances have changed for the good recently. Now I can see my way to a clearer future. Such a relief."

"But what has changed? Do you mean Prinny's gift?"

"Partly. First Nerida became engaged to George, then Ned told me he was looking about for some gainful occupation, and now…" he shrugged. "Prinny's gift is the icing on the cake. With the estate in Norfolk being enlarged, we can run Ryewolds the way it should be run. Our dependents there will be grateful to find their pleas for new roofs and pasture improvements will now fall on receptive ears. Not that I'm as bad a landlord as my father was, but it has been almost impossible to improve things when money was so tight."

Indignantly Helena protested, "I imagine you are an extremely good landlord. But I still say I wouldn't have been a charge on you. I could have *helped* you—"

He shook his head. "No man could ask a woman to marry him if he were in such straitened circumstances with all its incumbent responsibilities. Or so I thought until I nearly lost you."

Helena thought, "*He's just like me. Too darned proud.*"

"But now—" He broke off and got up to prowl restlessly around the room.

She began to understand that here was a man who had been sinking under the weight of responsibility. Certainly, he had had it thrust upon him. But he had willingly taken that weight and tried to turn it to advantage. Many another man in the same circumstances had shrugged, thrown up his hands, sold off anything unentailed, and run his entailed properties even further into the ground, leaving nothing for his children. Or perhaps he would have married an heiress. Ivor had done none of those things. He had not shirked his duty. He certainly was the honorable man she had always thought. She could trust him. She had known yesterday when he burst into that room that all her dithering was unnecessary.

She smiled mistily at him. He was still baring his soul and she tried to speak, but he stopped her.

"Yesterday when I realized Elverton had abducted you, my blood ran cold. I was desperate. I saw how much time I'd wasted in trying to get everything right. What use would doing the right thing have been if I'd lost you to Elverton? I vowed to myself then and there that if I could save you, that you would be all I'd want in the world."

Helena sighed. What woman could resist that?

Yesterday had changed a lot of things. Especially it had changed them.

He sat down beside her again. "It is incumbent upon you to say *something*," he urged.

"Oh, Ivor." Leaning toward him in an undignified and unladylike manner she rested her head on his shoulder and sighed thankfully. "Yesterday, I, too, saw that all my excuses were just that—excuses. I was not *really* convinced you had a *tendre* for Caroline, or anyone else. But she *is* the daughter of a close associate of yours. It seemed logical to assume that…anyway, I am a *governess*, although the stigma of my father's death and the threat of that promissory note from Elverton were the real barriers. I have too much regard for you to see you go through what I endured—that awful silence followed by hushed whispers at social gatherings." Her breath hitched.

"My poor darling." Then he murmured something indistinguishable and stroked her fingers. He began at the base and softly stroked in little increments upward to the tips.

Helena's heart tripped, and she forgot to breathe. A scalding blush suffused her skin from her face down to her toes. Had she really been going to throw away *this*? She must have been out of her mind. She peered up at him from beneath her lashes. His eyes were half-closed as he stroked her hand rhythmically. Then he lifted the hand to his lips, taking one of her fingers into his mouth. Everything inside Helena softened. She relaxed languidly back against the sofa cushions.

His smile glinted. "And?" he prompted softly.

"A-And…what was I saying? Oh yes. That wretched vowel. You see, Sir Ivor," she said seriously, knowing she was sinking fast but needing to explain herself first, "unlike Robert I knew Lord Elverton quite well, and I suspected that my father had used me as a—a gambling chip. Coming from such a despicable background, how could I ally myself with a decent family such as yours?"

Stafford folded both arms around her. "Helena, the problem of Elverton is now solved. He will never bother you again. And you have learned that your father loved you and did *not* want you to become involved with Elverton. So all we have left to worry about is to solve your muddled thoughts about being a governess." He grinned at her then leaned forward and began to nuzzle her earlobe.

"No, no." Her hand raised itself of its own volition and held tight to his lapel. "I decided yesterday that if I escaped from Elverton alive, I would stop worrying about being a governess. When I was locked in that room alone, I did a lot of thinking. I saw how silly I'd been to fret about how the rest of the world saw governesses. It's just that I don't *enjoy* being a governess so I haven't been thinking rationally."

He smiled and tipped a finger to her nose. "Neither have I since the day we met."

"Yes, but…" She trailed away.

"Come on, Helena. Tell me what's on your mind. We need to clear everything up so we can get on with living the way we deserve."

She licked her lips. "Well…several days ago when we were out riding, some of your friends asked to be introduced. You hustled me away and ever since then you've been rather...distant." She traced the button on his jacket until he clasped his hand over hers and held it still. "Ivor, you say my being a governess means nothing to you, but you cannot deny that you were most put out that morning."

He sighed and rubbed his forehead with his forefinger, a habit she had noticed before. "My dear, I would have been proud to make you known to them, but have you thought of the consequences? As I had not yet offered for you, and in fact had no chance of doing so for at least another six months, you might well have become the butt of their ribald conversation, especially since you were staying at Stafford House. I thought it best to insinuate that you were one of my sister's friends and that we were on our way to meet with Nerida. It was all I could think of on the spur of the moment. That particular group of men is not known for being discreet."

"Oh."

"Yes. Oh. Now, are you agreed that governessing is an honorable profession?"

She grinned. "Yes, Ivor. It is an honorable profession." She could hardly say otherwise since his mama had been a governess.

"It certainly is. As you can see, it has done our family no harm at all. On the contrary, I believe we were better informed than most children."

"Of course it did you no harm! I did not mean that...oh, you know perfectly well what I mean."

"Not always, my love. Sometimes you are enigmatic to the point of being obscure."

"I! I am enigmatic?" Helena exclaimed indignantly. "And just what do you call your behavior over the past two months?"

"Lovelorn," Ivor said, taking her firmly into his arms. "Lost, puzzled, angry, startled, long-suffering but most of all, shockingly lovelorn. Now Miss Helena Marshfield, answer me this. Are you or are you not going to marry me next month?"

Helena dimpled. "Next month?"

"Next month." Firmly.

"Oh, very well, Ivor. June sounds like a nice month to be married."

Epilogue

Helena Stafford stood at her bedchamber window at Ryewolds gazing out at the summery view. A green lawn stretched away to the right where it was bounded by a camellia hedge. In front of her a stone fountain absorbed the hot sun, and a lone throstle bustled and preened his way through a bath. Along the gravel path a persistent peacock stalked a blatantly uninterested peahen. Helena laughed aloud.

"What is it, darling?"

Two arms slid around her from behind, and she turned within their circle. She still melted when he called her 'darling,' but she was not so partial to 'Athena.'

"I didn't hear you come in."

"No. You were laughing at something outside. What is it?" He nuzzled her hair.

"Look, Ivor! Have you ever seen such a lackluster courtship?"

Ivor stared out the window and grinned. "Well *he's* not precisely lackluster. It's just too hot for him and he can't keep up. But *she's* definitely lackluster. I hope I never bore you like that."

"Never."

"Truly?"

"Now you're looking for compliments. You know perfectly well that...that...I am never bored, my love, and well you know it."

His hands slid down to her backside, pulling her against him.

"Good. It wouldn't do for me to lose my touch."

"Just as long as I am the only one who feels your touch, sir."

****

He knew she still had moments when she doubted his complete absorption in her to the exclusion of any other woman. He was working on making those moments fewer and fewer and was succeeding. But perhaps 'working' was not the correct word. It was hardly work to show her how much he loved her, how much he wanted her. Giving her pleasure also gave him pleasure, not something he had been familiar with. He had not realized that seeing the woman who meant the whole world to him undulating in his arms with soft little cries could give him an ache so fierce that it jolted his heart into a sort of thanksgiving.

She kissed his throat. "I'm sorry, Ivor. I didn't mean that. I know you would never behave like Cole or Lord Barringate. I don't know how their wives stand it. I would be destroyed."

"I know, my love. But you are different from those wives. Believe me, I knew a few of them some years ago, and they are every bit as licentious as their husbands are. Remember, instead, our closest friends who have made their own marital rules of shared goals and exclusiveness."

She nodded and smiled, and he turned her around so they faced the big mirror beside the window. His hands slid upward, gently cupping her breasts. She knew that from where he stood, he obtained a similar birds-eye view as he had the night of the Yardleys' ball. She now had her dresses made with lower necklines just to please him. He was a lucky man. The soft, gleaming skin he so adored was always freely offered for his delectation. In turn he made sure that his cravats were in less precise folds than in the past, because she had a passion for edging his cravats aside to dip her forefinger inside his shirt to stroke the skin of his throat and collarbone. He had no intention of sabotaging such an interesting habit.

"I was going to ask you, Ivor, whether we should suggest to Caroline and Robert that they might marry here at Ryewolds next year. Would that be acceptable to you?"

"My dear, please rid yourself of the habit of asking permission for things you wish to do. This house is yours now too. Naturally they will marry here if they wish it."

She leaned back against him, laying her hand over his where he stroked her breast. Turning her head, she nuzzled his throat.

Gradually his lady's memories of her years of servitude were fading, but she sometimes irritated him by asking his permission before making a decision. She was a strong woman. She would recover.

"I'm pleased that Josh Yardley thought they should wait until next year before marrying. Robert's leg had not mended enough for him to stand up at our wedding, but he will be able to stand straight and strong at his own wedding next year. And Caroline will by then be more mature. She is already assuming the mien of the wife of a budding politician and aide to the Prince."

They smiled together. Life was good. Life was

very good.

Ivor's arms tightened around her. He had everything he wanted, here in his arms.

****

Helena leaned farther back and tucked her head beneath his chin. Held in his arms, she had everything she wanted. Things might not always be smooth sailing, but they had a foundation of love to help them celebrate their successes and commiserate with each other when trouble came. Together they would raise a family and keep the love that had been so hard-won.

A word from the author...

Our family were all born in New Zealand and now live in Queensland, the sunshine state of Australia. Nobody else in my family writes, but in the latter part of the nineteenth century my antecedents published newspapers and were authors. Blood will out, as they say.

My specialties are poetry, novellas, song lyrics, and novels.

www.vonniehughes.com

Thank you for purchasing
this publication of The Wild Rose Press, Inc.

For questions or more information
contact us at
info@thewildrosepress.com.

The Wild Rose Press, Inc.